THE FURY

SOLOMON CHURCH
BOOK 2

MORGAN GREENE

D1521937

MERCURY BOOKS

Book Cover Design by EbookLaunch.com

ALSO BY MORGAN GREENE

Solomon Church
The Exile
The Fury
The Outcast

Jamie Johansson
Bare Skin
Fresh Meat
Idle Hands
Angel Maker
Rising Tide
Old Blood
Death Chorus
Quiet Wolf
Ice Queen
Black Heart
The Last Light Of Day
The Mark Of The Dead

The Hiss Of The Snake
The Devil In The Dark
The First Snow Of Winter
The Deepest Grave Of All

Standalone Titles
Savage Ridge
A Place Called Hope
The Blood We Share
The Trade

THE FURY

PREFACE

The Kosovo war was fought between 1998 and 1999 following the dissolution of Yugoslavia. The Kosovo Liberation Army battled for the independence of Kosovo from Serbia on behalf of the ethnic-Albanians against the wide-spread ethnic cleansings of their people.

In March of 1999, NATO eventually came to the aid of the KLA, forcing the conflict to a head. They launched Operation Allied Force, a relentless bombing campaign targeting key Serbian military targets, which lasted 78 days before the President Slobodan Milošević surrendered and withdrew Serbian forces from Kosovo.

Five hundred people were killed by the bombings, including many civilians. And by the time the conflict ended, the total death toll for the war was estimated to be somewhere between 12,000 and 14,000.

The vast majority of that number was comprised of

Kosovar Albanian civilians killed during the cleansings. The only universally accepted truth was the brutality of the war and the terrible cost of civilian lives.

On both sides.

ONE

KOSOVO, 1999

THE GROUND TREMBLED under the weight of the M-84 battle tank.

Church watched as it thundered down the road towards them at the head of a train of fifty tired Yugoslav soldiers. They marched behind the tank, aiming for a military checkpoint ten miles down the road. But it was here, in the Kosovan hills, that their band of Kosovo Liberation Army rebels would take this unit apart, further weakening the Yugoslav Army's grasp on this land.

Church readjusted his footing, his knees aching in his crouched position, and lifted his watch. It was a little before dawn, and the men coming towards them had been walking through the night. At approximately midnight, they'd launched an attack on a small Kosovan village, razing it to the ground. Another KLA faction had evacuated it just in time, and they were told that civilian casualties were kept to a minimum.

But at this point, even a minimum was too many. And though Church was doing his best to compartmentalise that bubbling anger in his chest, the men around him—the KLA fighters, the Kosovans who called this place home, who had watched their fields burn, their wives and daughters raped, their fathers hanged and their homes destroyed—were struggling to do the same.

The SAS weren't officially involved in the conflict at all. And though NATO had taken a hard stance against the Yugoslav Army's aims to destroy all remnants of Kosovo as an independent nation and reel it back into the fold, it was still a difficult and tumultuous political landscape to navigate.

But Church didn't care much for politics, and neither did the men around him. Captain Gareth West— Gaz to his men. Darren Davies—'DD', as they called him. Rob Lancaster, or 'Grandad' as he was known because of his white hair. They were the four-man team inserted deep into the heart of the war to try to tip the scales in favour of the KLA. They weren't a recognised military force—no more than a semi-organised group of resistance fighters waging war against the Yugoslav Army with old Soviet weapons and a deep-seated hatred to carry them through the darkest hours.

Little factions were doing all they could across Kosovo, but here, now, in these bushes, the man leading them was Darko Vida—and by the way his lips were twitching, by how hard he was gripping the M70 rifle in his hands, and by the murderous look in his eye, Church guessed he wasn't going to obey Gaz's word to hold until he gave the signal.

The tank rumbled closer, the men jogging wearily behind it, their battle gear—flak vests and helmets—clinking and rattling as they moved. There were two anti-tank mines buried fifty yards past their location, and the moment the tank rolled over them it would be relieved of its treads and all but disabled. Then they'd emerge from the bushes, hitting the Yugoslav unit from behind, taking them out before they even knew what was going on.

It perhaps wasn't the most honourable tactic, but there was nothing much about war these days that was honourable.

Church had only been in the SAS for a year, but he'd already come to realise that getting the job done was what mattered the most. Honour didn't much enter the equation.

Gaz crouched a little lower, his already small stature shrinking further into the copse of foliage.

'Hold,' he whispered, keeping his eyes fixed on the tank as it drew level with them, its huge diesel engine chugging viciously as it hauled itself along.

He watched it go by, counting the rows of men—twenty-five of them moving in the tank's tracks, shoulder to shoulder, two abreast.

Church did the same, knowing they weren't going to spring out until the men were well past.

Or at least, he thought so—until he took another look at Darko, the man exchanging glances with the fighters to his left and right—his brothers-in-arms, his friends, as good as his family.

Church watched him, and he knew he was going to say it before he even did.

'Now!' Darko cried.

And all at once the liberation fighters launched themselves from the trees, howling and screeching, opening fire directly into the ranks of the Yugoslav Army.

It was as though winning the night wasn't good enough for him. It was as though he wanted those men to know who was fighting them—who was killing them. He wanted to see it in their eyes as he brought death to them.

But Church knew that all they would succeed in doing was bringing death to themselves. Unless, that is, they intervened.

'Jesus Christ,' Gaz called, motioning them forward. 'Move. Move! Church! Grandad! The tank—now!' he shouted, pointing towards the M-84, which had ground to a halt twenty yards ahead, thirty yards short of the anti-tank mines, and was still fully functional. It was already swivelling its huge cannon back towards the fray. Gunfire chattered incessantly, the muzzle flashes cutting through the darkness as Darko and his men engaged.

Fountains of blood rose in the air, along with cries of anguish from both sides. Soldiers fell. Fighters took bullets. Some called out for their mothers. Gaz and DD jumped into action—the only two among the KLA fighters who seemed to have an understanding of what it took to win a gunfight like this.

They had no high ground, no cover other than the trees. They stayed there, picking off the Yugoslav soldiers with short, controlled bursts from their M16s.

'Smoke. Smoke!' Gaz yelled, tearing the pin from a smoke grenade and hurling it into the centre of the Yugoslav soldiers.

A frag would have been more effective, but it would have taken out as many KLA as it did Slavs—the men mixed up in a brutal melee of close-quarters shooting and stabbing.

And though Church was sure that Gaz thought they deserved whatever fate might come to them for charging in like that—as much as Church did—that wasn't the mission.

The mission was to help the KLA thwart the Yugoslav forces. To fight for the freedom of this place.

Church, still green around the edges, felt the seasoned hand of Grandad on his collar, dragging him up to his feet and shoving him into the open. They ducked under the swivelling barrel of the tank's cannon and ran down its length.

A squeak of steel told them the hatch was opening up top, giving one of the gunners inside access to the mounted .50 cal.

Before Church had even turned, Grandad had his pistol out, levelled at the back of the guy's head—and a well-placed round sent a spray of blood over the paint-work, the man slithering back down into his hole in a limp heap.

His eyes flashed to Church once more.

'Get up there,' he ordered him, kneeling and slapping the top of his right leg.

Church wasted no time, knowing what he needed to do. With Grandad's help, he stepped up—the old man launching him onto the roof of the vehicle. He scrambled over the cold steel, tearing a flashbang grenade from his belt. Pulling the pin, he dropped it through the hatch and turned his head away, covering his ears just in time.

A blinding flash leapt free of it, a deafening explosion accompanying a cloud of acrid smoke. Coughing and hacking, two more men began to emerge from the hole, and Church—on reflex—already had his pistol drawn. They were blinded, scrabbling for fresh air and freedom, and executing them like this seemed wrong on every level to Church.

But then Grandad's order echoed from behind him.

'Do it,' he called.

And Church shut that part of himself down, knowing this was the job. This was the life he'd chosen. And ultimately, this was the mission.

And then, without another second's hesitation, he pulled the trigger twice—putting down the first man instantly.

Before he turned his attention to the second, the man squinted up at him—hands raised, eyes wide.

But before he could beg for mercy, Church did what he was paid to do.

And he killed him as well.

TWO

PRESENT DAY

IT WAS ALMOST DAWN, and in those final moments where the night was holding its breath and the day was beginning to break, Church often thought back to all the times he'd seen the sun come up in his life—all the missions that had taken place during the darkest hours, all the men whose lives had been snuffed out in the minutes before dawn.

He pulled his head off the glass and sat upright in the front seat, readjusting himself, his back aching. He unfolded his arms, his weary eyes fixed on the road ahead.

'You good?' Julia Hallberg asked from the seat next to him.

He turned his head and looked at her, giving a solitary nod.

He didn't feel much like talking.

'You did good,' she said, driving them on through the English countryside. 'We've been chasing Belchik for years. But the guy—he's like a wet bar of soap. Nothing stuck to him—'

'The bullet did,' Church said sourly, realising quickly how definitive a statement that was. He cleared his throat and sat a little higher in the chair. 'Sorry,' he said. 'I didn't mean for that to be so...' He trailed off, unsure what word he wanted to choose.

'Cold?' Hallberg asked. She looked over at him and smiled, both hands on the wheel. It seemed large in her grasp. She wasn't a tall woman—she was slight, with dark hair pinned back and small, close-set, pretty features.

Church returned his eyes to the road once more. He'd been on the go now for around twenty-six hours and needed sleep. The whole mission had taken eight days in total, and he was exhausted. He eventually tracked down Belchik in Belarus, holed up in one of his mansions. It hadn't been as clean as Church had hoped, but he'd got the job done and gotten out relatively unscathed.

Unlike Belchik. After the DRC, Julia Hallberg's sting operation to bring down one of the largest trafficking rings across Europe had been in tatters.

She told him that he owed her. And at the time, he'd agreed.

But now, with this much blood on his hands, he was struggling with the debt—and when it was going to be paid in full.

What had gone from a noble notion of taking down evil men who'd slipped their heads from the noose had now become an ever-growing kill list.

And Church, seemingly, had become Hallberg's own personal off-the-books attack dog. She got him in and out of where he needed to go on Interpol's dime, but she kept her hands clean—and he knew that ultimately, if he got picked up by the local police, wherever he was, he doubted she'd ride to his rescue. Though, he couldn't say that for sure. She was… different. Nice. Nicer than she had any right to be doing a job like this. Making calls like this.

But getting caught by law enforcement wasn't the biggest risk. If he got put down—which was the far more likely scenario—he had no doubt his body would be dumped in a shallow ditch somewhere. No one would mourn him. No one would come to get him. He would just rot wherever he fell. And there was nothing he or Julia Hallberg could do about it.

Though that was a fate he'd accepted for himself a long, long time ago.

Eastern Europe held a lot of difficult memories for him—ones that he'd been keen to forget and ones he almost had, until the last few days. Now they were coming crashing back.

He stared down at his hands in the dark cabin of the smooth-riding SUV and squeezed them into shaking fists. This was the most comfortable he'd been in days —the safest he'd been in days—and yet his heart was beating faster now than it had at any point during the mission, and he wondered how much more he could bear, how much more physical and psychological abuse he could put himself through before he just cracked. Before he was unable to go on.

Hallberg's phone lit up then, on the dashboard—an incoming call—and she reached out, answering it. Church wondered who else knew about what he was doing. Who else would call at this time?

He pricked up his ears slightly—not wanting to listen in, but wanting to make sure that both he and Hallberg were safe from any blowback from what he'd just done. Which, for all intents and purposes, had turned into a big, bloody fucking mess. He'd lost track of how many men he'd killed. And that thought alone felt like a hot poker pressed to his throat.

Hallberg was Chief Operations Coordinator for the UK arm of Interpol, and that meant she had her fingers in a lot of operations—both domestically and cross-border. And as she and the man on the other end started speaking, he realised that the phone call wasn't about what they'd just done at all.

'Chief,' the man said. 'You awake?' The name on the phone said *Collins*.

Hallberg looked over at Church and raised a finger to her lips to signal for him to be quiet.

He knew better than to make noise anyway.

'Yeah,' she said. 'Just on my way to the gym.'

Church looked at the clock and saw that it was a little before six and thought that was a good cover. Very believable. No one could dispute that, and it gave a good reason to be in the car as well.

'Well, wherever you are—turn around,' Collins said.

Hallberg's brow creased. Church's, too, as he read the alarm in the man's voice.

'What's wrong?' Hallberg replied, keeping the car at a steady pace, unflinching at what might have been something big.

'A bomb just went off in Birmingham,' he said. 'Middle of an intersection full of morning commuters. We don't know the damage yet, or how many are dead. Emergency services are on the scene. But...' He trailed off, and Church read the look on Hallberg's face.

'They think it could be terrorist?' Hallberg asked.

'Yeah,' Collins—who Church guessed was her second in command—replied. 'But it looks like the same MO as the explosions we've been tracking across Europe.'

Church understood then.

While an explosion like this would be handled by the NCA, by Counter Terrorism, in normal circumstances—and surely would be now too—if it was cross-border, if it was linked to something going on inside Europe, then Interpol would be looped in. They would be the agency that made sure everybody had the same information, and that the investigations weren't double-tracking over the same ground.

Hallberg lifted her watch and looked at it as though doing the mental calculations from where they were, which, at that point, was somewhere west of Cambridge.

'I can be there in about ninety minutes,' Hallberg replied.

'Where are you?' Collins asked back.

'Just send me the details and keep me posted as the scene shapes up,' she replied. 'I'll be there as soon as I can.'

Collins knew better than to interrogate his boss and instead did what any good number two should do and said, 'You got it,' before hanging up.

They were already heading the right way, but now Hallberg sped up a little. After picking him up from the private airfield that he'd landed at, Hallberg had been driving Church back to the farm where he was staying—the farm that belonged to one of his former teammates in the SAS, one of the best men he ever knew. Mitch.

It was located in the Cotswolds, and it was fortunate that it was practically on the way. Hallberg could drop Church off and then continue north towards Birmingham, towards the site. And yet something was niggling at Church. He'd been away for days working this last mission, and before that it had been another one, and another one.

He felt like his feet had barely been on British soil for months, and this was the first he was hearing of any explosions—let alone a string of bombings across Europe, and now, seemingly, in the heart of England as well.

'I'll drop you home,' Hallberg said. 'Don't worry about that.'

Church sucked on his teeth for a moment, struggling

to resist the urge to ask a question he knew might open a door he didn't want to walk through. And yet, he couldn't help himself.

'What are these bombings?' he asked, suddenly more alert now, the heaviness of sleep cast from his eyes.

'The first one was in Austria,' Hallberg said, 'about three weeks ago, outside Vienna. The second—just outside Rotterdam in the Netherlands. And now this one here in Birmingham.' She shook her head as though to illustrate that they had no idea who was doing it. Or at least that's what Church was gleaning from the sound of her voice.

'And you've got no leads?' Church asked.

'We just don't know what they're doing it for. They don't seem to be in huge population centres. They're not trying to cause mass casualties, they're not trying to sow fear by hitting public transport hubs or public events. No known group has claimed responsibility for it, and there doesn't seem to be any discernible pattern. We're working hard, but the methodology doesn't match any known group or individual that we think would do this... Usually, we've got at least something to go on. But this time...'

'So it's a new player,' Church mused.

'Yeah. One who's got us running in circles,' Hallberg said back. 'Everyone's asking for answers that we don't have.'

Church nodded slowly, taking that on board.

'What?' Hallberg said, reading his focused expression. 'Had some epiphany already?'

Church shrugged. 'I don't know. But if you need an extra set of eyes on the site...'

Hallberg laughed at first, but then settled down to silence and considered that. 'One of our forensic guys did say that he thought the bomb looked homemade— but not... not modern. Not something that anyone who learned to build a bomb these days would use.'

'So you're thinking somebody ex-military,' Church replied, reading between the lines. 'Someone older. Someone who learned their skills years ago.'

'That's one theory,' she said. 'The report described the tactics as "guerrilla". Though what that means, I don't quite know.'

'I know what it means,' Church said.

Hallberg didn't respond to that.

'What are you thinking?' Church asked her after a few seconds.

She sank her teeth into her bottom lip. 'I'm just thinking how I can explain it.'

'Explain what?'

'Who the hell you are when I take you into the crime scene.'

Church curled a half smile, a sort of sardonic smirk in the darkness. 'You don't have to take me at all,' he said. 'I wouldn't mind going to bed.'

'Yeah,' Hallberg replied with a sigh. 'I don't think you're going to be sleeping for a while yet.' She looked over at him, her eyes fixing on his. 'I've got a feeling it's going to be a long day.'

THREE

TWENTY-FIVE YEARS AGO

CHURCH WATCHED with his hands draped over the rail of his rifle as the KLA fighters rounded up their dead and dragged them to the side of the road.

The smell of smoke and blood still hung heavy in the air as they separated them from the Yugoslav forces, stepping over the soldiers as though they were nothing to find their own men. A sea of corpses.

They had scarcely been twenty, taking on a unit fifty strong, and though they'd won the battle, their losses would no doubt affect the outcome of the war.

Darko's men were half of what they were minutes before, and the solemn looks on their faces told Church that once more they'd been reminded of the stakes—that the engagement could have gone any other way, that it could have been the end of them then and there. And it would have been, had it not been for Church and the others. Their prize had been the M-87 that they had commandeered. But at what cost?

'Darko!' Gaz called out, striding towards the man.

He was a few inches shorter than the Kosovan, and Darko made sure he remembered that as they squared up. He had a thick head of black hair and eyebrows doing everything they could to meet in the middle. He twisted his lips into an ugly grimace and looked down at the SAS captain in his face.

'What?' he practically spat.

'What the hell do you think you're doing?' Gaz snapped at him, shoving the man in the chest.

He probably had a good stone or two on the captain, but Church knew that Gaz was anything but a pushover —and if the KLA were capable of handling themselves, there'd be no reason for the SAS to be there at all.

'What am I doing?' Darko clapped back, taking a step before he righted himself and clenched his fists at his side, his desperation to take a swing at Gaz clear even in the darkness. 'I'm doing what it fucking takes,' he said. 'Not like you—crouching in the bushes, hiding, sneaking up from behind like a rat.'

'It's called having a fucking brain cell,' Gaz practically roared. 'We were outmanned more than two to one. That's why we didn't take them head-on.'

Darko laughed. 'Every fighter here is worth ten Slavs,' he said, spitting on the nearest corpse—a young lad who looked no more than twenty.

Another casualty of war in every sense of the word.

'Oh yeah? So then why the fuck are we here wiping your arses, eh? Answer me that.'

Gaz reached out then—his hand striking like a viper —and took a fistful of Darko's coat, pulling him close so that they were nose to nose.

'I will not stand for insubordination from the men under my command.'

'Yeah,' Darko said back, pressing his forehead against the captain's. 'And what exactly are you going to do about it?'

———

Darko and a few of his men split off from the group, taking the tank to a nearby village to stash it out of sight from forces that would no doubt come looking for it. When those men didn't reach the checkpoint by dawn, recon would be sent out to find them—and there was no hiding fifty corpses, which meant by the time that happened they all needed to be long gone.

Gaz announced they were hiking out, and that was good enough for Church and the others. They had 4x4s parked a klick away that would take them back to the makeshift KLA base—what had once been a wheat farm that was now the centre of the KLA's operations for this region. As Gaz cast an ugly look over his shoulder, watching as the tank rolled out with Darko and his three best cronies tucked inside, he quickened the pace.

DD fell into step beside him. The two were around the same age and had come up together. Gaz was an experienced hand and had been promoted just a few years before, and DD was the closest thing he had to family. Grandad was almost fifty and had served in the SAS for over twenty years, and that life—the hardness of it—had turned him grey. But Church didn't make the mistake of thinking that he was any less formidable than he had been at any point during his career. His white hair and white beard may have earned him the nickname Grandad, but anyone who underestimated him would be sure to regret that.

'How are you doing?' he asked roughly, catching up to Church.

He looked up at the man beside him. They were an odd fit—Church fresh to the service, Grandad the oldest hand here, and Gaz and DD somewhere in the middle.

They were just four men assigned to this faction of the KLA and one of who knew how many groups of SAS inserted to help the war effort. They weren't told anything except what their next mission was, and everything else was kept need-to-know in case they were captured and tortured. The brass called that plausible deniability. Church wasn't sure what he called it yet.

'Fine,' he replied to Grandad's question, casting a glance over his shoulder, making sure that the Kosovan fighters were behind them, silent and sad as they were to leave their fallen behind. But it was a long way to carry the dead home, and time to bury them there wasn't a luxury they had.

Grandad watched him carefully.

'Killing a man's not easy,' he mused, almost philo-sophically. 'Killing two's twice as hard.'

'Yeah? If it was that hard,' Church said, 'I wouldn't have signed up.'

Grandad cracked a little smile at that—the kind of sardonic smile that told him he knew Church was full of shit.

'Aye, maybe,' he said. 'But if you find it gets easier, let me know.'

'If it gets harder, you mean?' Church asked.

Grandad shook his head.

'No. If it gets harder, you know you're still human,' he replied, touching his finger to his heart. 'If it starts to get easier, that's when you know you're losing yourself.'

Church thought about that all the way back to the vehicles—and then all the way back to base.

They rode in the lead car with Gaz and DD up front, him and Grandad in the back. When they finally arrived —rolling into the airfield an hour later—Grandad groaned as he got out of the car, the old warrior's body not what it once was. Church went around and stopped next to Grandad, who was still, watching Gaz carefully. He seemed to have a sixth sense about these things. He noticed everything—the smallest changes in the air—and now he seemed fixated on their captain.

And as Church looked over too, he could understand why. Gaz was still on a tear, seething as he threw the car door shut and strode towards the main building—the building where Ismet Vida lived.

He was Darko's father, the mayor of the village they'd lived in—a village long since claimed by the Yugoslav forces, some two hundred kilometres from here. It was one of the first to fall, which meant the Yugoslav forces had more energy. They were fresher, more brutal then, and Ismet had witnessed what that looked like. He'd seen his wife's throat cut in front of him. He'd seen innocent men and women lined up in the streets and executed—pushed into shallow graves and lit on fire. And it was that that fuelled him now. That kept him fighting despite the seventy-odd years he had under his belt.

Church had always thought it was wishful thinking that Ismet had control of his son, Darko. But perhaps Gaz just refused to admit that out here, rank and station didn't mean what they should.

It didn't mean shit.

Grandad watched him go, turning to Church once he was out of earshot.

'I'm going to get some sleep,' he said. 'Wake me if shit hits the fan, yeah?'

He looked over and lowered his head, staring at Church from under his bushy white eyebrows.

'When Darko gets back, I've got a feeling it might. Hopefully that's not for a while—so Gaz has time to cool off. If not… you know where I'll be.'

He dropped Church a casual salute, then strode off towards their tent, and while Church figured his best move was to get some sleep too, his curiosity got the best of him.

Before he realised it, he was walking after Gaz, determined to see the show. DD seemed to have the same idea—or perhaps he was just anticipating that Gaz might need some backup—and walked with him.

As they approached the house, a pair of KLA fighters wearing heavy woollen scarves against the early-spring wind and sporting M70 rifles held their hands up to stop them.

'No,' one of them said—the one with the better command of English, though that was about as far as it seemed to extend.

Gaz stopped, lifted his hands to make sure they knew he meant no ill intent, and then demanded to go inside anyway.

'I need to see Ismet,' he said. 'Right fucking now.'

'Is not possible,' the particularly loquacious guard said back in broken English.

'Well you best fucking make it possible,' Gaz demanded.

The colloquial, mangled nature of that request seemed lost on the guard, and he just creased his brow and put his hand on Gaz's chest anyway.

'No,' he said, taking a risk that he understood what Gaz was asking.

'Take your fucking hand off me,' Gaz growled, grabbing the man's wrist and twisting it so violently that Church was surprised it didn't break—or maybe that was his intention.

The man crumbled, twisting to the floor, crying out in pain—but before his knee even touched the ground,

Gaz found the barrel of the second guard's M70 pressed to the skin just below his ear.

The man held it there as though the threat alone would be enough to stop Gaz, and Church watched with both trepidation and admiration as Gaz turned his head towards it—and then stooped to press his forehead to the muzzle instead.

'If you're going to fucking shoot me, shoot me,' he said. 'Otherwise get that fucking thing out of my face.'

Church wasn't sure if the man was going to take him up on it—but luckily, the door behind them opened instead, and an old man with a hunched back and a thick grey beard stepped out.

He was silhouetted by the dim light burning behind him, and it threw enough shards of illumination across the farmyard that Church could now pick out the faces of the rescued civilians around them.

He knew there to be several dozen seeking refuge here—stragglers who'd marched from their destroyed villages and found their way here just by chance. Or nomads the KLA had picked up on the side of the road, rescued from certain death if they'd met the Yugoslav forces instead.

They all stared on, frightened—none of them wanting to see more war, or more death.

The old man with the grey beard reached up slowly, wordlessly, and put his hand on the barrel of the M70 pressed to Gaz's head, pushing it down until it was pointed at the ground.

Gaz released the talkative guard, then met Ismet's eye.

'Your son almost got every single person out there killed tonight,' he hissed, his thick East London accent cutting through the Eastern European night.

Ismet drew in a slow breath and pulled his head back.

'I'm sorry,' he said. 'Darko... Darko's rage burns brightly.'

His English was good, if accented, and he spoke with a strange, poetic sort of rhythm.

'I instructed him to follow your orders. I told him that you were here to help.'

'Well, a fat lot of good that did,' Gaz grumbled. 'He charged headlong into fifty armed Slavs. And if we weren't there, you would have been burying a son come morning.'

'Then I'm glad you were,' Ismet replied, trying on a smile and reaching out for Gaz's shoulder. He shrugged it off as soon as the old man touched him.

'We're here to help, all right?' Gaz said back. 'I can't fucking do that with that twat son of yours trying to get me killed at every turn. Either he falls in line or he stays here at home with Daddy, all right? Now, I'm happy to tell him, but if I do, I don't reckon he's going to have any teeth left after we're done. So maybe you want to relay that to him, eh? Otherwise we'll just pack up and fuck off home instead, shall we? Leave you to this nice little war of yours and Darko can fight it any way he wants.'

Ismet stared at Gaz for what seemed like a long time, and as Church looked on, he felt the weight of eyes on him. He turned his head, looking around the frightened faces of the civilians, and spotted a young woman amongst them all.

She was in her early thirties, and she looked tired— as though she was living through a war. The light brown hair and dirtied skin made her blend in with the others around her, but her burning blue eyes shone in the night like two fire opals.

'You have my apologies,' Ismet said back to Gaz— Church only hearing it in his periphery, his eyes fixed on the blue-eyed woman across the yard.

'Were any of your men hurt?'

'No, thankfully,' Gaz said. 'But we're not taking that risk again. You tell Darko he falls in line, or we're done. Got it?'

'I understand,' Ismet said. 'And I will make sure to tell him. But...'

'But what?' Gaz said, already turning around and ready to walk away.

'But he is his own man. And this thing that burns in him—this fury... this fury at what has been done to his homeland, to his people—it is not easily extinguished. Not by me. Not by you. And not by the Yugoslav forces. He will fight until his last breath, and I don't know that there's anything that anyone can do to stop him.'

'Well,' Gaz said, hanging his head, 'that may be the case. But if he keeps going like he is...'

Gaz let out a gentle sigh, turning his back on the old man fully.

'His last breath is going to come a lot sooner than he wants it to.'

FOUR

PRESENT DAY

THE CITY WAS in turmoil as they arrived.

The distant howl of sirens echoed through the streets as they crept along. Hallberg flicked on her own lights as they wound through the centre of the city, mounting kerbs and navigating slowly around strings of grid-locked traffic as they made their way towards the site. At one point they fell in behind an ambulance and shouldered through in sequence, making good ground.

The sun was up by the time they arrived, and Church rolled down the window, smelling smoke and concrete dust in the air. The smell of a blast. A smell he knew well. It took him back—back to every mission he'd ever worked—and he closed his eyes against the images that flashed inside his head, steadying his breathing as they drew to a stop and Hallberg killed the engine.

She looked over at him. 'You okay?'

He nodded. 'Yeah, just tired.'

He stuck the heels of his hands into his eyeballs and pressed hard until it hurt, and then let out a long, sobering breath.

'Anyone asks,' Hallberg said, 'you're an ordnance expert. An outside consultant. All right?'

Church raised an eyebrow, looked over at her. 'Well, that's not a lie.'

'Yeah,' Hallberg replied. 'That's sort of the point. And if anybody asks any more questions, you tell them to ask me, okay? Don't tell them your name, don't tell them who you really are, and definitely don't tell them what we're working on.'

'I may look it,' Church said. 'But I'm not stupid.'

Hallberg smiled at him now, genuinely, warmly. A smile that brought him out of his blood-soaked head and into the present.

'I know,' she said. 'And though it's not a happy occasion, I'm glad you're here. You're a good man, Solomon, and I think you could really help—'

'Should we get on with it?' Church asked her. 'I would like to sleep sometime this week.'

Hallberg broke away and shook her head.

'Oh, I'm sorry, did I ruin the moment?' Church asked her.

She reached over and punched him in the shoulder.

'Well, fuck me for trying to be nice,' she said. 'You know there is such a thing as asset care, right?'

'That what I am?' Church said. 'An asset?'

'A big one. And a big pain in the—'

But she didn't get to finish her quip before there was suddenly a man at her window, knocking on the glass.

She turned her head towards him and let out a little sigh of relief.

'Collins,' she said, opening the door.

'Chief,' he replied, breathless.

He was in his late twenties, a thin guy in a black suit and the skinniest tie that Church had ever seen.

He'd garrotted men with thicker wires.

Church climbed out of the cab with some difficulty and arched his back, cracking it.

As Hallberg did the same and Collins began dragging her forward through the sea of marked cars and flashing lights—through the ambulances and the fire trucks, through the paramedics and the uniformed officers—Church surveyed the area, watching as black smoke continued to billow into the building.

'Morning,' Hallberg whistled, and Church looked over at her.

She gestured for him to follow, and he did, catching them up with a few long strides. People looked back, and upon seeing him, their eyes widened.

They stepped to the sides to let him through. He didn't look like any kind of officer—he wasn't in any uniform. He was in a white Henley rolled up to the elbows over his big, hairy arms. A pair of jeans faded at the knees with wear, and a pair of boots that announced his presence everywhere he went.

Unless he didn't want his presence announced.

Right now, he wasn't thinking about it at all.

Before him, the sea of people parted, allowing him through.

He scratched at his growing stubble and pushed his sandy-coloured hair—a little flecked with white now—back over his head, gaining ground on the detonation point with every step.

The blast site was cordoned off, and Hallberg approached it, ducking under the tape and into what remained of the middle of the intersection.

A uniformed officer held up his hand to stop Church. He was a tall man too, and yet seemed much smaller than the person he was trying to stop, even in his domed hat. He opened his mouth to speak, but then met Church's eyes and the word just seemed to die in his mouth.

'He's with me,' Hallberg called, grabbing the officer's attention, who promptly removed his hand from Church's chest and held it up to show that he meant no harm.

With a little huff of discomfort, Church ducked under the tape himself and strode into the road.

It was clear immediately that it had been a car bomb. It looked like it had been a Ford Focus, a newer model—a rental, he thought instinctively—the roof completely missing, the doors blown and bent outwards.

Next to it, a BMW SUV was a burned husk, and on the other side, what looked to have been a Skoda that had already been driving away was mauled from behind, the front half almost intact. The back half—just a blackened shell. All of the other cars parked around were much the same story.

Though the blast had been powerful, it hadn't been huge. Hallberg was right. Whoever had set it off hadn't been looking to inflict maximum damage. Church wondered what kind of explosive it was. How much of it.

Church began walking towards the cars, stepping between SOCOs in white coats and firefighters who were inspecting the area too.

He stepped between the BMW and the bomb car and looked from one to the other. There was something strange about what he was seeing, something somehow familiar, something like déjà vu rearing its ugly head in the recesses of his mind. He had seen cars like this before—but where? His time in Iraq, Afghanistan—he'd come across so many car bombs, but none of them quite looked like this, and he wasn't sure why. Where the dissonance was. What was niggling at him.

'Hey,' somebody called.

Church looked up.

A portly man in a windbreaker and a white shirt with a black tie that perched on top of his belly came striding towards him. He had grey, short hair and a neck that was wider than his head.

'Who the fuck are you?' the man called. 'You can't be here,' he said, beginning to shoo Church away.

He kept coming, and Church kept watching him. When he arrived, he reached out as though to try to push

Church away, but thought better of it, stopping a few inches short.

'Who are you?' he demanded.

'I'm a consultant,' Church said back easily.

'Not for me you're not,' the man snapped.

'For me,' Hallberg called out then, jogging over, leaving Collins behind. Her number two was watching them keenly, and Church knew that Hallberg would have some questions to answer eventually. He just hoped that, for now, his presence was of more help than hindrance to her.

'And who are you?' the portly man asked, narrowing his eyes at her now.

Hallberg fished her ID from inside her jacket and held it up. 'Julia Hallberg, UK Chief Operations Coordinator, Interpol.'

'So you do think it's connected then?' the man in the windbreaker said. He extended a hand. 'Sutton,' he announced himself as. 'NCA, SIO.'

Hallberg shook his hand warmly. 'Ah, Mr Sutton, good to finally meet you,' she said, giving him a respectful nod. 'I was hoping I'd run into you here.'

Church stared at him. The NCA was the National Crime Agency, the big dogs in the UK when it came to high-profile crime, terrorism, that kind of thing. The UK's very own FBI—or as good as. And SIO stood for Senior Investigating Officer, which meant that he was the head honcho for this particular investigation—especially by the way Hallberg already knew his name and was expertly stroking his ego—and the group of people behind him, all in matching windbreakers, were no doubt his team of investigators. The ones set to try to bring this bomber to justice.

Sutton shook Hallberg's hand and cast his eyes back to Church once more.

'This one's yours?' he confirmed.

Hallberg nodded.

'And who is he?' Sutton asked dubiously, cottoning on to the fact that Church had not offered his name, his title, or any kind of ID. Which, he had to admit, if the roles were reversed, would've got his back up too.

'Ordnance expert,' Hallberg said without missing a beat. 'Old friend thought he could lend a hand.'

'Not got enough qualified people at Interpol?'

'I do,' Hallberg said confidently. 'But they're either in Rotterdam or Vienna right now, and this one's the best I could do on short notice.'

The deprecation seemed to land well with Sutton, and he looked over at Church, smiling a little as though he was some big, brainless galoot. Some SIO he was, Church thought. He hadn't noticed the tattoo on the back of his right forearm—it was buried in the hair, but still clearly there. The flaming sword. Often mistaken for a winged dagger, and the origin and design inspiration was disputed at times. It was usually known to be Excalibur, but some said it was the sword of Damocles. Either way, whether you thought it was a winged dagger or the correct thing, anyone who'd seen it knew what it meant.

And if Sutton cared to look, it would have told him

that Church was no man to be laughed at. But he didn't, and Church was happy to fly under the radar, slowly moving his hands behind his back lest Sutton look down. And with the knowledge that he could have comfortably removed all the teeth from Sutton's head with one punch, he smiled back.

'I'm happy to sit this one out, if you'd prefer,' Church said, completely relaxed.

Sutton seemed to consider that one, and then turned back to the two cars behind him.

'No, no—if you think you've got some grand insight, please share. We could do with all the help we can get, *clearly*.'

Though the words themselves made sense, the delivery was what struck Church—as insincere, as though Sutton thought it was laughable that he was even there. What with the breadth of investigative skill and knowledge on offer in his investigative team. Who was this civilian, Sutton was probably thinking? Who thinks he's as clever as the NCA?

Church stared at the two cars for a few seconds in silence, and then looked back at Sutton.

And then he shrugged.

'Your guess is as good as mine,' he said.

Sutton bristled at that, licking his thin lips. His cheeks reddened and flecked with burst blood vessels.

He puffed his chest then and looked back at Hallberg.

'Get him out of here,' he said, 'and don't bring tourists into my crime scene again.'

With that, he turned on his heel and strode away, leaving Hallberg standing there, seething.

When Sutton was out of earshot, she looked up at Church. 'You really don't play well with others, do you?'

Church looked back down at her, noting how small she was—not even up to his shoulder.

He moved to shrug again, but Hallberg lifted a finger at him.

'If you shrug one more time—'

'You're going to give me a real telling-off?' Church asked her, interjecting with a little smile.

She measured the look on his face. 'I hope you're about to tell me that that little show of ignorance was just for Sutton, and you do actually have something useful to share with me about this?'

Church considered what he was going to say, and then decided that saying nothing was better. At least for now.

This site, this attack—it did feel somehow familiar.

There was something that he recognised, but he didn't know what.

A kind of sloppy precision. A kind of abandon that was rarely seen in attacks like these.

They took a lot of planning. They took a lot of ingenuity. And they took a lot of focus.

This bomb may have looked haphazard, maybe even like it had gone off at the wrong time, inadvertently, but Church knew it wasn't anything of the sort.

'How many died?' he asked.

Hallberg nodded at the BMW. 'Two in there—man and a woman—one in the Skoda, about eighteen more injured in the vicinity.'

'And the driver?' Church asked.

'Of the bomb car?' Hallberg said. 'We don't know yet.

'Several people are unconscious. Witness reports say people were fleeing, running in all directions. That panic started before the bomb went off. So maybe he armed it wrong, or it began to trigger accidentally, he tried to run, got caught in the blast, got knocked out while doing it. We hope he is and this is the end of it.'

'He's not,' Church said. 'He got out of this cleanly, and it went down exactly as it was supposed to.'

'Three dead doesn't seem like a very grand result for something like this.'

'It's not,' Church said. 'But I don't know why.'

FIVE

CHURCH WAS STANDING in the mouth of his team's tent, set up on the perimeter of the farmyard, next to one of the steel barns.

He was staring out at the refugees milling around. They had nothing to do, nowhere to go. Those who were strong enough physically, and those who still had the strength of will to fight for their country, were drafted into the KLA—sent to the makeshift training camp set up behind the main house: a row of hay bales with shooting targets pinned to them and a few makeshift foxholes dug for cover drills. But those who couldn't fight just sat around, staring into space, wondering if this was all there was for them anymore—and if, when the war ended, there would be anything more waiting on the other side.

And yet among the old, the women, the children,

Church couldn't find her. The blue-eyed woman in the darkness was nowhere to be seen.

'Sol,' came Gaz's gruff voice.

He looked up to see his captain striding towards him, incoming from the radio tent at the edge of their camp.

Church lifted his chin. 'Captain,' he replied.

Gaz motioned him inside, glancing over towards the main house as though making sure Ismet wasn't watching.

Church went in, and Gaz undid the ropes fastening the doors back, letting them fall shut, enclosing the heavy canvas tent. Grandad appeared and ducked inside without being called, standing arms folded with his back to the door, listening with one ear in case anybody was trying to overhear them.

'What's up?' Church asked, watching as Gaz paced slowly between their four cots. He looked pensive, as though collecting his thoughts.

'We just had word,' he said then. 'An officer in the Yugoslav Army has grown disenchanted with their war tactics. He made contact saying he wants out—that he wants to link up with the KLA, supply them intel in exchange for extraction.'

'Extraction?' Church said dubiously.

'He wants out of the country and out of the war for good. Him and his family.'

Grandad spoke up now, arms still folded. 'And at what point during this genocide did he grow a conscience? Because last I checked, they've been decimating villages for the best part of a year now. And it just seems funny to me that all of a sudden, just as the Slavs are starting to lose their grip on Kosovo and NATO is ramping up their efforts to push them back, that someone wants to flip.'

Gaz looked up at him. 'If you're thinking that he's trying to play all sides for the Slavs—find out where the KLA are holed up and what they're planning just to stuff them in the arse—yeah, I had the same thought. That's why I'm in here asking you, and not telling you.'

Grandad scratched at his white chin. 'You want us to make contact—see if he's full of shit?'

'The guy apparently requested to link up with somebody ranking in the KLA, which sounds a bit brazen to me. Though he seems to reckon if he can gain their trust, show them that he's serious, that's going to be his quickest ticket out of the country.'

'And you want us to go instead?' Church said now, glancing over towards Grandad. DD wasn't there, which meant he felt like Gaz was asking the two of them to take it on alone.

Gaz read their apprehension.

'Yeah, of course it's a risk, right? There's no one here in the KLA that we could trust to handle this the way we need it handled. Definitely not Darko and his fucking lot. And God, Ismet's got one foot in the grave anyway, which leaves... us. Except the problem is that the Slavs don't know that we're here, do they? Because we're not supposed to be. So that leaves us with a bit of a problem.'

Church and Grandad were both silent.

'You want me to spell it out for you?' Gaz said.

'In these instances, I usually find it prudent,' Grandad responded. 'Just so there's no misinterpretation.'

Gaz stared over at the most senior man among them —a man with more years under his belt than any of them. But a man who'd never risen to the rank of captain? Maybe he just wasn't ambitious enough. Maybe he just didn't want it. Either way, he knew what he was doing. Enough to make sure that he had what Gaz was asking him to do laid out in certain terms. Because if Church was right about what it was, then it was a big ask.

Gaz put his hands on his hips and let out a long breath.

'Right. I want you two to go out there. I want you to meet him. I want you to squeeze him. And if you think even for a split fucking second that he's full of shit, I want you to put a bullet in his fucking head and bury him. Alright? Is that clear enough for you, Grandad?'

'As a bell,' Grandad said back, not flinching. 'I just wanted to make sure we were on the same page.'

'Good,' Gaz said. 'I'll tell them to set the meet, and I'll tell them where. Once it's confirmed, I'll give you the details. Now—'

He strode for the door.

'You two boys get something to eat and have a nap. It's going to be a long night.'

———

Under the cover of darkness, Church and Grandad slipped out of the tent, geared up, and headed towards one of the 4x4s.

At some point during the day, Darko had arrived back, and though it seemed like Gaz had slept off most of his anger, Darko still seemed to have an axe to grind with them. He was standing outside the main house smoking, and spotted them headed for the cars. He walked over, flicking his cigarette onto the ground—the ember still burning, blue smoke curling into the air—and called out.

'Hey, where are you going?' he asked.

Church and Grandad paused and looked back.

Grandad sighed and clapped Church on the shoulder. 'Why don't you deal with this,' he said. 'Good learning experience for you. And remember—' he pointed at Church '—lie.'

Church gave him a little nod and turned back towards Darko.

He might have been bigger than Gaz, but Church had more than a few inches on him, and though he was younger, he didn't baulk as the man stepped close, making no effort to be friendly.

'Headed out?' he asked, looking at Church's kit.

His hands tightened around his rifle.

Headed out. That much was obvious, and he couldn't exactly say no. Darko might have been a brute, but he wasn't completely stupid. The question was formed to test whether Church was going to lie. He could say no, and Darko would know it. Or he could say yes, and Darko would press him.

'Yeah,' Church said.

'Where?' Darko demanded.

'We've been told about some Serbian soldiers—a couple of stragglers a few klicks out,' he said, shrugging. 'We're just going to go check it out. See if they're a scout team, defectors, or maybe just refugees that were misidentified.'

'Bollocks,' Darko said. 'Haven't heard anything about that.'

'Then maybe you should take the shit out of your ears,' Church said back lightly. 'We don't report to you.'

'Everyone here reports to me,' Darko said, putting his fist on his chest. 'Nothing happens here without my fucking say so. Alright?'

'Yeah, you can have that conversation with your dad,' Church said. 'But me? I don't get paid enough to stand here and get ordered around by you. So if you don't mind...'

He turned away from Darko and felt his hand on his shoulder—the grip tight. Church paused and looked back slowly, feeling like telling him to remove that hand would be redundant. His face said it all.

Darko let go and held up his hands, grinning at Church.

'Ah, big scary British soldier,' he laughed. 'Ooooh.'

He twiddled his fingers mockingly in the darkness.

'Remind me not to cross you, eh?'

'Hopefully you'll remember,' Church smiled back. 'Now run along to Daddy, huh?'

Darko backed up slowly, pointing at Church as though it were some kind of veiled threat—a way of saying *I'll remember this... you'll pay for it.*

And as Church watched him go, stinking of sweat and cigarette smoke, he hoped he *would* come back and try to make him pay for it. And that he'd have the opportunity to show him exactly what that would look like.

As he climbed into the 4x4, Grandad started the engine.

'Smooth,' he said. 'Not exactly how I would've handled it.'

'Well then maybe you should have handled it yourself,' Church said back, adjusting himself in the seat and pushing his M16—muzzle down—between his bouncing knees.

He'd been thinking about it all day. About whether or not he would see the morning. Whether or not they were walking into a Serbian ambush. Whether the guy they were supposed to be meeting—whose name they didn't even know, whose rank they didn't know, and whose loyalties they couldn't say—was just going to execute them the moment they arrived.

And yet Grandad seemed perfectly at ease with it.

'You're not worried what's going to happen?' Church asked as they rolled out.

'Tonight?' Grandad replied. 'Kid, I stopped worrying about this shit a long time ago. I've lived through more fights than I had any right to, outlived more good men than I had any right to. If this is my time, this is my time. This shithole is as good as any shithole I've almost died in so far.'

Church looked over at him with a little appre-hension.

'But don't worry,' he laughed. 'That doesn't mean I'm not going to fight to my last breath. It's not that I want to die. I just stopped worrying about it. What we do—this job? It's not for worriers. Not for those who fear death. You know that, don't you?'

But Church didn't answer. And Grandad didn't say another word about it.

They drove for two hours. The meeting point was a destroyed village twenty miles from anything else. It was called Gurtesh, and was no more than a few dozen houses surrounded by open, empty farmland. Nowhere to hide, Church thought as they got close. But it still seemed odd to him they had chosen this place.

Gaz assured them it was close enough to the Albanian border that NATO had full flyover, and that they'd made sure there were no Serbian ground forces anywhere near the village. As good a spot as any, he'd said.

Still, Church wasn't taking any chances—and it didn't seem like Grandad was either.

They parked five klicks outside and decided to hoof it in, arriving twenty minutes before the designated meeting time and taking up an overlook position above the ruined town square.

It was a cobbled space with an old fountain in the centre that had been decimated by what looked like a mortar shell. An old church stood at one end of the square, its steeple missing, huge holes in its roof, its walls barely holding on. And the surrounding buildings —which could barely be called that—some of them were still standing, others reduced completely to rubble and ash.

These small villages were evacuated when the invasion began, but when the Serbs arrived, they gave them no quarter—dropping all the ordnance they had on them, robbing the homes, the businesses, everything for anything of value. Food, clothing, arms and munitions, jewellery, money—whatever they could get their hands on. The places were cleaned out, and all they left in their wake was destruction. No hope of rebuilding.

There was no dignity to war, and this small village had seen the worst of it.

Grandad and Church took up residence in a home with a straight line of sight to the fountain—the meeting point there—and as Church stared out into the darkness, he wondered if their contact was staring back.

'Right then,' Grandad said, taking a knee next to the window and laying the barrel of his M16 on the sill. 'You head down. I'll stay here and keep an eye on you.'

'You're kidding,' Church replied, staring at the old man in the darkness.

Grandad shook his head. 'If we both go down there and they drop a mortar on us, we're pretty much fucked, aren't we?'

'Yeah, and if *I* go down there and they drop a mortar on *me*, I'm fucked.'

'Yeah, but at least that way I'll be able to kill whoever did it. Avenge you, you know?'

'Oh, that's sweet of you,' Church replied. 'You know, they should put that in a fucking birthday card.'

Grandad grinned at him. 'If you want to send an old man out there, slow and frail as I am, then I'll do it. And you—the young, strong new recruit—can cower up here in this—' he looked around the room they were in '—little girl's bedroom.'

It was half destroyed, but the pink bedspread and charred stuffed toys told Church he was dead on.

'Oh great, now you're pulling at my heartstrings,' Church said, harrumphing. 'Don't worry—I'll go.'

He gave Grandad a nod and turned towards the door. But just before he got there, Grandad spoke again.

'I really *will* keep an eye on you, Church,' he said, serious as anything now. 'Neither of us are going to die tonight. I promise you that.'

Church paused and looked back at him. 'I appreciate that. But you shouldn't make promises you don't know you can keep. You said it—this job's not for those not ready for it.'

Church left the building with his own words echoing in his ears and walked cautiously into the empty, broken town square, checking his watch. Ten minutes to go now, and he wondered whether he was still alone.

He could hear no sound from an approaching engine

—nothing to indicate that a car, a tank, or a plane was incoming. And all he could do was wait.

He stood at the fountain, checking the alleys and doorways around him, drumming his fingers softly on the barrel of his M16, held at low-ready, his eyes straining to pick out shapes among the shadows—but it was the crunch of gravel and broken glass that first told him he wasn't alone.

His rifle came up quickly and homed in on a shape emerging from a narrow road to his left.

A man stepped into the moonlight wearing a long, thick woollen coat, his hands in leather gloves, held high at the sides of his head.

The hair above his ears was shaved off, and across the top of his skull it was short. He had wide-set eyes and high cheekbones, a clean-shaven jaw and thin lips.

'Are you who I'm supposed to be meeting?' he asked. His English was good.

Church stared down the sights of his rifle at the man. They were trained on his heart.

'Well, you're pretty fucked if I'm not, aren't you?' he said back.

The man paused at his voice. 'You're English?' he called out, his brow furrowing, confused by Church's presence.

'Not quite,' Church said back. 'But close enough. Come out here where I can see you properly. And keep it relaxed. Nothing stupid.'

The man seemed hesitant now but walked out

further into the open. Only because he was at gunpoint, Church thought.

'Pull back the hems of your coat slowly and turn,' Church ordered.

Gaz had told them the terms of the meet stated the contact had to be unarmed—and if he wasn't, Church was in the right mind to shoot him then and there.

But as the man gave him a full look at his waist and belt, he could see that he wasn't carrying a weapon—at least not one he could easily reach for.

'Satisfied?' the man called back, completing his circle and dropping his coat.

'Not yet,' Church said. 'You've got thirty seconds. You tell me who you are and you give me something actionable, or I'm going to drop you right here and throw you in one of those mass graves along with all the Kosovans you killed.'

The contact stared back at him, taking umbrage at the comment.

'My name is Colonel Dragan Markovich,' he said proudly. 'And how do *I* know that *I* can trust *you*? That your word is worth anything at all, Englishman?'

'You don't.' Church kept his rifle trained on Markovich's heart. 'But the very fact that you're here tells me something about you.'

'And what's that?' Markovich asked back, narrowing his eyes further.

'That you're all out of other options,' Church said. 'And we're all you've got.'

SIX

PRESENT DAY

IT WAS past midday by the time they pulled into the courtyard of the farm.

Hallberg killed the engine and Church leaned his head back against the headrest, staring up at the stone building in front of him. At Mitch's house. They weren't housemates. Church lived in a small stone shepherd's hut a few hundred yards up the hill, just inside the tree line.

It was one room, modest, cold in the winter and damp and blistering hot in the summer. But not a soul in the world knew that he lived there, apart from the woman sitting next to him, the man in the house watching them through the windows, and his sister, who, strangely, he was thinking of at that moment. He always seemed to in the times where he didn't know what to do. Because she always did.

'You were talkative,' Hallberg remarked, staring out at the open grass field in front of them.

Church just hummed a response.

'Barely said a word all drive. And it was a long drive,' Hallberg said with a sigh, trying to lighten the mood.

'Sorry,' Church said. 'I'm just tired.'

'Yeah,' she said. 'But you were tired when I picked you up from the airport and you still talked. What's going on? As soon as you stepped into that crime scene, it's like a switch flipped in your brain.'

Church turned his head towards her slowly. 'Have you ever been in war?'

Hallberg stared back at him, paling a little at the question.

She cleared her throat gently. 'No,' she said.

He nodded. 'Talk to me when you have, and you'll know why I don't want to.'

She looked down then, apologetic almost, and Church reached for the door handle. As he touched it, Hallberg reached out and put her hand on his other wrist, squeezing gently.

'I may not have been to war,' she said, 'but I can listen if there's anything you need to talk about, okay? Anything.'

Church stared down at her hand.

Part of him wanted to take it and squeeze it, but a bigger part of him just wanted it off, wanted to be away, to be on his own.

'I'll bear that in mind,' he said, then pulled himself

free of her grasp and got out of the vehicle, turning back to look at her through the open door. 'Don't call me for a while,' he said to her.

She looked a little forlorn at that, but understood.

After the last few days, after what he'd just done, and then what she dragged him into, it seemed like she understood that he needed some time to put himself back together.

The strangest thing was, that Church never felt more at home than when he was in the shit, and that this— coming home to a quiet place—was the thing that he found the hardest.

And yet, before he returned to the battlefield, no matter what kind it was, he needed just a moment to himself.

A moment to miss it, almost.

Hallberg nodded to him once more, knowing that there was nothing else she could say, that there was nothing else to say, and waited for him to close the door.

He did, his stare unflinching, his eyes locked on hers, and then, slowly, she started the car and turned it around, heading towards the gate.

The front door to the farm creaked open behind him, and he heard the crunch of footsteps on the path.

'You're alive, then?' Mitch called out. Church didn't need to turn to look at him to know what he looked like. He was tall and wiry, greying hair and blue eyes.

'Just about,' Church replied.

He had told Hallberg he was exhausted, and though it was just a line, he really was tired.

'You want a cuppa?' Mitch asked, reading the tension in his friend. Even from the back.

Church turned to him, seeing him smiling, and though he'd already decided that he was going straight to his hut, straight to bed, he found himself walking towards Mitch instead.

Inside the farmhouse, it was warm. Mitch had a fire burning and filled the kettle, setting it on top of the wood stove for the water to warm.

Mitch settled into an armchair and Church took a spot on the sofa opposite.

'What's on your mind?' Mitch asked, reading his brother.

Church looked up at him, and though the knee-jerk was to say nothing, he knew that perhaps Mitch was the only other person in the world who understood what he was going through right now.

'Did you see the bombing on the news?' he asked.

Mitch nodded.

'I was there,' Church said.

'When it went off?' Mitch asked, a little surprised by that.

Church shook his head. 'No. After it happened—just after I landed—and Hallberg took me there. A little detour.'

Mitch let out a soft breath. 'And why would she do that? I thought the whole idea was to keep your involvement with Interpol quiet.' He shrugged to himself, the sting he felt from being left out of the operation that he was running with Hallberg still apparent. 'I mean, that was the reason that you didn't ask me to come with you, wasn't it?'

'It was,' Church said, putting his hands on his knees, wishing he'd turned down the tea now. But he hadn't, and he was here, and he needed to get his thoughts out. Needed to hear them aloud to straighten them.

'It's not just the bomb that went off in Birmingham,' Church said, 'the one that happened in Rotterdam, in Vienna. They're all linked.'

Mitch considered that. 'And Julia thought that it would make a good first date, taking you to the bomb site.'

Church sort of smiled, sort of grimaced at the same time. 'Leave that out, yeah?' he said, laughing sardonically. 'And no, she just wanted a second opinion is all.'

'And judging by how cagey you're being, you didn't want to give it?'

Church prided himself on how difficult he was to read, but Mitch seemed to have an uncanny ability to do it.

Maybe it was because they spent so much time together. Maybe it was because he and Mitch were so alike, had lived the same life, had been through the same shit, their minds working now in the same way— both broken in a fashion.

Church wondered what to say again, wanting to shut down, wanting to withdraw, wanting to run. But he didn't know how much longer he could keep that feeling that something was wrong inside him.

He needed to know if he was crazy or if there was

something there—something tangible, something worth obsessing over.

'It felt familiar,' Church said after a long time. The water was almost boiled now.

Mitch got up and went into the kitchen to fetch two cups. 'How so?' he called from the other room.

'I don't know,' Church replied as Mitch came back in, carrying them.

Two battered white mugs that had come with the house, their patterns or pictures long since faded, just dim afterimages on the porcelain.

'They all seem familiar,' Mitch said. 'When I think back, everything seems to sort of blend into one. Every gun I've ever held, every pack I've ever carried, every pair of boots I've ever worn through, every plane I've ever been in, every man I've ever killed, every body I've ever stepped over. It's no wonder that looking at that stirred some shit up inside you. It happens to the best of us. There's no escaping it.'

'It's not just that,' Church said, his brow creasing as Mitch filled the cups and brought him one. 'There was something more familiar about it—not just a flash of something that happened before. It was something I feel like I've seen, something I feel like I lived.'

Mitch stood above him, holding the cup in his hands, staring down at Church. 'Where?'

Church looked up at Mitch then, and wondered the answer to a question he'd never asked him.

Mitch was a little older than he was, had been in the service just as long. 'Were you in Kosovo?' he asked.

Mitch sort of bristled at that, as though it was a secret that he always thought he would carry with him to his grave.

'Maybe,' he said. 'Were you?'

Church couldn't help but smirk, meeting his cautious eyes. 'Maybe,' he said.

Mitch shook his head then and took a sip, wincing at the heat.

'Jesus Christ, that's hot,' he muttered, touching his knuckles to his lips and turning away. He put the cup down on the arm of the chair and eased himself down, ageing and tired, just a little further down the road than Church himself.

'I was there,' Church said. 'Fresh into the service, about a year. Total shit show.'

'Tell me about it,' Mitch muttered, leaning on his elbow, putting his hand over his mouth.

His eyes glazed over as he dug into his memories, thinking about it.

He seemed to come back to life then and looked up at Church. 'And you think that this bombing has some sort of link to Kosovo?'

'I don't know,' Church said back to him. 'But that's how it felt. I mean, the way that the KLA worked, the things they did, the way that they built their bombs and the way they used them. The way that they terrorised the Serbs for what they did.'

Mitch nodded slowly, though he didn't seem convinced. 'I understand,' he said. 'But do you really think that there's a link? That this is the work of the

KLA? That was twenty-five years ago, Sol. It's a reach. Hell, more than a reach, isn't it?'

Church had to think about that. He'd only just touched down from Eastern Europe, and though Belarus was a long way from Serbia, they were still Eastern Europe, had the same feel.

'Maybe I'm just projecting,' he said. 'I was in Belarus less than twenty-four hours ago. In the shit. So I don't know, maybe it's just stirring up old memories, you know?'

'Yeah, maybe,' Mitch said, his face conflicted, as though he were feeling the same pain, the same difficulty that Church was. 'I think there's only one question to ask,' Mitch said.

'And what's that?'

'Is it going to keep you up at night? This thing— thinking about Kosovo, this bomb, thinking that there's a link, that it's the same thing?'

Church just stared back at him.

Mitch risked another sip of his tea, and this time it seemed a little more palatable. 'It's probably nothing,' he said. 'But if it's eating at you, then let's take a look. We can work it through together, tease it apart, and once you see that these two things are completely uncon- nected, you can just get on with living.'

Church stared back, and had to admit he was thankful for Mitch then.

Just telling him to let it go, telling him that he was crazy, wouldn't help, wouldn't fix this.

No, not the way their brains were wired. Not the

way they were wired now. It would have eaten at
Church. It would have been a little black mass festering
at the back of his mind.

He would have gone to bed thinking about Kosovo,
not slept, thought about it all night. Creating links,
creating ideas that weren't there.

They would only dig him further and further into his
own head. At least this way, if he and Mitch started to
unpack it, he would see, as Mitch said, that it was
nothing—that he was just projecting.

It would focus him.

It would allow him to move past it, to put Kosovo
back where it belonged, in the locked box, in the abyss
of his brain.

And then he'd lock Belarus in a box just like it and
cast that into the darkness as well.

SEVEN

TWENTY-FIVE YEARS AGO

CHURCH AND GAZ stood at the edge of the field, watching as Darko and his men pumped bullets into the hay bales in front of them.

They had their fingers in their ears, waiting for the barrage to stop. Plumes of dust and hay erupted into the air, most of the paper targets that had been set up remaining untouched. Church had his own thoughts about their accuracy and efficiency, but it was clear what Gaz was thinking too, by the look of frustration on his face.

Church wouldn't have trusted any of them to hit a stationary target at twenty yards, let alone a moving one. And sure, you could blame the shitty AK knock-offs they were firing with—the M70 was hardly a prime weapon—but still, Church figured it was about ten percent equipment and ninety percent user error.

When Grandad gave them the wave to stop and lower their weapons, the men did so—a few holding out, wanting to empty their magazines.

Gaz removed his fingers from his ears and stretched out his jaw. He'd been clenching it, he was so unhappy with their performance.

'What were you saying?' he asked Church, his voice hushed.

Church cleared his throat. Before the men had started shooting, he'd been explaining to Gaz how the meeting the night before had gone.

'His name's Dragan Markovich,' Church said. 'He's a colonel with the Serbian Army.'

'What do we think? Is he full of shit? Trying to pull one over on us?' Gaz asked flatly.

Church wasn't sure yet. The man had been withdrawn and had provided just a few pieces of intel that NATO were already investigating—some plans for troop movement and supply lines, where the Serbian Army were going to push into next, and what kind of ordnance they had at their disposal. It was nothing NATO probably didn't already know, but Markovich was just testing the waters. If he gave up the prize too early, he would have no leverage. He was smart. Church had to give him that.

He'd provided enough information that NATO could make a positive step, but not so much that the Serbs would be dealt a killing blow right away—and they would know somebody inside their own ranks had flipped. It was a fine line for Markovich to walk. For

Church and for NATO, there was no risk. But for him, it was everything.

He'd watched as his own army had raided and pillaged, as they raped and killed. And if they knew he was trying to defect—trying to sell out his own people for the Kosovans—the Serbs would waste no time in doing to him what they had done to those people. To his family, too.

He was risking his life even meeting with Church and the KLA—let alone feeding them information they could use against his own people.

'He passed the sniff test,' Church said. 'He didn't try to shoot me in the back when I walked away, so that's a good sign.'

Gaz raised an eyebrow. 'You turned your back on him?'

Church looked over, a little indignant. 'Just a figure of speech, Captain.'

Gaz grumbled a little.

Looking out across Darko's men, Church thought he was probably thinking the same thing he was—that even with all the intel in the world, trying to organise this rabble into some kind of useful fighting force was a tall order.

'All right then,' Gaz said with a little sigh. 'Once NATO confirm that his intel isn't total dog shit, we'll set up another meeting and see what he really wants to trade. See how important getting his family out of this place really is. I'll keep you updated.'

His eyes lingered on Church then for a few seconds

—his face, the lack of lines there, his junior age perhaps —telling Gaz he wasn't quite cut out for a job of this magnitude.

But if that's what he was thinking, he didn't say it.

From in front of them, Grandad's voice echoed out: issuing move-and-cover drills to Darko's men.

'Half of you line up behind that foxhole over there on the left,' he said. 'Half of you behind this one. One man in each at a time.'

Darko's men all looked at each other as though the instructions were so complex they'd need an interpreter and a degree to work them out.

But eventually—begrudgingly, even—they started to divide themselves.

'Shooter on the right calls "cover",' Grandad said, pointing to the first foxhole nearest him. 'Shooter on the left lays down covering fire. Shooter on the right moves up, takes up defensive position.' He pointed to a lone hay bale halfway between the foxholes and the targets. 'When he's there, the second shooter on the left yells "cover". First shooter lays down covering fire while second shooter advances to target. Any questions?'

Seemed simple enough to Church, but as he looked at Darko's men, all stared at each other with dumb looks on their faces—realising that perhaps these basic military tactics were a little beyond them.

Darko, however, at the front of the line, seemed to understand well enough.

'Do we look stupid to you?' he called out.

Church didn't even think most of Darko's men knew

what he'd said, but they all fell in line, laughing behind him anyway.

Grandad looked over at Gaz as though unsure whether or not to answer that. Even if it was rhetorical, there was a pretty clear answer.

But picking a fight with Darko was the easy part. Getting them trained—which was the mission—was trickier.

'All right then,' Grandad said. 'Show me.'

Darko glanced over his shoulder at his men and, grinning, climbed down into the first hole—not even getting down onto his knees.

He just sort of crouched awkwardly, his entire body practically above the lip of the shallow ditch. He wasn't prepared to get down into the mud, then. This whole exercise was moot.

'Ready?' Grandad asked, knowing the answer was no. 'Go!'

But if he expected Darko to yell the word *cover*, he was mistaken. The man leapt from the hole with a fierce roar and charged straight towards the paper target, dropping his rifle to his hip halfway there and letting out a stream of continuous fire.

He kept advancing until he was just a few feet short and emptied the entire magazine into the paper target at point-blank range, obliterating it. He kept his finger pinned until the magazine ran dry and the mechanism clicked on an empty chamber, then turned and lifted his rifle over his head, victorious. His men raised their fists and whooped and hollered for him.

Grandad advanced on him swiftly, surprising Church —as he often did—with his speed.

He reached up and ripped the rifle out of Darko's hands before he even knew he was there.

'What the bloody hell was *that*?' he snapped at him.

Darko rounded on the man.

'What?' he barked. 'I got the job done. That's what you wanted, isn't it?'

'I wanted to teach you something resembling a skill that might keep you and your men alive,' Grandad snapped.

Darko looked down at himself then and patted his body as though emphatically checking for wounds.

'Huh. I seem pretty alive, no?'

'Yeah,' Grandad said, shoving the rifle into his chest. 'It's much easier when they're not shooting back. You try that out there, you're going to get yourself killed—and I'm not going to be around to wipe your arse.'

Grandad released the rifle then, and Darko let it fall to the ground between them.

He stepped over it, squaring up to the old man. He was three for three so far. The only one left was DD, and Church was sure he was probably starting to feel left out.

This Darko guy was cruising for a fight—desperate for one—and Church and the others were probably the only ones in the camp who were willing to give it to him.

They were trying to preserve a fragile peace, but it would only stretch so far.

Still, Grandad didn't deserve whatever Darko was desiring to dish out—and Darko definitely wasn't expecting what Grandad was going to give him in return.

Gaz nudged Church in the arm then.

'Go sort that out,' he said tiredly, 'before Grandad breaks his nose and turns this whole fucking thing into a bloodbath.'

Church surged forward, not needing any more encouragement.

He was the biggest of anyone there, and he found that usually worked one of two ways. Either it was a sort of nuclear deterrent—he was intimidating enough to stop others from wanting to fight just in case he got stuck in. Or the other way was that because he was big, men like Darko took that as some kind of biological affront, and they were desperate to prove their mettle. Or perhaps just the size of their balls.

As Church came forward, Darko's eyes flicked to him, and he was pretty sure he knew which way it would go. He put his hands up to try the civil approach, but before he could even open his mouth, Darko launched himself forward and slung a hook into his jaw.

Church saw it coming and managed to tense at the last second—but the blow still landed hard and sent him back a step.

He cursed himself, knowing he should've seen it coming.

Darko had told him he'd come for him just the night before, and Church had no one to blame but himself for not expecting him to make good on that threat. But Church was bigger. He was stronger. And it wasn't the first time he'd been punched in the face.

He regained himself just out of arm's reach and waited for his eyes to refocus.

He could taste blood in his mouth and watched as Darko stood there massaging his knuckles, looking out at his men. Here, he really was King Dick, and Church figured because he was Ismet's son and the leader of this band, no one was willing to put him in his place.

The one thing he didn't realise was that Church didn't give two shits about any of that.

'You get one of those,' Church told him, holding up a finger. 'Now—you want to get back in that fucking hole and do the drill properly, or you want to see what happens when you try for a second?'

Darko seemed to think about that for a moment—then decided.

Church could see in his eyes which way Darko decided. And was glad of it.

The man lumbered forward, winding up another haymaker, and slung it—aiming for Church's teeth this time.

It was a common misconception people had—that because Church was big, he'd be slow too. But he wasn't. And he ducked to the left, letting Darko's hand sail straight over his shoulder.

He could've cleaned him out right there—put him

down with a single punch, broken his jaw, cracked a rib. Hell, he could've put his heel through the side of the man's knee and made sure he walked with a limp for the rest of his life to remind him not to be such a fucking arsehole.

But giving someone the gift of humility was often more effective than pain.

So instead of putting his fist through his face, he threw it up across the man's chest and stood up behind him, throwing his left arm over his shoulder and around his neck, clamping him into a sleeper hold. Before Darko could even regain his balance, Church flexed his bicep, crushing the carotid artery in his neck and cutting off the blood supply to his brain. He could feel his forearm cut into the man's larynx, all but closing the trachea.

Darko couldn't breathe, and he wasn't getting oxygen to his brain—which meant he'd lose consciousness in seconds.

He seemed to realise that. Or perhaps he just had even less fortitude than Church gave him credit for—because he slipped into unconsciousness almost instantly.

Church fixed his eyes on Darko's men, who had all fallen silent—their laughter extinguished as quickly as Darko had been.

Unceremoniously, he let go and dropped the man to the floor in a heap.

Church took a step towards them and suddenly their rifles all climbed a few inches—not to attention, not pointed at Church, but halfway there. Church froze and looked back at them, not wanting to escalate further.

As sure as he was that he could take any one of them in a one-on-one fight—and even with how poor their aim was from this distance—all twenty of them firing at once… he was sure at least one bullet would find its target.

But luckily, Darko raked in a sudden breath and started hacking and coughing, clawing his way to his hands and knees as he came back to the world.

Holding onto his throat, he staggered to a wayward stance and took a few steps back towards his men before turning to face Church—making sure he was out of reach before he spoke.

He met Church's eyes now. The anger that had always been there still burned—but it was tinged with something else. Something Church hoped Darko would carry with him.

Fear.

Fear born from the knowledge that he wasn't untouchable.

'We were winning this war before the SAS arrived,' he spat, cutting the air with his hand. 'We don't need you here.'

He turned to his men and banged on his chest with a closed fist.

'We have God on our side. We fight for our home-land. We fight for our honour—and that is more than enough. But I wouldn't expect *you* to understand what that's like.'

Instinctively, Church felt his ire rise—his fists locking at his sides.

It seemed like Darko hadn't quite gotten the message.

Maybe he would break his jaw after all.

Humility hadn't seemed to set in yet. So maybe a dose of pain would help the medicine go down.

But before he could cross the distance, there was somebody else in between them. Church did a double take—the tunnel vision he'd had a moment before now filled with the face he'd been searching for for the last twenty-four hours.

The woman with the blue eyes was there, looking right at him.

Her hair was tied back, her face angular, her lips full and pink—cracked with dehydration.

She had her hands out at her sides as though protecting Darko, and Church, seeing this, let his hands open too.

No words passed between them, but Church understood the message clearly enough.

His gaze drifted beyond Darko and the men, and he saw the hunched figure of Ismet standing at the corner of his house, bracing himself against the wall. Church realised it had to be more than coincidence that this woman and he had shown up at the same moment.

She held her fierce look for a few moments longer, talking Church down with just those pale blue eyes— eyes that looked like they had seen a thousand years' worth of pain. Eyes determined to see no more.

And then she pulled them away and began pushing Darko back towards his men. And when he seemed to be walking under his own steam, she turned back once more, approaching Church.

He felt a little surge of nerves—fearing the dressing-down from this stranger more than anything Darko could have done.

'You shouldn't cross him,' she said, her English perfect but cut with the accent of her homeland.

'I'm not worried about Darko,' Church said back.

'You should be. If he knows he can't beat you in a fair fight, he'll find a way to do it that isn't fair.'

'Well, if he comes into our tent at night and tries to slit my throat, he'll be in for a rude awakening himself,' Church said—without realising just how cold that threat sounded until it had already left his mouth.

The woman in front of him steeled herself, lifting her chin bravely.

'You men and your determination to turn everything into a pissing contest,' she said. 'I'm just trying to save anybody from getting hurt. We're already fighting the Serbs. We don't need to fight each other too.'

Church noted her diction—the words with which she spoke—marking her as someone with a better education than a tiny village in the far reaches of Kosovo would afford.

'Your English is perfect,' Church said. 'I'm guessing you're not from here.'

'I'm from here,' she said back, the indignation clear

in her response. 'I just left to get an education. Is that a crime?'

'No,' Church said. 'It's commendable.'

'Oh, is it? Why? Because this place has nothing to offer? Because this place is so terrible?'

She gestured around at the sprawling farmland—the picture of pastoral peace and tranquillity. Beautiful on any other day. Beautiful on this one, despite the war.

'That's not what I meant,' Church replied.

She scoffed at him and shook her head.

'Just leave Darko alone,' she said. 'If you give him a wide berth, it makes all of our lives easier.'

'Makes *his* life easier, you mean,' Church said, looking up at Ismet at the corner of the house.

She followed his gaze to the old man, then looked back at him.

'Both of ours,' she said, turning her back on Church and striding away. 'Darko's my brother.'

EIGHT

PRESENT DAY

CHURCH'S SISTER was the only real family he had left in the world.

Nanna was older than he was and much, much wiser, and she never failed to remind him of that. She knew that if she didn't call, Church wouldn't call her.

So she made sure to call.

A lot.

Made sure to get him out of that hut, away from the farm and into civilisation.

He had been dead for 10 years, and she'd never forgive him for that. He hadn't known her daughters growing up, and Nanna was going to make sure that he didn't miss anything more.

Her youngest, Mia, had just turned 14 and was giving Nanna, like any teenager, absolute hell. Though she seemed to be managing it well. The superhero that she was.

She'd recently split up with a piece of shit husband, a cheater and liar, and now she was tackling raising her two teenagers almost alone.

Church had offered to pull off his fingernails, remove his teeth, and do all manner of other things that Nanna laughed at as though they were a joke.

Church was completely serious.

He told Nanna that nothing cleared a man's head like having a zip tie ripped tight around his testicles and left there for a few days. And while she said yes, that probably would have the desired effect, she didn't want to, quote, 'make things worse'.

Church didn't see how that was possible. But if there was one thing in the world he was afraid of, it was crossing his sister.

Church stopped outside her home, bringing his Land Rover Defender to rest in the centre of London, and got out.

Just months earlier, he had been in this exact spot overlooking the park. And had moved heaven and earth to get to Nanna, taking on a fleet of plain clothes police officers to get to her before his enemies had.

And now he was back here again, strolling up to her front door like it had never happened at all.

He shook the memories off, heavy as they seemed to be these days, and mounted the steps and knocked. Though before he even got his knuckles to the wood, she opened it, scowling at him.

'You're late,' she said.

'There was traffic,' Church replied.

'It's London. There's always fucking traffic. Leave earlier,' she told him, grabbing him by the arm and pulling him inside.

It wasn't a party, they were just having dinner, the four of them—Church, Nanna, Mia and Lowri. But she was right, he was late, and it hadn't been the traffic.

He took a few wrong turns, which he never did. Missed a few green lights, which he never did. And once, he had looked up and had no idea where he was. Which never happened. And it was because Kosovo was still invading his every waking moment. He could see the car bomb in Birmingham in perfect clarity in his mind and had been trying to understand what felt so wrong about it.

And there was a laundry list building for him.

Hallberg was correct. It hadn't been a grand result, not hundreds dead, but Church knew that he was also right that it had happened exactly as it was supposed to. That if the only people who died were in that BMW and in the Skoda, then they were the only ones that were supposed to.

Nanna led Church through into the kitchen, where she had a large glass of wine poured for herself, the bottle next to it, and without a word, she put it in the fridge and poured him a glass of water instead.

He'd been on the wagon for a while. Not that he'd ever titled himself as an addict, but there had been dark days, and many of them after he'd 'died'. So a rose by any other name and all that shit.

She leaned against the fridge and stared at him. 'How have you been?'

'Fine,' Church replied.

'How have you really been?' she asked.

He smiled a little. 'Getting by.'

She nodded at that. 'The girls will be glad to see you.'

'I'll be glad to see them,' Church said, not lying.

'They miss you,' she said. 'Now that they know you're alive, they want to get to know you. But prepare yourself; Keith told them what you used to do for a living. What you really used to do.'

Church stiffened a little. Was this guy trying to get his nuts zip tied?

'When I wouldn't tell them,' she said, 'they started asking him and well, to get them off his back... he said that you were in the service and well, just prepare yourself. They're going to ask today.'

Church felt his hands start to curl into fists.

The last thing he wanted to do was to talk about his career, not when he already couldn't get it out of his mind.

'But you don't have to,' Nanna said. 'I told them that you wouldn't want to, just... I wanted to let you know that they're going to ask.'

'That's fine,' Church said stiffly. 'I'll give them the short and sharp version.'

Nanna let out a long sigh. 'So...' she said.

Church read the apprehension in that word and looked up at her.

'Sorry,' he said. 'I don't think I'm going to be very good company today.'

'I'll let you in on a secret,' Nanna said, raising her eyebrows. 'You're never good company, but you're the only brother I've got, so I'm sort of stuck with you.'

Church couldn't help but smile at that. 'Yeah, well I'm glad you're my sister.'

'You should be,' she replied. 'I actually give a shit about you. Too bad it doesn't go both ways.'

'There's nothing I wouldn't do for you or the girls,' Church said, a lot more gravely than he had intended.

Nanna shrank a little bit. 'I know,' she said. 'I was joking. I know you love us. I know that you just...'

She sort of trailed off, but was saved by the sound of the stairs creaking.

They both looked over towards the door and the girls came into the kitchen.

Spotting Church and smiling, they walked over to him and hugged him. Almost awkwardly. He was still a stranger to them. This hulking legend that their mother had told them once upon a time had gone off to war and never come back.

And for the last ten years, that's what they believed.

But now here he was, back from the dead, and judging by how tentatively they approached him, a little bit frightening because of it.

'Why don't you go set the table, girls?' Nanna said.

'I'm just talking to your Uncle Solomon. Boring adult stuff.'

They eyed the pair of them, sensing the adult nature of the conversation, and though Mia, the youngest, lingered—seemed to want to ask whether or not Church had brought her something for her birthday, or perhaps lay one of the questions that Nanna had warned him about on him—Lowri knew better and steered her sister away towards the living room.

'I did bring her a gift,' Church said, taking a guess. 'I left it in the car.'

He realised then that it was sitting on the passenger seat.

He didn't have a clue what to get her, and with no bank account or debit card, his ability to shop effectively—and online—was null and void.

He also had no idea what teenage girls liked and all the things he liked he was sure that Nanna would be remiss for her to receive. And Mitch had been no help at all, either. Still, he had done his best and brought her a box containing a paracord lanyard that could be hung around the neck.

It wasn't much of a fashion statement, but what it did do was house a three-inch, pointed stainless steel hair stick that he had hammered out of a BBQ skewer he'd found in Mitch's shed. It sat neatly inside the lanyard with a rounded handle, completely hidden, but if drawn, was easy to plunge into the eye of anyone that might be giving her trouble.

Of course, he'd packed the spike separately, fearing what Nanna would say if he just handed it over to Mia.

He would give the spike to Nanna and allow her to decide whether or not Mia should have it. In his mind, all girls—especially in the city—should have some way to defend themselves. But he figured that just giving her a straight-up knife might have been a little too on the nose.

This way at least she could carry it and not think about it until she needed it.

Nanna stared back at him as he thought about it.

'That's fine,' she said, before he could even tell her what the present was. 'I got her something from you. Thought it might just be easier.' She whispered, holding her hand to the side of her mouth.

Church smiled at that, a little disappointed, but also understanding completely.

'Well, you can have a look at the gift and then decide whether to give it to her. It's probably not right anyway.'

He cleared his throat then, squirming under her gaze. She was the only person in the world who made him feel small.

'So...' he said, stumbling over his words.

Nanna was watching him intensely, decoding her brother as she always did.

'There's something weighing on you,' she said without warning.

'Then there's always something weighing on me,' he replied.

She pursed her lips and then took a sip of wine.

'What are you doing for work now?'

He began to shrug, but then stopped himself, knowing it wouldn't fly.

'Some contracting,' he said. 'With Interpol.'

'Contracting with Interpol,' she repeated back, separating the words. 'Sounds mysterious? Ominous? Dangerous? All of the above?'

He offered a brief smile, but no explanation.

'Right,' she said. 'You know I've only just got you back, right?'

'I'm not going anywhere,' Church promised her.

She took a bigger sip of wine this time, as though not believing that he could promise that. And he didn't think he could either.

'You're not involved in all this bombing shit, are you? I've seen it on the news. Vienna, Rotterdam, now Birmingham. Please tell me you're not tangled up in that, Sol.'

He didn't mean to react, but he did, and it didn't escape Nanna.

'You are, aren't you? Jesus.'

'No,' he lied. 'I'm not, don't worry.'

'Bullshit,' she said, putting the wine glass down on the counter and coming to the island in the middle of the kitchen, bracing herself on her hands.

There was no escaping her gaze. She had the same dark blue, almost slate-coloured eyes he did. And he couldn't help but wonder if his were half as scary as hers when they fixed on someone.

'Tell me what's going on.'

'I can't,' Church said.

'Why not?' Nanna demanded.

Church could tell her that it was privileged information, that it was need to know.

He could say all manner of things, but he thought for once, that perhaps the truth might be better.

Especially now.

Especially with her.

'I can't tell you,' he said, meeting his sister's eye. 'Because I have no fucking clue what's going on. And that's the problem.'

NINE

TWENTY-FIVE YEARS AGO

Dawn was fast approaching when the station came into view.

Markovich's initial intel dump had pointed NATO to an old police station that the Serbs had reappropriated into a small fuel depot.

There was a cache of weapons and ammunition there, and resupply trucks stopped on the way to what was the front lines. Destroying the place would sever an artery in the Yugoslav Army's troop circulation. Blowing its fuel tanks would mean the Serbs would struggle to get needed provisions to the front lines by land—and with NATO dominating the air above, it would give the KLA a chance to dig their heels in.

But this deep behind enemy lines, it was asking for trouble.

Markovich was in charge of supply lines in this

region, and this would be the ultimate test of his loyalties. If they were about to walk into a firing squad, the
Serbians armed to the gills and ready for them, they'd
know he was playing both sides.

If they managed to get the drop on them and take the
station out, perhaps—just perhaps—he was worth something after all.

They were in three vehicles and moving fast.

Church and the lads were in the lead car, and Darko
and what he described as his seven best fighters were in
the two trailing behind. Gaz had wanted to move as just
a four, but Ismet had insisted that Darko go with them—
that he get to witness the operation, that he get to learn.

And he'd promised Gaz that Darko was under strict
instruction to stay in line.

Ismet had promised Gaz that he was going to follow
orders this time, but judging by the look on Gaz's face,
he didn't hold out much hope. None of them did.

The station was dark as they approached, and they
killed the headlights more than a kilometre out, driving
by just the light of the burgeoning dawn.

When they reached the position they'd agreed on—
just behind a ridge that would keep them out of sight of
the station, a few hundred metres from it—DD pulled
the car in and they killed the engine, climbing out.

They hardly had an arsenal at their disposal, but they
had brought a couple of long guns with them, and both
Gaz and Grandad were crack shots. They opened the
back and pulled the rifles out—a pair of L96A1s—

assembling them with ease even in the dark, affixing the optics and screwing the flash hiders onto the muzzles.

As Darko and his men formed up, they looked at the SAS soldiers in front of them. Church and the boys were in unmarked gear—standard surplus green and black—bearing no insignia, no flags, nothing that would give them away as what they really were.

Darko's men, on the other hand, wore jeans and boots, hoodies, old flak vests—the fabric frayed and peeling around the pads, the Kevlar plates showing through the threadbare equipment.

They looked on at Church and the others with resentment—contempt for their gear, for their training, for everything they were—but knowing this couldn't be done without them.

Gaz held up the bolt-action rifle and weighed it in his hands, looking out at Darko and his men.

'This is simple,' he said. 'Me and Grandad are going to keep overwatch. You lot are going to fall in behind DD and Church. You do what they say. You keep quiet, you stay low, and you don't go until I say go. All right?'

Darko stared at him, nostrils flaring, but didn't argue. Instead, he just nodded.

'Good. Now let's do this before the sun's up and they see us coming.'

His eyes lingered on Church and DD, waiting for confirmation that they knew what they were doing. It had been a long car ride, and they'd discussed it emphatically—reviewed maps, reviewed intel, made sure this shit was locked down tight. And Church was confident it was.

Markovich had said it was just a handful of men holding onto the station—a couple of former police officers, a few soldiers. Less than a dozen, he had guaranteed. And it was between supply runs and deployments, which came no more than once a week. They wouldn't be expecting anyone to hit them, let alone the KLA. If they could catch them asleep, there would be no resistance.

The plan was simple.

Grandad and Gaz would pick off anyone on patrol before they got in. They'd engage quickly, sweep through, search and destroy. Find their targets—munitions stockpile, fuel tanks—and blow them up with the C4 Church was carrying in his pack. If they got more than they bargained for with the men inside, they would pull back into the open, draw the Serbian forces out, and then Gaz and Grandad would do what they did best.

DD made a swivelling motion with his hand that told Church they were moving out, and then set off over the ridge.

Gaz and Grandad climbed up with them, finding positions to shoot from some fifty metres apart—giving them both a clear line of sight down to the station but making it impossible for any ordnance to take them out at the same time.

As they headed down the slope, Church took it in. There was one main building—low-slung, single-storey, concrete. A Soviet-style block.

It wasn't pretty, but it meant they wouldn't have to deal with tight stairwells and multiple floors.

There was a fenced-in compound at the back where the fuel tanks were, along with a single tanker they used to bring it in.

There were a handful of vehicles—police patrol cars and a couple of military jeeps—but no tanks, and nothing that should give them any problem.

DD led them in at a fast trot, and as they closed on their target, Church heard Gaz's voice in his earpiece.

'Area clear,' he said. 'No sign of movement. Clear to engage.'

DD touched the call button on his shoulder ahead of Church and whispered into the mic hanging from his helmet.

'Roger,' he said. 'Engaging target.'

'Good copy,' Gaz replied.

And that was it.

There was no more hanging around.

They were aiming for the front door, which they'd been informed wouldn't be locked—and though Church and DD moved quickly and silently, the men behind them jogged along panting, unfit smokers one and all, brawlers on their best day.

DD closed up on the door and Church took up a position behind him, feeling the heat of Darko's breath on the back of his neck as he crowded around— desperate to get inside, feeling as though being exposed was worse.

Church didn't have a chance to tell him to back off,

to give him space, before DD took hold of the handle, whispered the word 'entry', and ducked inside.

Church went on instinct and reflex then—the muscle memory kicking in—stepping into the interior and finding an empty square reception area. The door leading deeper into the station, towards the bullpen and the cells, was wedged open with a brick.

They swept the room—just the two of them.

'Clear,' DD whispered.

No patrols outside. No one standing guard. Church hoped that meant everyone inside was asleep. They'd be able to get this done without a single shot being fired.

They moved forward, Darko's men jostling and grunting behind them as they ran reluctantly into the station as well.

As they got into the corridor, they slowed—DD crouching and holding up a fist to signal they should stop.

Church pressed himself against the wall behind him and waited, listening for whatever DD had detected.

Could he hear something rustling in the distance?

A single bulb was burning at the far end of the corridor, making the whole place about as bright as it had been outside—a sort of pale light that stopped your eyes from focusing properly. But it was by far not the worst place Church had done something like this.

A toilet flushed then, somewhere beyond the wall ahead.

DD lowered his fist, returning it to the barrel of his rifle.

Church willed someone not to step into the corridor, but he knew doing that was only tempting fate—and a moment later, a man wearing a battered police jacket—dark blue with a furred collar—stepped into the corridor, buttoning up his trousers.

He looked up, bleary-eyed, down the corridor, and at first didn't seem to see them in the gloom. He blinked a few times, squinting and taking a step forward, checking whether he was still asleep or dreaming it. But then he realised that he wasn't.

His hand leapt to his hip, as though searching for a weapon that wasn't there. Despite his police jacket, he was wearing just a pair of underpants, and he was completely unarmed—which meant there was only one thing he could do.

'Shit,' DD said, as the man began to fill his lungs—knowing that the shot would be as loud as his call for help, but there was no other choice.

'Contact!' DD called out, loud and sharp, squeezing the trigger and putting three rounds into the guy, centre mass.

He convulsed backwards and tumbled to the ground.

'Shit, shit, shit!' DD yelled, standing up and turning round to head for open space. 'Fall back!' he shouted—but there was nowhere to go.

Church turned to go, but instead of finding space behind them, he found Darko and his seven men—all crowded so tightly into the corridor that it was a wall of bodies that couldn't be moved. A backstop that both Church and DD were going to get executed against.

'Fucking hell,' DD snapped, turning back towards the corridor and the man he'd just killed.

There were shouts echoing from all around now—the clamouring of bodies scrambling from bed and to arms.

'Move, move, move!' DD ordered, surging forward —the only direction they could go.

Church put his hand on DD's shoulder to let his brother know that he was right on his six, and they advanced together.

There were doors all down the length, and they stopped at each one, throwing them open and scanning the inside for any targets. The first two were empty storerooms—interrogation rooms, offices—and they kept moving. Darko and his men came up behind in a solid mass, aiming at everything and nothing, as though combatants were about to drop from the ceiling or pop up from the ground.

There might have been ten of them moving through that building, but there were only two who were going to accomplish this task. And Church couldn't help but wonder, deep in the back of his mind, whether this was what Darko wanted—that he wanted to push them into the jaws of death. Wanted them to die here and now so that he and his men could finally be rid of the chokehold he thought the SAS had over his people.

Church quashed that thought as DD threw open another door—and Church saw movement. DD opened fire and Church went with him, sweeping the room from right to left as DD took it left to right, carving out a path of bullets, putting down two men.

They seemed to be sleeping in what had once been the break room and kitchen area.

'Clear,' DD called, pulling back and moving on—near frantic now. Moving this fast, this recklessly, was suicidal. But there was nothing else for it. No other options. They had to get this done, and they had to get it done now—or at the very least, find another way out of this building.

There was a door at the end, just past the toilet the first Serb had come out of, and all they could do was blast through it.

'Popping stunny!' DD called, motioning Church past.

They moved like a well-oiled machine. Church pressed himself to the steel door at the end, cracking the handle and opening it a few inches while DD got to a knee and slung a stun grenade in across the tiles. He popped a second just after, and Church listened for the first detonation. It boomed beyond the metal and he threw the door wide, allowing DD to hurl one into the other side of the room.

Church pressed himself against the wall and DD flattened himself almost to the ground—which meant the one Serb waiting with his weapon trained on the door, blindly firing the moment it opened, sent a bullet straight over DD's head and into the chest of one of Darko's men.

He careened backwards and hadn't even touched the

ground before Darko's men launched forward and hammered their triggers. Church and DD could only hold themselves in cover as a stream of bodies moved over the top of them, an explosion of muzzle flash and fire filling the station.

Church opened his eyes and looked inwards, seeing a dozen bodies, all clamouring for cover. This had been the bullpen where the officers had sat at their desks— now repurposed into what looked like the main sleeping area. Darko's men filed in, a few of them taking fire, falling, stumbling, throwing themselves towards the nearest desks. Weak morning light filtered in through the high-set windows around the edges, and blood arced through the shafts, spraying the walls and the dusty glass with crimson.

Cries of pain echoed down the corridor as DD and Church finally got to their feet and pressed inward, wondering what the fuck had just happened—and if there was anything they could do to clean this mess up.

But before they even managed to make it inside, it was all over. There had been maybe six men in total. The rest—women and children.

Their families, Church thought.

The men had jumped up to defend their home, the women and children diving for cover—and as the gunfire ended, Darko's men claimed victory, their ranks thinned a little.

They cheered and held their rifles up, almost invisible in the heavy cloud of smoke drifting through the air.

DD looked around, listening to the sobs of the widows, and put his hand on his helmet.

'Jesus Christ,' he muttered, reaching to his shoulder. He touched the talk button and gathered himself before he spoke.

'Building secure,' he said slowly. 'But Gazza… it's a mess down here.'

'Say again,' Gaz ordered.

'It's clear,' DD said. 'But it's not good.'

'En route,' Gaz replied. 'Hold fast. And for fuck's sake, don't let Darko and those idiots do anything stupid.'

'Yeah,' DD said, turning to Church, the sombre look in his eyes. 'It's a little late for that.'

TEN

PRESENT DAY

CHURCH WAS SITTING at the kitchen table in his cottage, a sheet laid out across the entire surface, with three disassembled weapons in front of him.

At the back of the table was an HK417 battle rifle. In pieces to his left, his L119A1 Close Quarters Combat Carbine rifle, a compact fully-automatic rifle with a 10-inch barrel, commonly known as the C8 CQB. And on his right, and currently in his hands, was his disassembled Glock 17.

Taking care of his weapons was something that he'd always done.

The phrase 'take care of them and they'll take care of you' was drummed into him through his military career, and he had to admit it was one of the only universal truths that he completely accepted without any objection. Though it wasn't just good practice—it was also a form of meditation.

He didn't have to concentrate on what he was doing, but it took time to do right, and the repetitive, focused work gave him room to think, allowed his mind to detach from his body and begin to unpack everything that just seemed to be blended into one swirling mass inside his brain.

When his phone started ringing on the table next to him, he paused, the wire pipe cleaner inside the barrel spring of the Glock. He looked down at the small screen of the old flip phone and read the number, recognising it to be one he knew—one of the few who had his number to call.

He lowered the spring slowly, wondering what it was that she wanted, and reached over, opening the phone and setting it down, putting it on loudspeaker.

'Fletcher,' he said, almost cautious.

There was a little prickle on the back of his neck. Why was she calling him?

She never called.

Not unless she needed something, at least. And right now he didn't know what it was he could give, or that he wanted to give anything.

Anastasia Fletcher was a journalist he met in the DRC ten years ago for the first time, and one with whom he'd formed a tentative friendship. She'd helped him take down Walter Blackthorne and the rest of the unit that double-crossed him, but he didn't know if friend was the right word to call her.

Their relationship was more transactional, and if she was calling him, that meant she was looking to transact.

'Solomon,' she said brightly. 'How are you?'

'I'm fine,' he said, not bothering to ask how she was. It was all superficial anyway.

'I just thought I'd check in,' she went on after a few seconds.

'That's kind of you,' Church replied gruffly, again not offering any routine to the conversation. He wasn't much for the light patter. If she wanted something, he would rather she just came right up and said it.

And she seemed to sense that.

With a long sigh, she got down to brass tacks. 'It's not a social call,' she said.

'I'm shocked,' Church replied, setting the spring down and leaning closer to the phone, listening to her soft, quickened breath.

She cleared her throat a little and then said, 'Have you been watching the news lately, or are you still living in a cave?'

'The cave,' Church replied, playing dumb.

'Right. Well, I don't know if you've seen, but some-body seems to be blowing things up around Europe. And now in the UK too.'

'I heard about the bombings,' Church said absently. 'I didn't realise that was your kind of story.'

'My kind of story,' Fletcher said back, 'is any kind of story where there's a deeper truth being kept from the public.' She said it almost defensively. Defiantly.

'Right?' Church said. 'And what deeper truth do you

think is being kept from the public this time? And more importantly, what do I have to do with it?'

'Well,' she said, 'as many contacts as I have, you're one of the only ex-military special forces type guys that I know.'

'"One of"?' Church replied to her, raising his eyebrows.

'Well yeah, I tried Mitch first,' she said with a laugh. 'But he didn't pick up, so I guess I'm stuck with you.'

He thought about what Nanna had said in the kitchen, how Fletcher was using almost the same words.

'Yeah, that seems to be going around,' he said with a little laugh. 'So what exactly is it that you're trying to get out of me?'

'I don't know yet,' she said. 'That all depends.'

'On what?' Church replied. Apprehensive as he was about sharing war stories with his sister, with Mitch, with anyone, he was even more apprehensive about doing it with a journalist—especially one liable to splash his words across a dozen web pages.

'When did you start in the forces?'

'In the army or the forces specifically?' Church questioned her, trying to ascertain what it was she was getting at.

'Let's say forces, just for the hell of it,' she replied.

Church found that interesting, but he didn't know why yet. 'Ninety-eight.'

She let that hang for a moment, as if noting it down. ''98. Okay.'

And she hedged. Church leant sideways, putting his

elbow on the table, hand on his forehead and leaning his weight on it.

'You want to just get to the point?' he said.

'Kosovo.'

Church sat up now and stared at the phone, his eyes wide, heart beating a little harder. 'What about it?'

'I'm investigating the role that NATO played in the Kosovo conflict. Officially, they entered the war in March 1999, when Operation Allied Force started, but I think that, unofficially, they were there before that.'

'Do you?' Church said. 'That's strange.'

'Strange why?' Fletcher said.

'Because if NATO said something officially, I'd be inclined to believe it.'

She laughed unabashedly. 'Oh, would you? And all governments only say the truth and do exactly what they promise. And they definitely, definitely don't do things they say they're not going to. Hey, have you ever been to the DRC, by the way? I hear it's lovely this time of year.'

'Yeah,' Church said with a little sigh. 'I guess we're not fooling anybody these days.'

'No,' Fletcher said a little more sternly. 'We're not. So?'

'So what?' Church asked.

'Well, if NATO were unofficially involved in Kosovo before March 1999, my research is leading me to believe that perhaps they weren't the only ones.'

'You want to spell it out for me?' Church pressed her.

'You want to stop playing dumb?'

'Who says I'm playing?'

Fletcher laughed at that again. 'You're going to make me say it?'

'I am,' Church told her.

She let out a long breath. 'God, you know having a conversation with you is like pulling teeth, right?'

'I've been told,' Church said.

'Kosovo. 1999. Prior to the official launch of Operation Allied Force, prior to the bombings—were you in Kosovo? Were the SAS there?'

Church didn't know what to say, didn't know if he could say anything. He knew he shouldn't.

'What would it matter if the SAS was there?' Church replied. 'Hypothetically.'

'I don't know yet,' Fletcher said. 'I'm just digging and I need to know more. And everybody I've spoken to so far has been about as helpful as you are being right now.'

'Well, maybe that's a sign to leave it alone,' Church said.

'Yeah, in my experience,' Fletcher replied, 'it's usually a sign that I shouldn't leave it alone. That there is something buried. Something to exhume.'

'There are lots of things buried in Kosovo,' Church said. 'A lot of things that shouldn't be buried. But I don't know if you're going to like what you find if you go digging around there.'

She seemed to glean context from his words, from

the coldness of them, from the death and the weight that
they carried.

Church was the one then who couldn't help but ask
a question. If this was eating at Fletcher from one side,
he had to admit that it was eating at him from the other.

'What do these bombings have to do with Kosovo?'
Church asked lightly, trying to pass it off as idle
curiosity.

She chuckled a little under her breath. 'Well,' she
said, 'if you tell me yours, I'll tell you mine.'

Church considered that for probably longer than he
should have. Probably long enough to give away the
game.

'I don't know anything,' he told her. 'And as terrible
as the Kosovo war was... I'm sorry to disappoint you,
Fletcher. You wasted a phone call,' he said, reaching for
the spring of his Glock 17 once more. 'Because I wasn't
there.'

ELEVEN

TWENTY-FIVE YEARS AGO

By the time Gaz and Grandad arrived, Darko and his men were already sorting out the dead.

He'd lost two of his own—but more Serbs. Six in that room alone, plus the three that DD and Church had taken, made nine total, leaving just their wives and kids alive.

As they began separating the dead, dragging them away and investigating the rest of the station, it became clear that the haphazard shooting had been no better today than it had been on the range—and that at least three of the men they'd shot were still breathing.

This, though, seemed to please them more than anything.

It was hard to know what to focus on—what to try to stop.

Deeper in the station, Darko's men had discovered

the cell block, and the shouts of indignation drew Church that way like moth to flame. As he stepped through the heavy doors and into the concrete corridor, he could see what Darko and his men were shouting about.

There in the cells were prisoners. All dead. And not by humane means.

They'd been tortured to death. Church could see missing fingers and fingernails, kneecaps broken. Teeth pulled with pliers. Eyes so bloodied and swollen that no doubt they'd been beaten to blindness.

These men had suffered a fate worse than death, and Church could see no single killing blow—just a combination of savage beatings, starvation, dehydration.

The Serbs had taken distinct pleasure in ending the lives of the KLA fighters they captured, and Church didn't have to be a genius to see what was coming next.

As the first of Darko's men surged back towards the bullpen and the wounded Serbs, the thought seemed to spread like swarm intelligence: what the Serbs had done to them, they would do back—two-fold.

Church went after them and was about to call out and intervene when Gaz appeared and let out a quick whistle, grabbing Church's attention.

Church took another look at Darko's men, watching as they gathered up the wounded soldiers—much to the protests of the wives, who clutched at their bloodied bodies—and began dragging them towards the cell block by their arms, by their legs, the third by his hair.

He called out, clutching at his gut shot, and left a trail of blood as one of Darko's brutes dragged him along.

'Jesus Christ,' Gaz said, looking around the room.

Church pulled his eyes away from what was about to happen and set them on his captain.

'You find the fuel tanks yet?' Gaz asked, knowing full well that Church hadn't, considering where he was standing. Gaz reached up and snapped in front of Church's eyes to focus him. 'Hey—on mission,' he said. 'Church. Fuel tanks. Yeah?'

But Church's eyes had once more drifted back to the pleas for mercy coming from the Serbian soldiers.

Executing them would be one thing—but Church couldn't imagine what Darko's lot were about to inflict.

Gaz reached up then and grabbed him by the top of the flak vest, pulling him down to his level.

'Oi,' he said. 'Not our fight. Not our concern. All right? This—what's going on between the KLA and the Serbs—it was happening long before we got here, and it'll be happening long after we're gone. All right? We take these tanks, and we get the fuck out of here. The faster you do that, the faster they'll have to stop.'

But it was then that Gaz's words of pragmatism and wisdom ran dry.

Another of Darko's men—a tall guy with a thick beard and close-set eyes—seemed to forget all about the wounded soldiers and what might be fair wartime revenge, and instead turned his attention to the group of grieving widows.

He scanned them, inspecting each as though they were cattle at a market—and to him, they were.

When he seemed to find one he liked, he walked towards her without any ceremony and reached down, grabbing her by the elbow. He tried to hoist her to her feet, and when she shoved him off, he struck her. A quick blow—knuckles across her face, open-handed— but enough to send her spinning to the ground. Enough to open her skin and make blood trickle down her cheek.

He reached down again—and though she tried to fight him off, she knew it was hopeless.

Her eyes cast to the other women there, who all clutched at their children, hiding their heads away from what was about to happen.

They looked on, knowing there was nothing they could do. No way they could fight. Their husbands dead, their lives and bodies at the mercy of these brutes.

And as Darko's man took her by the wrist and began hauling her towards the corridor—towards one of the storerooms they'd passed on the way in and the privacy they would afford—Church could stand by no longer.

Instinctively, he drove his wrist upwards, pushing Gaz's hand free of his collar, and swept towards Darko's man. Before the man could even look up, Church put his fist through his face—so hard that he felt the orbital bone at the side of his right eye crunch under the blow. The man bowled sideways, immediately unconscious, and hit the floor in a limp heap.

The woman fell to the ground and curled up into a

ball, as though expecting that Church was simply marking his territory. Claiming her for himself.

But the word that left his mouth wasn't one of cruelty.

'Run,' he said, low enough that Darko's men—who had now looked up from their position at the door to the cell block, watching the show about to unfold—wouldn't hear.

The woman ceased shaking and turned her head towards Church as though she hadn't heard him right. He flicked his eyes towards the door leading from the bullpen into the car park behind the station, and she followed his gaze—seeming to understand, but perhaps not quite believing it.

There was a footstep to his right, and Church looked up, expecting to see Gaz there, ready to chastise him—but it wasn't. All he saw was a fist.

He couldn't react before it hit him square in the mouth, almost taking him clean off his feet.

He stumbled back, crashing into one of the desks and sending it sliding across the grey tiles.

He looked up to see Darko coming forward again, unleashing another punch. He pushed himself forward, parrying it with his forearm and slinging a left hook into Darko's gut instead. The man doubled up over it, then reached up, clawing at Church's face—raking his nails down his cheek and jaw. Church felt them break skin and felt his fist lock reflexively in response, ready to send a vicious uppercut into Darko's chin, ready to end him then and there, take his head clean off his shoulders.

But before he could, Gaz was between them once more, shoving him away.

Grandad, reading the situation—knowing what needed to be done and what would happen if he didn't —took Darko by the arms, locking him up so that his elbows were by his ears, and twisted him towards the exit, taking him out of play.

Church watched him go, watched as Grandad released him, shoved him away and held him back— keeping him at bay while Gaz did what he needed to do and secured the peace.

'You may be right,' Gaz hissed at him, 'but this is not our war, Church—and the man you just hit is not our enemy.'

As Church registered a warm trickle of blood running down his face, he couldn't help but sneer at that.

'Yeah? Doesn't feel like it,' he said.

Gaz sighed, keeping his eyes fixed on Church. 'Yeah, well—while you're in here fighting for one life, thousands more out there are dying. You may think this is where the real battle is, but it's not. It's all around us. And the quicker you deal with those tanks, the quicker we get the mission done, the faster we can end this war. Not just for these people—for everyone. For the whole fucking country. You get it? What we're doing here—it doesn't matter. But what we're doing with Markovich? That matters. It really matters. What he can do for us, the information he can provide—that has the power to make a real difference. That has the power to end this before it goes any further. And you need to get your fucking head on square and realise that.'

'We have the power to end it,' Church snapped back. 'NATO. They could do it today. They've got jets in here —why don't they?'

'Are you mad?' Gaz said. 'We're on Russia's doorstep. NATO launches a full-blown invasion, it could start World War goddamn Three. And that's not to mention the civilian casualties. Look around you, Church. Even here—what have you got? Ten soldiers holding on for dear fucking life, living meal to meal, struggling to feed their kids. And how many more places like this are out there? And you think NATO should come in and carpet-bomb the entire fucking country? How many women—how many kids—are they going to fucking kill doing that? You're in here risking your life to save one of them, and then you suggest NATO turn around and kill thousands more? Tell me how that makes any fucking sense, Church?'

He lowered his head to catch Church's downturned eyes, demanding an answer.

'So we just let this shit go on? We look away? You let Darko's men torture people to death? Let them do this?' He gestured to the woman at his feet, crawling slowly towards the door. 'It may not tip the scales in the grand scheme—but I'm not going to stand by and watch it happen.'

Gaz gave him a hard look, not seeming to have an answer for him.

The woman picked herself up now, getting to her knees as the two men continued to stare at each other. And then she sprang up and bolted for the door—running for the freedom Church had offered her.

But she only made it halfway before a single shot rang out.

Church and Gaz both ducked and looked at the source—seeing Darko's pistol raised from the doorway to the corridor. Grandad wasn't quick enough to stop him. Wasn't expecting it.

The woman running for the door cried out and then sprawled forward, reaching up her spine with her left hand, groping for the hole in her back.

She landed on her knees—and then her head hit the tiles with a dull crack, and she lay still, blood pooling under her body.

Gaz was holding onto him before Church even tried to move, and Grandad restrained Darko now. Too little. Too late.

'That was a mercy!' Darko called. 'You saved her from one fate—but you can't save these people from the other. You tell me which is worse, huh?' he went on, as Grandad wrestled him backwards. 'You decide!' his voice echoed from the corridor, 'Because these people here—they either know the pain they caused us, or they know death. But they'll know one of them before we leave this place!'

Church just stared at him, never hating a man so

much in his life—but knowing that, ultimately, far short of murdering Darko and his entire group, he was right.

They couldn't be stopped.

And here, in this place—in this war—no one was innocent.

And perhaps the greatest mercy of all was a quick death.

———

Thick black columns of acrid smoke rose into the air behind him as Church made his way alone towards the ridgeline, leaving the police station behind.

Markovich made contact with NATO not long after the raid began and said that he wanted to meet again—and it had to be now.

Word, it seemed, had gotten out before everyone had been killed, that they were being attacked, and Markovich was looped in.

Perhaps he wasn't expecting such swift action from NATO, or perhaps he was ready to take another step towards their deal. Either way, Gaz relieved Church of the explosives in his pack and told him to get on the road as soon as possible.

It was a long drive to the rendezvous, and though Church thought that DD or Grandad or Gaz himself would have been a better choice—more experienced—Church figured Gaz removing him from the Darko equation was killing two birds with one stone.

And he was right to. How it would all play out in

there, he didn't know—but he trusted Gaz to make sure that if they weren't going to leave anyone alive, then it would be done right.

As right as it could be, at least.

He found the first 4x4 and climbed in, taking hold of the wheel and resting his head against it. He closed his eyes, listening to the slow pulse of his heart in his head, and wondered—replaying that scene over and over in his mind, asking himself if it could have gone differently and how. What he could have done. How he could have stopped it. Whether there was any way he could have saved those people, those women, those children.

But he didn't know. And had he pushed any harder, maybe he would have been the one taking a bullet in the back.

Gaz was right about one thing. The faster they ended this war, the better. And that's what he told himself as he cranked the engine and slingshotted the truck forward in a cloud of dust.

He drove for hours until he reached Gurtesh, the village that he and Markovich had first met in, pulling the car in the same place that he and Grandad had parked it before.

Once again he hoofed it in, and he reached the ruined square. He slowed, spotting Markovich—this time in the open, waiting for him. The man was sitting there in the weak spring sun, on the edge of the ruined fountain, hunched forward, his elbows on his knees, his long woollen coat draped around his hips, spilling into the basin behind him.

He looked up at Church as he approached—not smiling, his expression blank.

'I wasn't sure you were coming,' he said, sitting upright, putting his hands on his thighs now, running them along his trousers as though to dry sweating palms. 'I was expecting something else.'

'Like what?' Church asked, catching his breath, the M16 heavy in his arms after the run.

Markovich shrugged. 'A bullet.'

Church cracked a wry smile at that. 'Yeah, unfortunately, I think you're probably a little too important for that.'

'Important?' Markovich asked, raising an eyebrow.

Church cursed himself for using the word. 'The fate of this region might rest on your shoulders,' he said. 'If your information is good enough. And if it is…'

He trailed off, letting Markovich fill in the blanks.

'My family,' Markovich replied.

Church gave one single nod. 'We need to turn the tide of this thing,' he said then, as Markovich pushed himself to a weary stance. 'And to do that, we need something concrete. Something good.'

Markovich sucked air between his teeth. 'Well, you certainly don't waste any time,' he said. 'I'll give you that. Hitting the fuel depot like that—it took balls. And it's got the Serbs scrambling.'

'Good,' Church said.

'I don't know about that,' Markovich replied. 'For this?' He shook his head slowly, contemplating it. 'For this there'll be blood. And lots of it.'

'There's already blood,' Church replied sourly, picturing the woman with a hole in her spine, bleeding out on the floor of the police station. 'Too much of it.'

Markovich took stock of his expression and let his words drift away in the cool air.

The town around them was silent.

After a few seconds, Markovich tilted his head back and looked up into the featureless morning sky—pale blue and endless. 'You know, when you look up and you see this, you can almost imagine there's no war going on at all.'

'Yeah. Almost,' Church said, noting the silence, the lack of gunfire, the lack of explosions and smoke. He imagined this place, where they were standing, before the war. What it would have been like.

Whether there would have been market stalls lining the cobbles where he was standing.

Whether there would have been children playing in the fountain, people throwing in pennies to make wishes. Whether young couples would have stopped at cafés on their first date. Whether parents would have walked through the square, swinging their children between them.

Whether on Sunday mornings the church bells on the steeple that was no longer there would have rung, and everyone from the village would have drifted towards it—coming together as one community before the war.

And then Markovich said something that Church wasn't expecting.

'You know, I used to live here.' Markovich lowered his eyes, a sort of wistfulness in them. 'This is where I'm from. Where I grew up. My wife, too.' The words caught in his throat a little.

That's why they were here. Gaz hadn't chosen the place at all. Markovich had. Because he knew the place. Knew the lay out. He had the homefield advantage, would have a chance of escaping if things had gone sideways on their first meeting.

'Our house,' Markovich went on. 'It was over there, at the edge of the village.' He pointed towards a destroyed building to their right. 'There's not much of it left now.' He chuckled a little. The saddest sound Church had ever heard. 'It was falling down before the war. But now …' He shook his head, thinking of it.

Church could imagine, too. The whole town was in ruin.

'We moved to Pristina years ago,' Markovich said, 'but we always planned to come back. To leave the city, to raise Rena here. In the countryside. Like we were raised.' A brief flicker of a smile reached his lips and the extinguished itself just as fast. 'In another life,' he finished, clearing his throat.

Church drew a breath, steeling himself. 'I assume because you wanted to meet, you've got something for us,' he said. 'Something real.' He wondered if Markovich could hear the hope in his voice.

Markovich looked at the man. 'I do,' he said. 'Just like you, I want this to be over quickly. I want my family out, and I want them out now.' He turned around and picked up two brown paper files from the edge of the fountain, holding them up—one in each hand.

Church looked back at him. 'I can't do that. Not yet,' he said. 'Not until I see.' He reached out for the files, but Markovich pulled them back a little, as though to hold them out of reach.

'I need some kind of assurance,' he said.

'You can have it,' Church replied quickly. 'If the information you supply leads to the end of this war, then your family will be safe.'

'And all I have is your word?' Markovich asked him.

'My word means a lot,' Church replied, meeting the man's eye.

Markovich rolled his lips into a line.

He didn't really have much choice but to trust Church—and knew that if he walked away without handing over the information, all he'd succeeded in doing was betraying his country once for no payoff.

He had no other option but to go along with this—to take the stranger in front of him at face value.

'What are they?' Church asked, looking at the files.

Markovich looked at the one in his right hand. 'One is evidence of the atrocities that have been committed against the Kosovan people—and the names and faces of the men who ordered them. The other,' he said, turning his head to look at his left hand, 'are blueprints for a major Serbian munitions factory and depot. If you had to choose what's more important—justice for those already fallen, or saving those yet to fall—which do you choose?'

Church's grip tightened on his rifle. 'I'm hoping you're here to give me both,' he said gruffly.

'I am,' Markovich replied. 'But I just want to know the man that I'm dealing with. I want this war to end—and I want to see the men responsible for all of this death and destruction swing.'

Church lifted his chin a little. 'And do you count yourself in that, Colonel?'

'More than you know,' Markovich replied, softening a little, his shoulders sagging. 'But I hope… I hope this can be my redemption. Or a step towards it, at least. Tell me, soldier—how many men have you killed? Five? Ten? Fifty? For causes you believe in, in your heart?' He tutted and shook his head. 'War is hell, no matter what way you spin it. So let's stop it. Together.'

He lowered the files then and pinned the one in his right under his left elbow, holding out a trembling hand towards Church.

Church stared down at it, wondering if he could trust this man—knowing that if he didn't, that he was right. This hell would just go on and on and on.

And with that thought burning in his mind, he took a step towards Markovich and extended his hand too.

TWELVE

PRESENT DAY

A MID-2000S BLACK Toyota RAV4 rolled to a stop outside an upmarket apartment block in the 13th arrondissement in Paris.

It came to rest at the kerb and remained perfectly stationary with the engine off. But the driver didn't disembark.

The vehicle sat in place, completely still for twelve minutes. Then the driver's door opened and a man stepped out. He was wearing a black jacket and a black hoodie. Sunglasses. A baseball cap pulled down low over his face. He left the driver's door open and walked casually towards the back of the car before disappearing along the street.

One or two commuters stopped to look at what was happening. One called out, but the driver didn't respond.

A woman began to approach the car, the door still open, looking inside.

And then, as the front door to the apartment building opened and a portly man in his seventies, accompanied by his wife, stepped down onto the pavement, the RAV4 exploded.

A ball of white flame leapt from the interior, blowing all of the windows out and rending the roof, the blast powerful enough to engulf the elderly man and his wife entirely, the shockwave so strong it destroyed the camera recording the footage they were watching.

The feed went dead and Church looked up from the screen of the iPad, right into Julia Hallberg's eyes across the kitchen table in Mitch's house. She reached over and paused the video, allowing Church to keep hold of the iPad in case he wanted to watch it again.

He didn't need to.

'This was two hours ago,' Hallberg said. 'And it's the first clear look we've got at the bomber. But as you can imagine, we've had no luck pulling facial recognition from this footage, and there were no prints in the car. Everything wiped clean before he got out.'

'Which, in itself, is something to go on. If he was so keen to make sure the car was clean, then it means that his fingerprints are in some system somewhere,' Church said. 'He's on record—either he's a felon or has had some kind of government involvement. Police, military, that kind of thing.'

'We already figured that much out,' Hallberg said

tiredly, staring at Church. 'I was hoping you might be able to offer something we don't have.'

'Like what?' Church asked her.

She let out a frustrated sigh. 'I'm really starting to get bored of this act, Church,' she said. 'As well as the man and woman coming out of the building, the lady checking on the car was also killed in the blast. And six others inside the building were all injured, including a lady getting her mail just inside the reception. She's in a coma, with a bleed on the brain. Doctors say she'll be dead before the day is out. And it's really beginning to piss me off that you know something about this that you're not telling us,' Hallberg snapped.

It was a new mode for her—she'd always been cool and collected.

But Church could tell now her patience had worn out.

'I don't know what to tell you,' he said.

'Honestly, it doesn't matter if you don't know what it is,' Hallberg said. 'Tell me anything—tell me every-thing. We finally had the report back from forensics on the bombs. It confirmed that they were all the same simple construction. Plastic explosive, simple timed detonator with bridge-wire charge. The explosive's chemical signature is a perfect match to Russian plastic explosives—Semtex—the detonator something out of a Soviet war museum.' She reached over and began flicking through screens on the iPad, showing him the report. Pictures of the remains of the detonator. Pieces of plastic that didn't look like anything to anyone else—

but to Church, they were familiar. Too familiar, even. Like random parts of a puzzle that someone who'd never built couldn't identify.

He knew exactly how they fit together. Where they'd go.

He had seen explosive devices exactly like this. Hell, he'd used them himself.

And there was just one word that kept rearing its ugly head in his brain, kept screaming at him.

Kosovo. Kosovo. Kosovo!

'We've got someone using Russian explosives, targeting specific people in Europe, on British soil, killing them with no concern for collateral damage— and you know something about it. And you're not telling me. So you're as good as killing these people yourself,' Hallberg said, digging into him. 'So this is it. This is your last chance,' she said. 'You tell me what you know now—or what you think you know—or we're done.'

Church measured her for a long time.

If he did tell her, then what? How would that go?

It would open a can of worms he didn't think he could close again. The things he'd done there... The things his team had done. The way it all went down. The loss of civilian life on both sides. The word *mess* didn't begin to cover it.

It was hell.

And if the next words from his mouth were that the SAS were in Kosovo, then that would unleash an avalanche of shit that would come crashing down on the

British Army and British government alike. And he wasn't going to be the one to do that.

No. His unit may have double-crossed him and left him for dead. But a handful of bad eggs didn't define the entire service—and the service had been his family and his home for two decades. He wasn't about to betray that now. Not for Hallberg. Not for anything.

'Fine,' she said after a few more seconds, pulling the iPad towards her and holding up her hands, as though to illustrate that she was washing them of Church and all of this. 'You know, I expected more from you,' she said. 'I didn't know what—but more than this.'

Church looked back at her. Mitch, sitting to his right, was as silent as he was.

She glanced at both of them, then scoffed, picked up the iPad, and stood up.

'Thanks for the tea,' she said to Mitch, about as curt as Church ever imagined she could be.

Then she took one more look at him and just shook her head.

'We're done,' she said. And with that, she strode towards the door and slammed it behind her.

Only when they heard the engine of the SUV start and she drove away did Mitch speak.

'She didn't mean that,' he said. 'She'll be back. She'll call you when she needs something.'

'I know she will,' Church said absently, still staring into space, still thinking about how the pieces of that timer fit together. The plastic explosive of Russian origin. The nature of the bomb. And something about that figure—the way he walked, the way he moved.

Church didn't know who it was in that cap and hoodie. But he knew he'd seen that walk before. Striding toward him.

It was a powerful, dogged walk. A self-right-eousness he knew well.

A familiarity with violence and an uncaring for human life.

If he hadn't been sure before, he was sure now.

There was a link—more tangible than he'd been willing to believe, closer than he could have imagined—between what was happening now and what happened to him in Kosovo twenty-five years ago.

But what was the purpose? What were they trying to achieve?

He had half a story. And he knew that no matter what happened next, he needed to find the rest of it.

'So, now that she's gone,' Mitch said. 'What do you really think?'

'I think...' Church said. 'That the past has a nasty habit of not staying buried.' He turned his head to look at his friend, Mitch staring back at him, his eyes just as hollow as his own. 'And that my ghosts are finally coming back to haunt us.'

THIRTEEN

TWENTY-FIVE YEARS AGO

CHURCH KILLED the engine outside the KLA camp and hunched forward, stretching his back, rolling his shoulders one way and then the other.

He'd been on the road for almost eight hours in total, and along with the trip out to the Serbian police station, he was feeling it. Every potholed, rutted mile. With a sigh, he pushed open the door and stepped out, trudging back towards camp. The hour had grown late, and it looked like Ismet's house was full of light and sound—Darko's men in there no doubt celebrating their victory today.

Church grimaced at it and turned his head away, heading towards their tent, slowing only when he spotted the woman with the burning blue eyes watching him from across the courtyard. She was outside Ismet's house, washing what looked like sheets in a wooden tub by hand. This old farm was devoid of a lot of modern amenities, it seemed.

As she spotted him, she got up and walked over, drying her hands on the dirtied apron covering her long dress.

Church watched her approach, her eyes only seeming to brighten as the light of the day continued to fade, somehow alight in the golden afternoon sun.

He wasn't sure what to say, but it didn't seem like she was interested in introductions, and instead just reached up for his face and took him by the chin, pressing her thumb and fingers into his cheeks, turning his head left and right, inspecting his split lip and the scratches on his face courtesy of Darko.

'Get into a fight with a cat?' she asked plainly.

Church reached up and batted her hand away gently. 'Something like that,' he said.

She put her hands on her hips and stared up at him. 'I realised I never learned your name yesterday morning. I thought about that after you left—that if you died, I wouldn't even know who you were.'

'That bothered you?' Church asked.

She shrugged. 'Darko's needed a smack for a long time—I just thought it'd be nice to know who exactly gave it to him.'

'I gave him one more today,' Church said gruffly.

She restrained a little smirk. 'Did you now?'

He struggled not to smile back at her.

She extended her hand towards him then. 'Marsela,' she said, and turned her head, motioning to the house. 'You've already met my father and my brother.'

'I have,' Church replied, following her eyes, listening to their raucous laughter as though they hadn't tortured and murdered anyone that very morning.

'Solomon,' he replied back.

'Huh. Like the king,' Marsela said. 'It's a strong name. Your parents must have had high hopes for you.'

He harrumphed at that, the face of his father briefly flashing in his mind. 'Yeah, maybe,' he said, keen to change the subject.

'Come on,' she insisted, as though reading his apprehension to want to talk—but seemingly insistent on it anyway. Was she really that bored here? Church glanced around the empty yard and decided that yes, she probably was. Or at least she was looking for some kind of distraction from the reality of it all.

She reached out and grabbed him by the sleeve, pulling him to the right of Ismet's house, where an old manual water pump sat at the edge of the farmyard, a steel bucket waiting underneath.

'Those need to be cleaned,' she said, gesturing up at his face as they walked, her grip tight enough on his shirt that it became clear it wasn't a suggestion.

She let go as they got to the pump and reached for the tap, pumping it a few times to get the water running out in a thin stream. She turned the bucket over and pointed at it, instructing Solomon to sit.

Tired and stiff, he eased himself down onto it, watching her as she pulled a rag from the waistband of her apron and held it under the stream. She turned back to him then and began dabbing at his cheek, not really taking much care or interest in how gentle she was being. Cold droplets of water spotted his trousers and his collar as she pressed the rag against his skin, squeezing the liquid from it.

Church didn't think she was trying to hurt him—but perhaps she just thought him incapable of feeling anything at all.

'Tell me,' she said, 'Solomon—'

He couldn't help but hear the emphasis she put on it.

'—why do you choose war?'

He looked up at her, the question catching him by surprise. But he could see that that was her aim all along. Not to introduce herself, find out his name, but to ask—ask why he was here. Why he was really here.

'I didn't choose war,' he said back. 'War chose me. It always has.'

Her hand paused at his cheek, and she seemed to dig a nail into one of the scratches on his face, pressing into his flesh through the rag.

The pain was sharp and sobering. He looked up at her—at her hard expression. She'd once been beautiful, he thought. But now war had stripped that from her.

Almost.

'It's not that I want to,' he said. 'I just can't stand by and do nothing. I never could. Not while people are getting hurt.'

She let her hand drop slowly from his cheek and looked down at the blood on the rag. 'So you kill,' she said. 'To save?' She scoffed a little and shook her head. 'That's an interesting morality.'

He watched her inspect his blood. 'Yeah, I've been thinking that too.'

'Well, maybe that's the problem,' she said, folding up the rag and wringing it out before she returned to his cheek, scrubbing roughly at the marks her brother had given him. 'You think with this,' she said, reaching up and tapping him on the forehead between the eyes with her index finger. 'Instead of this.' She let her hand drop and she pressed her palm to the middle of his chest, holding it there, feeling the beat of his great heart even through his flak vest.

'If I think with that,' he said slowly, reaching up and resting his hand on her wrist, unsure if he wanted to hold it there or pull it away, 'I think there'll be even more blood on this ground, not less.'

Darko's face flashed in his mind then—the desire to tear him limb from limb, festering deep inside Church, right below where Marsela's hand was resting.

She searched his eyes then for a hint of what he meant—or perhaps she already knew, and instead was searching for something to tell her that she was wrong.

'Where does this all end?' she asked, after what seemed like a long time.

'When they tell me it's over,' Church replied, closing his eyes and peeling her fingers from his breast.

'And you'll die for this place if you have to?' Marsela asked, almost a whisper now. She turned her hand over, loosely clasping it around his.

He stared down at it, knowing that if he wanted, he could envelop her hand in his—that he could squeeze tightly enough that he would crush it completely. Her innocence, her frailty, struck him all at once.

'If I have to,' he said, 'I will.'

But he wasn't sure he even meant it. He certainly didn't want to die for this place—for men like Darko. But it wasn't just men like Darko who were out here. Marsela pulled her hand free now and ran the tap over the cloth again, squeezing all remnants of crimson from it until the water dripping through the fabric ran clear.

'Do you ever think of running?' she asked him.

'Do you?' he replied.

Her eyes leapt to his. 'Always. Every moment of every day. But my brother, my father…' She looked over at the house now, the raucous laughter within—her family, and what Church was sure was all that was left of it. How many friends, how many cousins, grandparents, had she lost? Her mother? How many siblings had she had before this all started?

'Your father would forgive you,' Church told her anyway, not wanting her to meet the same fate. 'He's a good man. Your brother…' He trailed off, and Marsela smiled again.

This time, there was no pleasure in it at all.

'You don't need to say it.'

'No. I don't,' Church replied.

'And what about you?' she asked, twisting the rag, strangling it in her grip, wringing the water from every thread. 'Are you a good man?'

Church thought about that as she lifted it to his lip and moved it gently across the cut there.

It was tender—but he could barely feel the pain as he considered the weight of her question.

'I thought I was,' he said, the words coming to him almost subconsciously. 'Now? I don't know anymore.'

Marsela's hand stilled. 'Perhaps it's better to think about it at the end, when you have your whole life to look back on. Here…' She shook her head. 'There are no good men here, I don't think.'

He reached up then and ran the tips of his fingers over her pale, soft knuckles, enveloping her hand in his.

This time, he didn't think of crushing it. This time, he thought of shielding it—of protecting it from whatever was coming next. That if he held her, if he held on and never let go, then perhaps the fate that seemed to be awaiting them all here would somehow not find her—but him instead.

With her other hand, she slowly cupped his face, resting her palm on the claw marks that Darko had left.

He closed his eyes then and turned towards it, hiding his face in her palm.

And without another word, he felt her fingers on the nape of his neck, guiding his head—slowly, quietly—into her breast.

And there she held him.

For how long…

Church didn't know.

FOURTEEN

PRESENT DAY

MITCH WAS RIGHT, Hallberg did call again.

And though Church was reluctant to pick up the phone, expecting her to berate him, she didn't.

It was the opposite. It was nearly midnight when she called, and Church lifted the front of his ear, lying in bed.

'Solomon,' she said with a sigh. 'I'm sorry about the other day.'

'It's okay,' Church said. And it was, he understood, and she was perfectly within her rights.

'It's just there are people dying, you know, and, and I want to help, but I just... I don't know how to catch this guy. He's a ghost. And all of our checkpoints, all of our searching, everything. It's just, it's just coming to nothing. So please, I'm not telling. I'm asking if you know something, just tell me. We need to catch this guy.

He's not going to stop. He's going to keep killing people. And so far it's just been three or four ... but what happens when it's thirty or forty or a hundred? I don't begin to think that I can understand how you feel about that, with what you've seen. What you must have done ... but I know how I feel and I know that I'll do anything to stop it. But I need you to help me, please. I don't understand what it is that's holding you back. But please don't make me beg.'

Church's grip tightened slightly around the phone, his heart beating a little harder.

He thought he'd probably have preferred to be berated than to listen to a genuine plea for help.

And now he had a decision to make.

He could lie there, staring at his ceiling, and tell her that he knew nothing.

He could lie to her and probably sever their relationship forever—and perhaps that was the best thing?

Perhaps just cutting her off and crawling back into his hole, into his self-imposed exile was the best thing for it. But they weren't so different. She said she couldn't let it lie. She couldn't just allow it to go on, allow people to be killed. And he didn't think he could either. And especially knowing who that person was, who the bomber was, impossible as it was, that it could be that same man that he'd stared down before, that same man that he'd seen inflict harm on others without any conscience.

A man who had everything taken from him, and a man who was willing to die for his home.

He didn't want to say the name, not even in his own head, but he could picture his dark features clearly standing across the farmyard from him.

'I don't know,' Church said, his voice small, catching in his throat. 'But I think you should look at Kosovo.'

The words came out stunted and strained, and to him it felt like a betrayal as large, or perhaps even larger, than the one he'd faced himself.

It was as though he was driving a knife into the back of his own career. Misplaced as his loyalties may have been, it was something that he could never shake and didn't think he ever would.

'Kosovo?' Hallberg asked. 'As in the Kosovo war?'

'Yeah,' Church said in the darkness, whispering as though someone, anyone, might overhear.

'What the hell does the Kosovo war have to do with these bombings?'

'That much I don't know,' Church replied to her. 'But that's what it feels like to me. That's why I didn't say anything, because I didn't know. But it just, that's how it feels, okay? I can't explain it, but the bomb, the bomber, it just all seems too familiar, like, like something was left unfinished there and now it's... now it's coming back.'

She didn't reply, and Church didn't blame her.

What he was saying was barely making sense even to him, but they were the words in his head, the words that had been on the tip of his tongue for what felt like the longest time.

'Okay,' she said. 'That's something, and I'll start looking into it. And don't worry, I'll leave you out of it, I promise.'

Church nodded, not really able to say anything else, but he did appreciate that.

'But look, I don't know how much information I'm going to be able to dig up and how quickly on this. If you know more, if you can find out more, if you can … God, if you can find out who this guy is and what he's trying to do, then please, we need all the help we can get. His timeline is accelerating. There's two bombs been set off inside a week and who knows when the next one is coming. In his head he's obviously got some kind of list he's working through and now he's speeding up. Is there anyone you can reach out to? Anyone who you might think knows more than you? Knows what's going on?'

Anastasia Fletcher's face appeared in his mind, but he didn't say anything.

'I know it's a lot to ask,' Hallberg said. 'But if you know something, if you were there, if there's anyone else that you can reach out to who was there at the same time, then maybe—'

'Okay,' Church said, cutting her off, not wanting to hear any more begging. 'I'll see what I can do.'

She let out a long, rattling breath. 'Thank you, Church,' she said. 'If you can help us get this guy, you'll be doing more for me than you know.'

'I'm not doing this for you,' Church said.

'No, I know—I didn't mean that, I just meant...' She trailed off then.

'It's okay,' Church replied. 'I know what you mean and... I'm sorry.'

'Sorry for what?' Hallberg asked.

'For everything,' Church said, closing his eyes and pulling the phone away from his ear.

He hung up on her before she could say anything else, and lay there in bed alone, listening to his heart thud soft and fast in his ears, knowing that he had to reach out to Fletcher.

That he had to dredge a part of his life out of his past that he promised he never would.

And that when it was all laid bare, that it would expose him for who he really was and, more frighteningly…

For who he'd always been.

FIFTEEN

TWENTY-FIVE YEARS AGO

IT WAS guerrilla warfare at its core.

Gaz had received word from Markovich that the munitions depot they were about to hit had seen an influx of Serbian army. This was what he'd meant when he told Church there would be reaction for hitting the police station.

Now the Serbs had redoubled their forces, and Markovich said several dozen were likely to be holed up at the munitions depot, expecting some kind of attack.

Which was why they were going in in the dead of night—and why they too had mustered a larger force.

Church didn't like the plan in the slightest—and neither did Gaz. But orders were coming down from the top, and they needed to continue to loosen the Serbian grip on Kosovo—and this would deal a major blow to the entire army. NATO were coordinating all across the region, and it couldn't wait. They needed to keep hitting the Serbian army before they could organise any kind of real retaliation.

Darko had assembled every last man that he had, and they were all jostling, antsy for the fight that awaited them.

There was a mix of nerves and excitement from his men—some of them confident that they'd come through this, others doubting they would, and a few who just didn't look like they cared either way.

All they wanted was to taste Serbian blood—and they didn't really care what that cost them.

Though this time, at least Church hoped it wouldn't be costing him anything.

Seeing what had happened at the police station, Gaz had made the decision that they wouldn't be going in together—but separately instead. If Darko wanted a shootout, then that's what he'd get.

He was to lead the men in an all-out frontal assault on the building while Church and Gaz slipped in the back, found the stockpiles and dealt with them. Hopefully. If they were dealing with a KLA onslaught from one direction, they wouldn't be expecting or prepared for the SAS to be going through the back door at the same time.

Or at least that was the plan. Whether or not it would come off that way, Church didn't know. But now there was no backing out of it.

Gaz took a few steps towards Darko. All of them were formed up in the car park of an old disused service station about a mile down the road from the depot itself. He clapped Darko on the back and forced a grin. In the darkness it looked strange and malformed, Church thought—and by the way Darko was looking at him, he thought the same thing.

'It's all you,' he told the head of the KLA force. 'Your operation, your men, your command. You want to kill them all, kill them all.'

Darko ran his tongue over his bottom lip as though looking for some coded message there—but there was none. What Gaz was saying was perfectly true—it didn't really matter much what Darko did as long as his men put up enough of a fight to occupy the Serbs long enough for them to achieve the mission.

And by his expression it looked as though he realised that's what they were suddenly: cannon fodder.

And he was glaring at Gaz as though it was Gaz's fault—as though he was marching them into a firing line when this was what he'd been asking for all along.

Grandad had been dead right when he'd said it after Darko had sprung from that foxhole and charged the enemy blindly, emptying the magazine into the hay bale point blank—it was a hell of a lot easier to play tough when there was nobody shooting back.

Now Darko didn't look so sure.

In fact, it looked like his balls had shrivelled back up inside his body.

And though Church didn't want to see anybody die tonight—if Darko was included in that list of those who didn't come back—he wouldn't be shedding a tear.

Darko gave Gaz one more look up and down, and then motioned for his men to climb into the four-by-fours they'd brought, leaving one behind for Church, Gaz and the others.

They watched them mount up and roll out, waiting for the imminent gunfire to erupt. Hell, their plan was as stupid as it was simple. Charge the front gates, ram them through, park the cars side on, take cover, and then just shoot at anything—at everything—that moved, and hope by the time the last man fell they were still standing.

They watched them tear out of the car park, and then Gaz signalled for the guys to climb into the remaining 4x4.

He started the engine—but not the headlights—and wheeled it in a circle, slowly jostling up over the kerb and into the scrubby fields that surrounded the service station. He guided them forward until the lights of the depot came into view in the distance, and then killed the engine, allowing them to roll to a stop, turning the truck side on so that the driver's door was facing the depot.

It meant that if they had to make a run for it, the driver could get in first and get the engine started. It was as efficient as possible in preparing for a quick exit—though Church hoped that it wouldn't come to that.

But in these situations you never knew which way it was going to go.

In silence they disembarked and made their way forward—spread out a few metres apart, moving in a line as they came up on it. DD had bolt cutters in his pack and would be dealing with the fence when they reached it. Church had two kilos of C4 in his. And Grandad was stocked up with smoke grenades and spare mags. And Gaz was running point—outfitted with night vision goggles and a thermal scope. The shot-caller in this. The scout.

Church had to give it to him. He admired the man— knew that he wouldn't ask any of his men to do anything that he wasn't ready to jump to do first.

They had no idea what was waiting for them—and if anyone was going to get picked off, Gaz was making sure that it was him. So much so that he even handed off the keys to the vehicle to DD before they reached the fence.

He crept up first, motioning the men down, and knelt in front of it, taking out the thermal scope and scanning the back of the compound.

Darko's men had to make a loop of the place first in order to reach the front, and no doubt he'd be arriving any moment—and it seemed that's what Gaz was waiting for.

There was a flare of engine noise in the distance and then the crunch of metal on metal. Church envisioned them blowing through the gates and into the compound, and then shouts of alert rang in the night, gunfire following it swiftly.

Tyres screeched and bullets ricocheted off steel plate as the fight began—but all of them had their eyes fixed on Gaz. It was his word—and that word was now go. He motioned DD forward, and the man sprinted up, drop-

ping to a knee and hacking through the fence with precision. Grandad came next, with Church bringing up the
rear, and the three of them filed through the hole with
Gaz holding the corner of the fence back.

They made a beeline for the corner of the building.
It was a huge steel-clad warehouse. To the left were a
row of M87 battle tanks along with armoured personnel
carriers and two trailer-mounted 88mm anti-aircraft
guns. This wasn't just some small munitions depot—
this was serious—and Church really was beginning to
feel like what they did here might actually have an
effect.

They'd all memorised the plans from Markovich and
knew what they had to do.

There were three main storage areas, and Markovich
had told Church that it would likely be split into small
arms, large arms, and airborne ordnance—and he just
hoped they'd brought enough explosive for all three.

Gaz and DD pushed in first, heading for the fire exit
at the back of the building. It was padlocked from the
outside, and Gaz wasted no time gesturing to DD for the
bolt cutters. He made short work of the chain—but the
door would be another story.

He motioned for DD to turn around and pulled the
heavy pry bar from his pack.

Church and Grandad formed up behind, covering
their flanks while Gaz drove it in between the door and
the jamb and started levering it.

'DD—give me a fucking hand, yeah?' he muttered
under his breath, the words strained.

DD took hold and pulled too, the pry bar beginning to bend under the force, the two of them giving it all they had. They could of course take some of the plastic explosive that Church was carrying and press it into the frame, set off a quick door charge to blow it open—but doing that would tell the Serbs that the attack wasn't just coming from the front, and that's the one thing they wanted to avoid.

With a final yank, the door bolt twisted and bowed, the frame giving, and the thing flew open. There was a moment of silence—a yawning chasm of black beyond the door—and then a red light flared to life above it and a deep wailing alarm began to sound.

'Jesus Christ, Gaz—this wasn't on the fucking plans.'

And though they could stand around all night and discuss it, the reality was that they might as well have just pulled out a megaphone and announced that they had arrived.

Gaz swore and looked around at the men.

'Alright—contingency,' he said. 'Church—pack, now.'

He didn't need to be asked twice, tossing his pack to Gaz, who promptly ripped it open and pulled out the C4.

'Grandad—give us some cover,' he ordered, while he separated the parcels of plastic explosive, slotting one into the thigh pocket of his cargo pants along with a timed detonator. He passed the second similar section of the explosives to DD and then pushed the third into Church's hand.

'I'll take small arms,' he said. 'DD—you're in Warehouse Two. Church—you take ordnance. Good? We're in and out. Set charges for thirty seconds on my mark. Then we rendezvous outside the fence and make a break for the car. Quick as you like, lads,' he said, giving them all a nod.

There was no time to lose—and none of them confirmed—their understanding implicit as they all began to move.

'Grandad—watch the door. Make sure no one fucks us in the arse here.'

The white-haired warrior gave a nod and held his position just inside the door as they all ducked inwards.

They were met by a long corridor spreading out in both directions.

Church was heading right towards Bay Three, DD and Gaz going left towards Two and One, with Gaz giving himself the tallest order, the longest time inside, the furthest to run, the greatest risk—and the greatest chance of not making it back.

Church took off in the other direction, looking over his shoulder to see Grandad watching him go—not quite sure what the stern look in the old man's eyes meant. Perhaps a sense of apprehension—maybe even a flicker of fear there—but he couldn't think of that now.

Church thundered forward, searching for the door that said Bay Three, and when he found it, he threw his shoulder through it and dove inside.

The space was huge—and in front of him, pallets and pallets of shells and bombs—enough to level an

entire country. He paused to take it in for a moment—
and that brief hesitation almost got him killed.

He saw the muzzle flash first and heard the bullets
dance off the casings of the munitions around him a
millisecond later. He ducked instinctively—a barrage of
fire raining down from the high catwalk around the top
of the warehouse.

From Markovich's plans, Church knew that there
were a set of offices suspended above the warehouse
floors—and no doubt that's where the Serbian forces
were trying to make their stand from. But Church had
one thing on his side—and that was the explosives in his
pocket—which, even if he just shoved them between the
bombs he was hiding behind, would set off a chain reaction large enough to take out everything in this room
and blow the roof a mile into the sky.

Hell, it might have brought down the entire building
itself—but doing anything under fire was no easy task.
It was dark, and he stared down at his shaking fingers,
clenching them a couple of times as the bullets kept
hitting.

He fumbled the detonator into the explosive,
pressing it deep into the plasticised material, thumbing
the timer until the numbers appeared. He pressed the
button, the digits climbing by ten each time, and when
he got to thirty he stopped, reaching to his shoulder and
touching the talk button linked to his comms, breathless,
heart pounding.

'Captain—I'm in trouble here. Charge is ready to be
set.'

There was no response, and Church could no longer discern where the gunfire was coming from. It echoed through the whole building, the sound bouncing around. Was it coming from the front? Was it coming from behind? Was it coming from Storage Bay One or Two? He didn't know.

He touched his shoulder again. 'Captain, come in,' he called. 'Captain?'

But it was no good. He had to make the call himself.

It was Grandad's voice he heard then.

'Hold fast, Church,' Grandad said. 'I'll find him.'

But Church could tell from the strain in his voice that he knew more than Church did—that they were in trouble. That Church couldn't sit there forever. The Serbs were beginning to spread out along the catwalk, and soon they'd flank him, be right above him, and he'd be fucked.

He got to a knee and painted a vertical line of fire up the wall, raking it over the catwalk in front of the men, sending them scarpering back towards the office. He chased them there, trying to pick off who he could, and clipped one in the darkness—but there was no light and he couldn't see what he was shooting at, not until they shot at him first.

'Fuck it,' he said, ducking back behind the stack of bombs, thumbing the timer up to ninety seconds now instead. He hit the big red button and watched as it began to count down—a minute and a half until this place went boom and became the biggest fireball in Western Europe.

He shoved it between the bombs and took one last look at it, watching as it ticked down to a minute and twenty-five, wondering if that was too short a time to do what he needed. But there was nothing that could be done now—and they weren't going to get another go at this.

He jumped to his feet and let off another stream of suppressing fire, making a dash back through the door, chased by bullets all the way there. He ran into the corridor with such pace that he bounced off the opposite wall, pain lancing through his shoulder as he righted himself and began sprinting back towards the exit, hearing now what Grandad had—the firefight erupting from Bays One and Two.

Church slowed slightly as he reached the first door, panting hard, trying to keep the count in his head. Just over a minute, he thought, as he followed the sound of fire, ducking into Bay Two, scanning the upper reaches of the room for the aggressors. He saw them instantly—more of them than he'd faced. Lots more. This was the centre of the building where the Serbian forces had been clustered, and it looked like half of them were shooting down from the upper windows at Darko's men while half of them had turned their attention to protecting the thing they were here to protect.

Church spotted Grandad taking cover behind a crate on the left, and on the right he could see DD slumped against a wooden box, clutching at his ribs. Church wasn't sure which way to move, but before he could make a decision, Gaz was next to him, shoving him out of the way and sprinting forward.

'Cover me!' he ordered, and Church jumped to it, lifting his rifle, sending a stream of bullets towards the strobing muzzles above. Gaz sprinted towards DD and slid across the oily concrete to his man, slamming his hand against his stomach to staunch the bleeding.

He was hit. There was no doubt about that.

'Cover! Cover!' Gaz called, not even bothering to look back as he threw his hands under DD's arms and began dragging him towards the door. Grandad popped up now too, and joined the fight—and while Church and Grandad pinned them down, unsure if they were hitting any of their shots or all of them, Gaz tried to bring DD home.

Were they hitting anything? It was impossible to tell in the darkness—but it didn't matter. They had to keep firing. Church's magazine ran dry, and without even needing to look, he reached up and ejected it, grabbing another from his belt and slotting it into place. He knelt, pulling back on the bolt to chamber the first round and then fired again—no more than a second and a half between the intervals.

Gaz was halfway there now—and they couldn't let up. Grandad began backing towards the door, intersecting the line between Gaz and Church, the two of them laying down enough fire to keep the Serbs at bay.

Or so Church thought.

Suddenly, Grandad called out in pain, sagging backwards—almost to a knee—but not stopping his attack.

He reached to his hip and steadied the rifle in the crook of his right arm, spraying bullets wildly into the air as he staggered backwards, turning and making a dash for the door himself, limping and dragging his left leg.

Church saw it then. That they were finished. That this was it.

There were too many of them. They had no cover. They had the low ground.

There was no way they were going to survive this.

Not unless some miracle happened in the next three seconds.

And then it did.

The shockwave came first—then the noise. The fire halted above as the whole building shook, the explosion from Bay One making the walls bow and bend with the force.

Gaz's charge had blown.

He turned away from the blast, covering his ringing ears, closing his eyes against the shockwaves, losing his count altogether. But he knew it couldn't be far—and if they weren't out of the building in the next few seconds, there wouldn't be a building left to get out of.

By the time he looked up, Gaz was there, panting and yelling at DD to get his fucking legs under him.

But the man was shot, he was hurt, and he was in no fit state to walk.

Church dropped his rifle and let it swing on the neck strap, reaching out for Gaz's pack and hauling them back through the doorway and into cover.

Thick black smoke had filled the corridor now. It

choked Church as he tried to pull Gaz and DD upright. A moment later, Grandad dragged himself through the door, leaving a bloody handprint on the frame. Together, Church and Gaz managed to get DD to his feet and draped over Gaz's shoulder.

The smaller man, despite his stature, wasted no time in dragging and marching DD towards the door—and even in the half-light of the corridor Church could see the blood streaming through his fingers.

But it wasn't just DD that was hit.

He turned to Grandad now—the man holding onto his hip, his fingers dug into a bloodied hole just inside his pelvic bone.

'It's not as bad as that,' he said, lifting his chin towards DD, 'but I am going to need a hand.'

Church looked at the man and then back down the corridor towards Bay Three. How long did they have?

Not long enough.

And without asking, he hooked his hand between Grandad's legs and threw him over his shoulders.

'I'm not crippled!' he protested.

'But you are slow,' Church replied, taking off at a run, reeling in Gaz and DD just before the exit, pushing on Gaz's pack to make him go faster—to get him out of the building and out of the blast radius.

He didn't need to be told. Gaz understood—and was yelling every swear word Church knew and some he didn't.

Church knew it was any moment now—and when his charge went off—unless they were far enough away, they'd be torn apart by it. They made a mad cap for the fence, but the Serbs weren't letting them go without a fight. They were beginning to spill down from the offices now and onto the warehouse floor, their footsteps echoing down the corridor behind them.

'Put me down, for fuck's sake,' Grandad snapped, and Church obliged, tearing his pistol from the holster on his hip and levelling it at the open door behind them.

He and Grandad began to back up, arm in arm, their weapons raised—and the moment they saw movement, the first hint of a body—they both opened fire, peppering the inside of the doorway with rounds, trying to give Gaz and DD the best chance of making it outside the fence.

There were shouts from their right then, and Church turned, levelling his pistol that way instead. But under the security floodlights pinned to the side of the building, he could see that it wasn't more Serbian fighters—it was Darko and his men.

Church didn't think it was possible—but he was actually glad to see Darko in that moment.

'Cover us!' he shouted, pulling Grandad around and setting off after Gaz and DD. Darko and his men hung there awkwardly under the light—and as Church cast another glance over towards them, he could see their rifles hanging low at their hips, none of them making any effort to do what he'd asked. And all at once, he knew that he'd made a grave mistake.

A shot rang out behind him—and he felt the bite of the bullet in the back of his left leg.

He called out, his knee buckling—and he and Grandad fell, sitting ducks. Church spat flecks of red-hot spittle between his teeth, looking up towards Darko. He began easing backwards out of the floodlight now and into the darkness and the safety it afforded—recusing himself from the order Church had given and from the fight altogether—letting events take their course.

Perhaps it was the rage Church felt from that which gave him a sudden, heightened sense of what was going on—or the shout of the Serbs advancing from behind—how far away they were, how many, and where they were going to be. Because when Church rolled over, he barely lifted his pistol before they were between the sights. He caught the first in the middle of the chest, the second in the shoulder, following it up with another round in the head.

The two men were dead before they hit the floor—and the third, surging out with them, began to scatter, turning and scrambling for cover. Church fired on him, and the man hit the ground before he made it ten feet.

Grandad was limp next to him, blood trickling from above his eyebrow. When he'd hit the floor, he'd landed on his head and was out cold—which meant the only way he was getting out of it was if Church was carrying him.

He twisted onto his side and shoved himself to a knee, forcing his leg to bear his weight. Despite its protest, he managed to get to something resembling a stance, pulling Grandad up with strength he didn't think he could find—and once again hoisted the man onto his shoulders. But halfway he failed—and Grandad just sort of slumped onto his back, draped over him like an old rug.

'Why are you so heavy, you old fuck?' Church snarled, pulling down on his wrists so that Grandad's chin was resting on his shoulder.

He loped forward, looking towards the corner of the building, looking for Darko—knowing he wouldn't be there—waiting for more Serbs to come out behind him, for more gunfire, for the bullet that wouldn't hit him in the leg—but in the back. The bullet that would kill Grandad. The bullet that would kill him.

And yet—despite the fires of hell calling his name—they saved his life.

Because just then—just before he died—his timer hit zero—and the entire building went up in a column of fire.

Bright enough and hot enough to turn night to day—and everyone inside to ash.

SIXTEEN

PRESENT DAY

Anastasia Fletcher was not dressed for the countryside.

Church's Land Rover Defender was parked in the middle of the field about ten miles from Mitch's farm, and he watched with some amusement as she pulled her BMW coupe off the country lane and jostled through the gate and onto the grass.

She pulled up a few feet inside the hedgerow and killed the engine. Looking around with a bewildered expression on her face, she opened the door and climbed out unhappily. Wearing a pair of jeans and a low-slung pair of dolly shoes, she looked over at Church, wrapped up in a woollen jacket, and put her hands on her hips.

'Really?' she called, her voice echoing through the cool air.

Church didn't reply. He just stared at her and

restrained a smile as she began making her way across the grass, walking in a pantomime fashion as though she were trying to sneak, lifting her knees up high and searching for parts of the ground that weren't soggy.

Church didn't think it would help to shout to her that there were no such parts to be found.

She squelched her way forward and when she was almost to Church, he walked out to meet her.

'You know when you dropped me coordinates,' she said, 'I thought, oh, that's mysterious. He must be serious. But I figured it would be a multi-storey car park, a service station, hell I would have even settled for a lay-by! So, do you want to tell me why it is you've got me traipsing into the middle of a soaking wet field?' She stared up at him, her dark hair pulled back to the nape of her neck, her pale skin shining in the morning light, her cheeks rosy with the approaching winter.

'Hands,' he said, motioning for her to lift them out to the side.

'What?' she laughed back, shaking her head at him.

'Put your hands out,' he said, with no hint of humour.

Her brow creased, but she did as she was asked, standing in a T-pose.

Church patted her down, moving from her wrists, up her sleeves, down her ribs, feeling in her pockets, avoiding the more intimate zones, but ensuring that any phones or recording devices stashed in her jacket were removed. He was taking no chances.

He took her mobile out of her pocket and held it up,

turning around, setting it down on the Defender's bonnet a few feet behind, checking first to make sure that nothing was recording before he returned to Fletcher.

'That's a little bit overkill, isn't it?' she asked.

'I want to make sure this is off the record,' Church said gruffly.

'It is. I told you that. You don't believe me?'

He just looked at her.

Fletcher stared up at him, trying to ascertain why he had such a conflicted look on his face. And they'd get there, but first he needed to confirm that if she used anything that they discussed here, that it wasn't coming back to him.

'You said you had something for me,' she said, keen to get on with it. 'I assume it's about Kosovo, if you're going to all this trouble.' She glanced around. 'I mean, I get being cautious, but seriously?'

'Seriously,' Church said back. 'It may not matter to you, but it matters to me.'

She held her hands up. 'Fair enough. So why'd you drag me all the way out here? What's going on?'

'I need to know what you know about the bomber and about how it's linked to Kosovo,' Church said.

'I've got some questions for you first,' Fletcher jumped in, stopping him in his tracks. 'Firstly: were you there?'

There was no squirming out of the question this time.

'I was,' Church replied.

'When?' she asked. 'I need dates.'

'We got there in January 1999. Joint op with NATO. Before they were officially involved.'

'Until when?'

'End of March. Just after the bombings started.'

'With the SAS,' Fletcher confirmed.

Church just nodded at that.

'How many in your team?'

'Four,' he said.

'Were you the only team? Were there others? How many?'

'I don't know. I know we weren't the only ones. But how many, I couldn't say.'

'And what did you do when you were there?' she asked.

'A lot,' he said. 'Too much.'

She scowled, the frustration clear in her face. 'This won't come back to you,' she said. 'I'm not going to quote you.'

'I know you're not,' Church said. 'But still, there are things you need to know and things you don't. Things that aren't mine to say.'

She sighed loudly. 'And what is yours to say, Solomon?'

'Well, you ask me and then I'll decide,' he replied. 'But this needs to go both ways. I need information too.'

'Yeah? What kind of information?' she said, hands on hips again.

'You said that you're investigating the role that

NATO played in the conflict—Operation Allied Force—but what does that have to do with the bomber?'

She considered him for a moment. 'And why is that so important to you?'

'Let's just say I've got a vested interest,' he replied.

'Cryptic,' Fletcher said back, raising her eyebrows.

Church shrugged. 'You want to know what I know? I want to know what you know.'

She stared up at him and then bit her bottom lip. 'You're helping Interpol, aren't you?'

Church kept his poker face.

Fletcher nodded, taking his silence as a sort of confirmation.

'And I assume that if you're here asking me about NATO, that means that I'm a step ahead of them on this, which quite frankly, is worrying,' Fletcher said.

'And what exactly are you ahead of them on?'

'The bombings,' Fletcher said. 'They struck me as a little weird. Not enough collateral damage, not enough casualties to be terrorism—'

'They felt more like targeted attacks,' Church finished for her.

'Right?' Fletcher said. 'Big question is who were the targets? I started digging into the names and well, what I found was interesting.'

'And what did you find?'

'Well, that was the thing—nothing,' she said. 'The names on the casualties list seemed to have a sort of veil up around them.'

'What do you mean?' Church asked her.

'Not all of the names were released immediately, and when they were, they weren't returning anything. I couldn't find the usual information from public directories like you would with regular civilians. So I did some digging, called in some favours, and in each of the attacks someone that died was either still working for NATO or formerly worked for NATO, and always in senior positions with top secret clearance. That's why there wasn't much information to find on them—it'd been removed from public record. It was weird, almost as though the authorities were trying to keep their deaths quiet, or at least bury the link between the victims.'

'But you found the link,' Church said, watching her. 'Kosovo.'

Fletcher nodded. 'Yeah. In every attack, at least one of the victims was someone who had some clout during the conflict, someone who had the deciding say on launching Operation Allied Force. Which, as I'm sure you know, has been the biggest black mark on NATO's record for the last twenty-five years. It's hard to brand yourself as a peacekeeping organisation, as a force of defence and support when you murder 500 civilians by carpet bombing them in their homes.'

Church folded his arms. 'Yeah,' he said, leaving it at that. 'So you think that whoever this bomber is, he's going after the people who gave the go-ahead for Allied Force?'

'It's just a theory right now,' Fletcher said. 'But there's a story there for sure. This guy, whoever he is, has an axe to grind. And he's grinding it. I'm going to keep digging, keep poking, but it's hard to do when you've got nothing to go on—and I hope that's where you come in. If you can give me some details, help me tie together the parts of the puzzle I already have, when I start making phone calls and start demanding answers, if they think I already know half the story...'

'They might be more inclined to give you the other half,' Church said.

'That's my hope,' Fletcher replied. 'And if not, well, maybe you'll give me enough to write something anyway, enough to bring what NATO did back then to light. Enough to make people understand what really happened.'

'I didn't take you for a war journalist,' Church told her.

'I'm not,' she said. 'But if there's a government trying to cover up the shit they did, or, hell, multiple governments conspiring to do just that, then that's the kind of journalist I am.'

Church smiled a little.

He had to give it to Fletcher. She was fearless.

Poking any bear took balls, but poking one as big as NATO? There were so many stories of journalists shaking the wrong trees and paying the ultimate price for it. And Fletcher had almost done just that in the DRC.

But here she was again, shaking with abandon, and Church respected the hell out of her for it.

'I know it's probably going to fall on deaf ears,' Church said, 'but I think you should be careful—You know, if you push too hard, you might find these people you're going after, they push back.'

'Noted,' Fletcher replied, looking up at him. 'And you should be careful, too.'

'Yeah, and why is that?' Church said.

'Well, if you were there,' she said, 'in Kosovo, if you were involved in Operation Allied Force, if you had a hand in making that happen, then there could well be a target on your back as well. If this guy, whoever he is, is determined to make everyone responsible for Allied Force pay...' she said, turning to look out across the frigid, soaked field, 'well, just don't be surprised if you find your name on that list as well.'

SEVENTEEN

THEY DROVE like hell to get home.

Grandad was able to staunch his own bleeding and sat in the front seat while Church knelt in the back, keeping his fingers firmly in DD's ribcage. The man groaned and swore all the way back, but kept consciousness—the tough son of a bitch that he was.

By the time they got into camp, the first flecks of dawn were lighting the sky, and Church hoped that all four of them would live to see the sun come up.

Gaz exited the car and they carried DD, now just clinging on to consciousness, into the camp.

'Help! We need help!' Gaz yelled as they arm-and-legged him toward the main house.

The lights inside came on and the door opened—Ismet's two guards flooding out along with Marsela and the old man himself, no doubt waiting up for them to return—or not.

'We need to get him stabilised,' Gaz said, breathless as they carried DD towards the threshold. 'And then I'll call for Medevac.'

Marsela stopped them as they entered the house, coming under the hallway light, and looked down at DD, opening the hole in his shirt to look at the wound.

'There's no time,' she said. 'Get him into the kitchen. We've got to treat this here. He'll never make it to an evacuation.'

Church looked up at her then.

'Are you a doctor?' he asked—surprised they hadn't gotten that far—and was surprised when she returned his gaze and nodded.

'Almost. I was well on my way before the war start-ed,' she said, motioning them to follow her. 'But that's a story for another time.' She was already running to the kitchen sink and rolling her sleeves up. She began washing her hands as they slid DD onto the table and she went to work.

Grandad staggered into the kitchen after them, clutching his hip, his leg soaked with blood, and Marsela looked up at him.

'God, you too,' she said, already unfastening DD's flak vest.

Grandad waved her off. 'I can wait,' he said. 'Fix Darren first.'

Marsela looked at Church then, her eyes drifting to his leg.

It was tightly bandaged and he could just about bear his weight on it, so he didn't think it was anything more than a flesh wound—hopefully a through-and-through. He hadn't looked at it yet and wouldn't until he was sure that DD was going to pull through.

Marsela's eyes rested on the bloodied gauze around his thigh and then lifted to his—but he said nothing, just shook his head—and she understood.

Tend to DD first.

It was an hour before she'd pulled the bullet fragments out and stitched him back together—but was insistent that Gaz get DD that evac anyway. But just as he was about to turn towards the door, DD's hand shot out and grabbed him by the wrist.

Gaz looked down at it—the pair of them covered in his blood—and then lifted his gaze to the man on the table. He had one eye open, his teeth gritted.

'Welcome back to the land of the living,' Gaz said. 'Thought we'd lost you there.'

DD just stared back at him. 'I'm not done,' he said, tightening his grip on Gaz's arm.

Gaz bared his teeth and sucked air between them, appraising his brother's condition. 'I don't think that's your call to make, mate,' he replied.

'No evac,' DD said again, mustering as much weight in his words as he could. 'I just need a day or two and I'll be back on my feet.' He rested his head back then and closed his eyes, and Gaz looked at Marsela for some kind of confirmation. One way or the other, she didn't want to—or perhaps wasn't able—to give it.

It was up to Gaz to make that call, and he didn't know which way to jump either. He turned his attention to Church, as though searching for some kind of answer.

It was the first time Church had ever seen Gaz falter —not know which way to jump. What decision to make.

Marsela didn't waste more time, though. 'Help me move him into the living room,' she said to Gaz and Church, motioning for Grandad to approach the table and climb on. 'We're not finished yet.'

Church and Gaz did without a word—and DD, though he groaned in pain, didn't make any sort of protest, and allowed himself to be carried out of the kitchen.

They laid him on the sofa and he let out a long, rattling breath.

Church turned back to the kitchen while Gaz lingered for a moment longer, resting his hand on DD's shoulder.

'You did well tonight,' he said. 'It went sideways on us—but you put your shift in. Get some rest, all right.'

DD just gave him a vague nod and then turned his head away from the light coming in through the window.

When Church returned to the kitchen, Grandad was sitting on the edge of the table, one hand hooked into the belt of his trousers, pulling them down a little to expose the bullet wound—the other lifting the hem of his shirt.

Marsela was working out of an old Soviet first aid

kit—the hooked stitching needles fit for shark fishing—
stout and blunt.

'You're lucky,' she announced to Grandad. 'Doesn't
look to have hit anything important. But this is still
going to hurt like hell.'

'They always fucking hurt,' Grandad grumbled
back. 'It's not the first time I've been shot.'

Marsela looked up at him as she picked up the
bloodied forceps she'd used to deal with DD and carried
them towards the sink to wash them. 'Well,' she said,
'you think you would have learned by now then.'

Grandad let out a little laugh—and then winced at
the pain it caused him.

Church lingered by him, favouring his good leg, and
folded his arms. 'Maybe you are getting slow, old man,'
he said.

'Yeah, yeah,' Grandad replied. 'They've been telling
me that for ten years and I'm still here. And correct me
if I'm wrong,' he went on, closing one eye and squinting
at Church, 'but you also got shot, didn't you?'

Marsela stopped her washing and looked up quickly
at Church then.

'Just a graze,' he said. 'Nothing serious.'

'I'll be the judge of that,' Marsela announced,
finishing with the forceps and coming back to Grandad.
'You want something to dull the pain?' she asked him.

'Like anaesthetic?' Grandad asked back.

'More like vodka,' she said.

He chuckled again. 'You know what? I wouldn't
turn it down.'

Twenty minutes later he was limping towards the front door—keen to head back to the tent, get some well-earned sleep.

And then it was Church's turn. Gaz was still in with DD, making sure he stayed breathing. He knew that he should have called that evac—but knew why he hadn't.

Church understood that if they called NATO and fed back up the chain about what had happened—about how injured they'd all been—about how close it had been—then there was a good chance that NATO might pull the plug and extract them all.

They were here as a team of four—and if they were no longer a team of four—then the operation could be scrubbed altogether. Probably would—and Gaz seemed to want to avoid that at all costs—wanted to stay here—wanted to finish the job.

And Church did too.

'On the table,' Marsela ordered him. 'Take that off,' she said, pointing to the bandage.

'It's actually the back,' Church said, pointing to the rear of his thigh.

'Well then, you'd better turn around and bend over for me,' Marsela said, not restraining a smirk as she put her hands on her hips. 'Trousers,' she ordered, pointing down towards the floor.

Church sighed a little as he turned round, unfastening his belt.

'You know, usually this doesn't happen till at least the second date,' he quipped.

'Well, this is the second time I've had to treat your wounds, so maybe it does qualify.'

Church glanced over his shoulder at her.

She was standing close enough behind him now that he could smell her skin—the faint scent of orange and citrus rising from her hair. She stared up at him with those electric blue eyes, and then he convinced himself to look away.

He pushed his trousers down to his knees and did as he was told, leaning forward over the table, resting on his elbows as she took a look at the wound.

'Well, it's not a graze,' she said. 'But it doesn't look like it's hit bone. The angle looks like it's a through-and-through, and...' she moved her head around his leg, finding the exit wound. 'No bullet stuck in there. You're lucky.'

'Yeah, I feel lucky,' Church grumbled, thinking of how close they'd come to not getting out of there at all.

'A quick stitch,' she said. 'I'll clean and bind it, then. You'll have some discomfort, but I'm sure that's something you're no stranger to.' She set about lining up the thread and needle, but she didn't manage to get it into his skin before the front door burst open and Darko stormed in.

He took one look around, glancing into the living room, seeing Gaz and DD on the sofa there, seeing Church bent over the kitchen table with his trousers down, and whether it was just one of those things or all of them together, it was enough to make him erupt.

Reflexively, Church grabbed his trousers and pulled them back up to his waist, turning to meet Darko before he even reached the table.

'What the fuck do you think you're doing?' he snapped at his sister. 'My men out there are bleeding, injured, and you're in here treating them?'

Church held his ground, ready to intercede if he felt the need to, but Marsela seemed more than capable of dealing with her brother.

'Outside. Now,' he snapped at her.

'I'll go when I'm ready,' she said. 'I'm working.'

'You work for me,' he snapped at her, pointing to himself. 'And I said my men—our people—they need you right now. These fucking guys can wait,' he demanded, flicking a wrist at Church.

'I don't work for you,' she said. 'And I understand what our people are going through, but these men are here fighting for our people, and they deserve my help as much as anyone else,' she answered, facing him defiantly.

His hand flashed too quick for Church to get there in time, and he struck his sister across the face—not with the intention to hurt her, but just to shock.

Her hands leapt to her cheek but he wasn't done yet, and Darko seized her by the hair now, as though to drag her out to help his men if she wasn't going to listen to his demented logic.

But while Church wasn't quick enough to stop the slap, he was quick enough to stop this, and before Darko could even turn his attention to him, Church had him by the wrist and with one quick, powerful movement he seized his hand and jerked the two in opposite directions, listening with some satisfaction to the audible snap of what he thought was probably the scaphoid bone.

Darko reeled back, shrieking in pain, fishing for his pistol on his right hip with his left hand, trying to drag it from the holster, no doubt to execute Church then and there.

But before he even managed to get a hand on it, Gaz was in front of him, holding his arm in place.

'I wouldn't do that,' he said. 'Looks like you put a hand on a woman and paid the price for it.' He held Darko's eyes, and Darko stared back at him before turning his attention to Church once more, realising that here and now he was injured—and it was two on one—and if he escalated this further he'd only give them an excuse to finish him or at the very least break something else. And if there was one thing a rat had, it was a sense of prevailing self-preservation.

So silently, he tucked his naked little tail between his legs, dragged his hand free of his weapon and held it up. Seething, he backed towards the door, disappearing through it and into the brightening day.

Church turned back to Marsela to ask her if she was okay, but instead of gratitude he was met with a baleful scowl.

'Great,' she said frustratedly. 'Now I'm going to have to fix his fucking wrist.' She glowered at Church.

Church blinked at her. 'I'm sorry. I didn't mean to—'

'You didn't mean to what?' she said. 'Injure him? Break his wrist? Because it looked to me like that's exactly what you were trying to do.' Her cheek was reddening, glowing brightly now in contrast with her eyes. Her expression softened after a few seconds and she shook her head. 'I understand what you were trying to do, but... but it's not going to make things better. It's only going to make things worse. Here,' she said, handing the needle and thread she was still holding to Gaz. 'I'm sure you've stitched your men up before. You take over.' She grabbed up the first aid kit now and headed towards the door. 'I've got to go and treat my brother.'

And with that she promptly disappeared.

Gaz just stared down at the needle in his hand and then up at Church.

'Jesus Christ, Solomon,' he said. 'How many times I gotta tell you? The peace with the KLA is paramount to the success of this mission. God... if the Serbs found out we were here, it would be a political shitstorm of an unknown magnitude. The KLA don't want us here already. But if you keep picking a fight with Darko, then he's not going to have to kill you. He's just going to have to make one phone call. One word about who we really are and what we're really doing here and we're fucked. All of us. And if that happens, that's on you, Church.' He pushed the needle and thread into Church's hand. 'You can stitch your own fucking leg up—and maybe the pain will get you thinking straight, hey?' His eyes lingered on the big man for a few more seconds. 'But you know what?' he said, with a long, road-weary sigh. 'Somehow, I doubt it.'

.

EIGHTEEN

PRESENT DAY

FLETCHER'S WARNING rang in Church's head.

She was right: the bomber had been going after not just the men responsible for Operation Allied Force, but their families too—he seemed to have waited for that moment.

He could have taken the responsible individuals out at any time, but he didn't. He specifically planned it so that the blast would kill not only them, but everyone they loved, as well. This wasn't just some vendetta. This was a deeply personal mission of revenge. A mission to make not just things right, but to hurt. To make them bleed. And if there was one way to make Church hurt, to make him bleed, it was by going after Nanna and the girls.

He raced from the Cotswolds straight into the centre

of London, this time missing no lights, taking no wrong turns.

His focus was a laser beam. Now, for the first time in what felt like an age, he knew what he needed to do and where he needed to be. And he made it happen, thinking of every possible outcome, planning every possible contingency. The Glock 17 strapped to the side of his seat could be in his hand in less than half a second, and if he saw anything wrong, it would be.

The tyres squealed as he pulled onto Nanna's street and drove along in the gathering darkness, barely missing rush hour on the early side, the fast winter night closing in.

He parked quickly and got out of the car, the bite in the air not fazing him. As he scanned the surroundings, making a note of every car, checking every shadow, every darkened doorway for anything amiss, he saw nothing move and strode powerfully up Nanna's steps, knocking on her door with the heel of his hand. He waited, moving his weight from foot to foot, determined not to stagnate, and then knocked again.

After a few seconds, the hall light came on a moment later and Nanna came to the door, scrabbling with a latch. She opened it to the chain and, seeing it was Church, her brow creased.

She closed it, unlocked the chain and then opened it fully, not inviting him in before he stepped over the threshold.

He glanced up the stairs and then poked his head into the living room.

'The girls, are they here?' he said.

Nanna closed the door behind him and put the chain back on, locking it. She wrapped her arms around herself, and when Church turned back, she looked almost ashen.

'What's going on?' she said.

'The girls,' Church replied. 'Are they here?'

'No,' Nanna said. 'Mia's at a friend's house and Lowri's out.'

'Get them back now,' Church almost snapped at her.

'Tell me what's going on,' Nanna said firmly, stretching out her hand to illustrate that things were going no further until she had an explanation. 'You're scaring me, Solomon, and I'm not going to call the girls until I know exactly what's going on.'

Church stopped and looked at his sister. He wished she would just do what he said, but he knew that she would be immovable as she always was.

He let out a long sigh. 'It's the bomber,' he said.

'What about him?' Hannah asked quickly.

'What do you know about the Kosovo war?' he said then, hoping that he wouldn't have to make this a long explanation.

Nanna hedged, shaking her head. 'I know that it happened after Yugoslavia split up. I know that it was a shit show—ethnic cleansing, genocide, all that stuff.'

'Right,' Church said. 'And it ended when NATO interceded and launched Operation Allied Force. They carpet-bombed the country, killed more civilians than they did militants, forced the Serbians to surrender.'

'Okay. And what does that have to do with me and the girls?'

'I was there,' Church said. 'One of my first missions, working alongside the KLA against the Serbs. But...'

'But what, Solomon?'

'But my involvement went deeper.' He couldn't believe he was saying it. Couldn't believe he was finally saying all these things out loud. And not just for the first time today.

'I was working with a Serbian defector,' he said. 'We delivered intel to NATO that gave them the targets that they needed to strike. And we think that the bomber is someone that was involved. They're targeting high-level NATO personnel who gave the go-ahead for the bombings, who were involved, who were responsible for Operation Allied Force.'

The what little colour remained in Nanna's face drained from it. 'And that includes you?' she asked.

'I don't know,' Church replied. 'But I'm not taking any chances. I was there, and I'm not saying Allied Force wouldn't have happened if it wasn't for me, but it might not have happened quite so soon.'

'And now you think that whoever set off those bombs is coming for us. For me, for the girls?'

'I don't know,' Church said. 'But if he is, then I'm going to make sure you're safe.'

Nanna nodded slowly, knowing not to laugh, knowing that it wasn't a joke and that Church wouldn't be there if it wasn't serious.

'Have you seen anything strange? Noticed anybody unfamiliar hanging around, any cars parked outside, anything like that?' he asked her.

Nanna went blank for a moment, as though racking her brain for the information, and then she shook her head. 'No, I don't think so. Nothing like that,' she said. 'But I go to work, I come back. It's… you know, you—you don't look outside.'

'No, you don't,' Church said understandingly, moving past her and into the living room. The light was off, and he kept it that way, walking towards the blinds, putting his fingers between them and splitting them just a little, scanning the street once more.

'You're scaring me, Solomon,' Nanna said, coming into the living room. 'Do you really think that there's a threat against us?'

'I can't say,' Church said. 'But the bomber has access to information he shouldn't have access to, knows how to get to people. He's been planning this for a while. These killings, they're not random. But when he sets those bombs off, he's close by. He does it himself—wants to see it.'

'You don't sound shaken by that fact,' Nanna replied, reading the tone of his voice.

'It means if he has a plan to come after you, if he has the intention to carry it out, then he's going to be here.'

'And that's a good thing?' Nanna asked.

Church reached to his hip and unholstered the pistol he'd brought from the side of the seat. 'It is,' he said, looking back at his sister. 'Because I'm going to kill him before he even gets close.'

The sound of an engine cutting out in the darkness brought his attention back to the window then, and Church looked out, scanning the street once more, comparing it to the mental image he'd taken when he pulled up.

Everything was the same—except wait, no, there was another car now. A hatchback. Innocuous-looking. A few years old. He'd heard from Hallberg that the vehicles that had been used in the bombings had been stolen. But nothing fast, nothing that stuck out. Older, invisible cars. Like this one.

Church fixed his eyes on it, waiting for the door to open, for the person to get out and head into a house. But they didn't. They just sat there in the darkness, the headlights off, the engine out, still behind the driver's seat, as if waiting, watching.

He could almost feel their eyes set on Nanna's house, and a cold fury bubbled up inside him.

Church backed away from the window and racked the slide on his Glock, chambering a round, meeting his sister's eyes for just a moment before heading for the door.

'Wait here,' he said. 'Lock it behind me.'

In any other situation, she might have argued, might have protested, might have told him that she knew better. But for all the times that was correct, now, she didn't. This was Church's domain, and what he was about to do, Nanna could have no part in.

He headed down the hallway and into the kitchen, aiming for the back door, slipping out into the garden without hesitation. He jogged through the enclosed courtyard there and then unlatched the back gate, ducking into the narrow walkway between the houses.

It led out at the end of the block behind the car that he'd seen, and he made no effort to slow his pace, practically sprinting to the end and rounding the corner. He held the pistol trained on the ground roughly ten feet in front of him, his finger on the trigger, his elbow close to his ribs, hiding its presence but keeping it in a ready position. He was on the street now, and making up ground on the car. He crossed the street, out of the streetlights and into the shadow, and stepped onto the grass verge outside the pavement, using the darkness to his advantage.

The car loomed closer, and he did his best to get a look at whoever was inside, but couldn't. They were just a dark shape, a dim glow illuminating the silhouette, but nothing else. Church wondered if it was the glow from the display screen of a bomb timer.

He wasn't taking any chances, and he wasn't wasting any time.

He lunged from the shadow, put his left hand on the driver's door and tore it open. Seizing the driver by the collar, he ripped him clean out of the car and shoved him onto the ground so hard that the man made an audible squeal. But it wasn't the squeal of a hardened soldier, Church realised suddenly as he brought the person into the light. He stared down into the frightened eyes of an eighteen-year-old and saw that he had the muzzle of his pistol jammed into the soft patch of skin under his ear.

The kid's eyes widened and Church felt the sudden wetness against his knee. He looked down and realised the kid was pissing himself. He stood up, legs splayed on either side of the boy, his hands still on his collar. The smell hit him then—cannabis. He looked down at the kid and then at the pavement around them, seeing the rolling paper, seeing the tobacco and small pieces of cannabis strewn around, realising what had happened.

This was no bomber. This was just some kid looking for a quiet place to roll himself a spliff, and Church had frightened him so badly that he'd wet his pants.

'Fucking hell,' Church muttered, standing up and drawing his pistol upwards, pushing it into his jacket.

The kid was in tears now, his hands by the side of his head, palms to the sky.

'I'm sorry, I'm sorry, I'm sorry,' he mewled.

Church took a few steps back, looking down at him, and then glanced over towards Nanna's house.

She was standing there in the doorway now, staring out at him.

And all he could do was stare back.

NINETEEN

TWENTY-FIVE YEARS AGO

ALMOST A WEEK PASSED after Church broke Darko's wrist and Marsella had tended to him, and he'd been walking around camp with a permanently pissed-off expression since, his wrist bound and splinted.

She'd been giving Church a wide berth since the incident and he hadn't even really been able to catch her eye to apologise—though he wasn't quite sure what for.

Church didn't think that anyone could love Darko, even if he was family, and yet Marsella seemed to, despite it all.

Church was unsure what to do and couldn't determine whether or not she was avoiding him simply to try to keep the peace between the SAS and the KLA, as fragile as it was, or if he'd really overstepped some boundary and burned whatever 'relationship' they had.

Church's leg had healed up for the most part and

knitted back together, and though it still hurt every time he put his foot down, he was walking without a limp now—and running, albeit with some difficulty.

Granddad was healing as well, and though he groaned and swore every time he sat up on his cot and got to his feet, he seemed to be almost back to fighting strength as well.

DD was a different story. The bullet had taken its toll, and though he was up and moving about, he was a shadow of his former self yet, and it would take weeks, if not months of rehab until he was able to fight once more at full strength.

Still, he refused to let Gaz tell NATO what had happened, refused to be the reason that the whole mission was scrubbed, and assured Gaz that when the time came, he could do what needed to be done.

Though Church thought that Gaz was putting off whatever came next, waiting for a moment where that could be the truth. They'd been biding their time, it seemed, and there'd been little hint of how much effect their attack on the munitions depot had really had.

Almost like none at all, from where they were standing, Church thought.

But he wasn't plugged in to NATO's grand plan to stop this war, or privy to what conversations were going on between them and Gaz—though as Gaz strode towards him now, he thought that might be about to change.

Gaz slowed and motioned Church away from the tent, out towards where the trucks were parked and they could have some privacy. Church could see him carrying a sat phone and was unsure whether or not he'd just had orders from on high or this was something else. He skipped the pleasantries, and the moment he thought they were out of earshot, he started talking.

'Just had word,' he said. 'NATO are planning something big. And they want Markovich to get them the exact location and building plans of Yugoslav mission command here in Kosovo.'

Church stared back at Gaz, processing that. As far as he was aware, Yugoslav command was set up in Pristina, in the heart of Kosovo, far behind what was the effective front line of the Serbian forces as they pushed the Kosovans back towards the Albanian border.

An air assault in the middle of the city would be the exact thing that Gaz said they wouldn't do. It would be bombing civilians—and yet that would seem to be the only option.

'They're going to launch an airstrike,' Church said.

'Said I don't know,' Gaz said back. 'They don't tell me shit. Just that they want those plans from Markovich —which is a big fucking ask.' He held the phone out to Church then. 'Which is exactly why you're going to do it.'

'Me?' Church replied, staring down at the phone. 'Why me?'

'Because you're the one that Markovich trusts. You've been his POC, you've looked a man in the eyes.'

'That hardly means that he trusts me,' Church said back.

'Yeah, well, he's expecting a call from someone to set up a meet, a drop-off, and soon.' Gaz shook the phone at him.

Church looked at Gaz, inspecting the conflicted look on his face. If this was a big ask, then it meant that there was a distinct risk to Markovich—which was probably why Church had to be the one to ask him to do it, rather than him being told by some anonymous contact at NATO.

'Are we getting his family out?' Church asked.

Gaz seemed a little sideswiped by the question, as though it were totally irrelevant to the mission.

'That's not our call,' Gaz replied. 'Just convince him to get the plans and hand them off to us. That's the job.'

'He's risking everything,' Church said.

'He is,' Gaz replied. 'And that's war. We're all risking everything. Now call him and get it done.' He didn't offer the phone to Church any longer, just pushed it into his chest.

Church took it and watched as Gaz walked away, shaking his head at the borderline insubordination that Church had just given him.

Church looked down at the phone in front of him, the number already on the little green screen, and let out a long breath. Markovich had proved his worth so far, and he'd done it off his own back, with just a vague promise of freedom ahead of him. And Church knew exactly what question he was going to ask when he gave him his next orders—and it was a question that he didn't have an answer to.

He hit the number to dial for Markovich, wondering what he was going to say, and looked up, scanning the camp once more for any sign of Marsella. When the line connected, he still hadn't found her. There was silence on the other end, as though Markovich was frightened to speak first.

'Markovich,' Church said quietly. 'My name is Solomon Church. We were never formally introduced, but we met several times in Gurtesh—the little village with a broken fountain.'

'I know where Gurtesh is,' Markovich said back, almost coldly. 'You're calling me? Why?' He was suspicious, and rightly so.

'NATO needs one more thing,' Church said, already feeling like he was lying.

There was a pause for a few seconds as Markovich considered his position.

'What is it?' he asked bluntly.

'We need intel on Yugoslav military command in Pristina. Building plans, information on who's there and when, employee lists. Everything you can get.'

'You want me to steal the blueprints for Yugoslav military command in Pristina in the middle of the fucking war?' He scoffed, the indignation clear in his voice. 'It cannot be done. The plans are in Pristina. They're in Yugoslav military command. How the fuck do you expect me to get there and get them? They're paper copies in the fucking archives room in the basement! I suspect you know how many soldiers are between here and there right now. There's no way I could get in there without somebody seeing me—without a hundred people seeing me. And what about my family? I've heard nothing from you. I've heard nothing from NATO about them—about their safety, about our supposed deal. And now you ask me this?'

'I know, I know,' Church said back. 'I'm sorry. It's being... it's being organised,' he lied. 'And I have been told if you do this, that— That—' He hated himself for saying it, for building up to lying like this. 'That it's the last thing,' he said. 'I promise you that you do this and... and that's it.'

'My family will be safe,' Markovich confirmed.

Church ground his teeth. 'Yes,' he said. 'You do this and your family will be safe.'

There was silence for a few more seconds, and then Markovich sighed.

'I will call you when it's done.'

'I'll be here when you do—' Church replied. But before he could get the words out, Markovich hung up.

Church lowered the phone and let out a long sigh, turning around to see Gaz standing behind him with his arms folded.

'I know that was hard, Church,' he said. 'But you did good. And that's a good lesson for you.'

'I lied to him,' Church replied. 'If he's caught...'

'Well, then you better make sure he's not,' Gaz told him. 'You wanted to make a difference. You wanted to move that needle... this is it, Church. This is an opportunity to take out Yugoslav high command. This is a chance to end this war—to stop it here and now.'

Church didn't reply to that.

He just held out the phone to Gaz, who shook his head.

'No, you keep it,' he said. 'And let me know when Markovich calls—because if he wants to save his family... I'm pretty sure he fucking will.'

TWENTY

PRESENT DAY

CHURCH FELT AS TIGHTLY wound as he ever had before.

He tried to explain what had happened to Nanna, but she wasn't buying it. Not one iota.

He couldn't tell her they weren't in danger, couldn't tell her that he was going to fix it, couldn't tell her anything.

Except that he was going to try.

And he didn't like that that was all he could offer.

He'd scarcely got back into his Land Rover Defender before he made the decision. Playing defence was no longer an option. The way he'd almost put a bullet through that kid's skull showed him beyond a shadow of a doubt that this was getting to him, and with Hallberg trying desperately to figure out where this guy was going to hit next, it didn't give him much confidence that they'd find him before he got to Hannah and the girls.

Which left him only one option.

He needed to find the bomber first and deal with him once and for all.

As he drove back towards the farm, he called Fletcher. And as though waiting for his call, she answered after the first ring.

'Solomon,' she said. 'Have you reconsidered? Finally decided to come clean?'

'Not exactly,' Church replied, 'but I'll make you a deal.'

'Oh, sounds tantalising,' Fletcher replied. 'I'm all ears. What kind of deal?'

'Exchange of information.'

'What are you thinking?'

'I'm thinking you tell me where the bomber's going to hit next. And I'll grant you an exclusive interview with him,' Church replied.

There was silence on the line.

'Bullshit,' she said after a few seconds.

'Not if your information is good,' Church said. 'I think you were right with what you said, and I'm not willing to risk my family to keep secrets. There never should have been secrets at all. So if you can point me in the right direction, if you can put me on a collision course with the bomber, I'll make sure that you get a one-on-one interview with him before I hand him over to the authorities.'

'That's an interesting proposition,' Fletcher replied

quietly. 'But what makes you think that I know where he's going to be?'

'Because I know you,' Church said. 'And I know you're good. If you know that he's working his way through a list of NATO officials, then I bet that you've put together a list just like that. Am I wrong?'

'Let's say you're not,' she replied. 'For argument's sake. What's this going to look like? Because if you start shooting, I don't want whatever crimes you get charged with coming back to me. My record's clean— just about—and I'd like to keep it that way.'

'It won't come back to you,' Church replied. 'You have my word on that.'

'Your word,' Fletcher parroted back to him.

'My word,' Church said. 'It's worth a lot.'

She harrumphed a little, considering it.

'Okay, if you can promise me that you'll get me in a room with this guy before you hand him over, let me get my story before he disappears into some black hole, then you got yourself a deal.'

'Good,' Church replied. 'Just tell me where I'm going and I'll tell you when I've got him.'

'Okay,' she said. 'I'll be in touch. Out of curiosity, when are you intending to launch this capture mission?'

'Yesterday,' Church said. 'So don't drag your feet.'

She laughed a little. 'Noted. I'll be in touch.'

And with that, she hung up and Church drove on through the city, his hands so tight around the steering wheel his knuckles were white in the darkness of the cab.

By the time he reached Mitch's farm, Fletcher had already sent him a voice note with the name and an address of a retired NATO exec now living in a farm in Northumberland.

'He's the only other one on UK soil, the others are all in Europe. I have no idea where the bomber is going to strike next or who, but this guy—Gordon Whitmore— he was one of the top guys when Allied Force was launched. He would have been one of the men sitting in that closed room, weighing up the pros and cons, the value and cost of civilian lives in order to force Serbia's hand. And without his signature, without his go-ahead, the bombs never would have fallen and 500 civilians never would have died. So if the bomber was hell-bent on making everyone who made Allied Force a reality pay, then Whitmore is definitely on that list. Good luck.'

Church and Mitch sat across the kitchen table from each other, prepping their weapons and gear as Fletcher's note played between them.

Mitch eyed Church as he thumbed rounds into the magazine of his L119A1 carbine.

'Did you really tell her that you'd give her an interview?' Mitch asked him.

Church nodded, finishing his own magazine and slotting it into his weapon.

'I did,' he said.

'And you're actually going to do that?'

Church looked up at Mitch, pausing his preparations. 'If he survives that long.'

'And is that our intention?' Mitch asked. 'Capture?'

Church didn't shrug, didn't do anything, just stared at his friend.

'I haven't decided yet,' he said.

Mitch smiled just a little.

'Sure,' he said. 'Whatever you say, Sol.'

They got on the road and drove north, the pair of them in flak vests, armed to the teeth, both of them with sidearms, Church with his carbine, Mitch with his HK417. A longer-range weapon, but deadly in the hands of a seasoned shooter at any distance. And that's exactly what Mitch was.

It took them hours winding north through the night, but sometime around 3 a.m. they approached the gate of Whitmore's farm. It was out in the sticks, down a long private lane, surrounded by what looked like hundreds of acres of empty farmland.

When they reached the gate, it wasn't some old rusted field gate. Two huge wooden slabs with steel frames sat between stone columns, a tall wall running on either side, a camera mounted to the right above a keypad.

They slowed as they approached, and Mitch instinctively killed the lights short of where the camera would see. He backed up a little bit, pulled onto the verge at the side of the lane, killed the engine and stared out into the darkness.

'Are we just going to walk up to the front gate?' he asked. 'Ring the bell?'

Church scanned the area.

There was woodland either side of them, and he

knew that no matter how much money Whitmore had accrued during his career, stone walls like that wouldn't run the entire perimeter.

'No,' Church said. 'Let's get in for a closer look. Scout the area, see if we can't set up somewhere to stake the place out. We can stash the car and come back.' He looked over at Mitch. 'This might not be a quick thing. It might be days, weeks before the bomber arrives. I don't expect you to—'

'Cut that shit out,' Mitch interjected. 'I'm here, aren't I? Long as it takes,' he said, putting his hand up for Church to take.

He did so, clapping his palm against his brother's.

In his mind, he'd envisioned doing this on his own. This was his past, his mistakes come calling, and his responsibility to fix them. But there was something in Mitch that recognised that too. As though he was vicariously making up for his own misdoings by helping.

And Church had to admit, it felt good having backup.

They left the car, dawn still a long way off, and headed into the woods. They walked a few hundred metres and then cut back towards the fence, moving quietly only by the residual light bleeding down from the sky through the bare treetops.

Winter—it seemed like it was on an unavoidable collision course now, and Church could feel the chill of the air through his fleece. Still, heavy layers hindered movement and made sound. He wanted to be light and fast, ready to jump if the time came.

They approached the fence and hopped over it, Church pushing down the barbed wire for Mitch to swing his leg over, and then Mitch doing the same.

In the field they moved quickly between sleeping cattle. It seemed like Whitmore had become a hobby farmer, and a herd of long-haired Highland cows were lying all across the meadow. They picked their heads up at the new arrivals, but thankfully made no noise as they passed.

The farmhouse loomed in the distance, dark, and Church could see that it was an old stone building that had been renovated, a steel barn set to its right, and to its left a huge garage with several cars on the wide driveway before it.

The ground rose up ahead of them and they adjusted their course to give themselves a better look down at the place. As they reached the crest, they both instinctively lowered themselves to their elbows and knees and then down onto their bellies, the cold, damp grass soaking them immediately.

Church reached to his belt and unflapped the small case there, pulling out a night vision monocular, pressing it to his eye, scanning the farm buildings. Mitch brought his rifle to his shoulder and looked through the optic instead, reaching up and flicking on the scope, which hummed quietly as it came to life, giving him night vision too. They both scanned individually and then in unison, lowered them.

The farmhouse itself was set in an open space about

a hundred metres from the tree line and the front gate that they'd parked near.

A sweeping driveway led up to the building, and though there were a handful of vehicles parked out front, it didn't seem like anyone was home. Not a single light was burning, which for a house this size seemed odd. Usually there would be an exterior light, a hallway light, something left on.

And yet it was utterly still. Abandoned, it felt like. Church's heart beat a little harder as he stared down at the place.

'Something doesn't feel right,' he muttered.

'I was just thinking the same,' Mitch said. 'You want to go down there?'

Church licked his lips, thinking about it.

They had trespassed on Whitmore's land—how much further did he want to push this?

And yet that feeling of unease was unignorable.

'Yeah, let's do a loop,' Church said. 'Make sure this place is buttoned up. Maybe they're just on holiday,' he offered, not sounding sure of it himself.

'Yeah, maybe,' Mitch replied, his response equally as unsettled.

They got to their feet and started down the hill towards the building, moving in a curve so that they approached up the driveway, getting the best view of the house. They both stopped as they reached the concrete, the pair of them freezing when they saw it: even in the darkness, it was clear that the hulking front door—eight feet tall and nearly four feet wide—was open.

Their rifles came up instinctively and they moved shoulder to shoulder, scanning their flanks, closing in on it, not needing to discuss what came next.

If the door was open, that could only mean one of two things.

Either Whitmore knew that he was on the bomber's list and had fled as quickly as humanly possible, not bothering to shut it behind him—or he didn't know he was on the bomber's list and they were already too late.

They stepped up onto the porch way and paused, listening for any sounds coming from inside. There was nothing, no movement, the air still around them, the only sound the quiet breaths of the two men standing at the front door.

They exchanged a quick glance and then Church nodded that they were going in.

He took the vanguard, his weapon much better suited to close quarters engagements, and as a pair they moved into the house, Church heading for a door to the right and going to the frame covering the room, nodding to Mitch who then moved to the next. They did that, sweeping the house room by room until they cleared the ground floor.

They headed up, stepping slowly, cautiously on each step, as though anticipating the worst. Church was almost hoping for it. Hoping to find the man they came here for.

But as they kept going, Church knew that the house was empty, that Whitmore had gone either on his own accord or under duress. It wasn't the bomber's MO, but that didn't mean things couldn't change, that they wouldn't, that he wouldn't progress, that his anger, his rage, his need for revenge wouldn't devolve into something more personal. He always ensured that he was close enough by to see that his devices worked. So was it a far cry to think that at some point, given the opportunity, he'd graduate to an even more intimate method?

As they finished the sweep, the last room checked off, Church and Mitch both let out a little sigh, partly in relief, partly in disappointment that they had indeed been too late.

'Fuck,' Church muttered under his breath. 'Place's a ghost town.'

Mitch looked around slowly and then lifted his head. They were standing in the master bedroom, the last room they searched, the en suite, and he looked over towards the bed.

'It's still made,' he said.

Church looked over at it too. Mitch was right. They hadn't jumped out of bed in the middle of the night and made a run for it, that much he knew for sure. So why, if they'd left in the light of day, hadn't they locked the place up at least? Or perhaps they had...

A thought occurred to Church then, and his hands tightened around the weapon.

'Let's do another sweep,' he said to Mitch.

'There's no one here, Church,' Mitch replied. 'We checked the whole house.'

'We're not looking for Whitmore,' he said. 'We're looking for ordnance.'

Mitch stiffened a little, drawing in a breath. 'All right,' he said, understanding.

If the door was open, maybe it wasn't Whitmore that had left it open, but the bomber who'd opened it instead. If Whitmore was expecting an attack, then he likely wasn't going to go anywhere in public, wasn't going to make himself a target. Which meant only one thing: if the bomber wanted to take him out, he'd have to do it right here.

They moved through the house once more, splitting up this time. Mitch took the downstairs while Church moved through the first floor, this time checking for what Church expected to be a sizeable enough chunk of C4 to bring this whole place crashing down. And just as Church was about to give up hope of finding anything, heading down the stairs towards a waiting Mitch, he stopped, his heels creaking on the steps.

He looked around himself, realising that this was the centre of the house, that the thick stone walls of the place meant that any blast that went off in a bedroom to kill one target would be contained—not directed to the others. No, if there was going to be a single payload to bring as much destruction as possible, it would be set right here. It would take out the central supporting wall and probably bring down the entire building. Church motioned underneath them, and Mitch understood, and without wasting another second, they both descended the stairs and doubled back underneath to the cupboard there.

The moment they opened the door, Church saw it.

A chunk of plastic explosive. Big enough to blow the roof off the entire house.

'Jesus Christ,' Mitch muttered, pushing Church out the way and kneeling down. He lifted it gently from its spot nestled against the supporting wall and pulled it towards him, inspecting it in the darkness, the only illumination coming off the dim green screen of the detonator fixed to it.

It displayed one word in grainy black text: 'Armed'.

Church saw, by the nature of the construction, that it was exactly like the others. Simple. Reliable. But the one good thing about simple devices like this was that they were easy to disarm. All you had to do was slide the detonator pins out of the explosive and you separated the charge from the payload.

But Church didn't waste any time watching Mitch do that, because he'd already come to another conclusion. Just like the other devices, this one was remotely detonated. The short-range RF receiver would trigger the explosion, which meant one thing—if the bomb was here, so was the bomber.

Church strode to the front door as Mitch's words echoed behind him.

'Disarmed,' he said with an audible sigh, standing up. 'Church?'

He heard his name distant behind him, barely registered as he stepped to the threshold and stared out across the darkened, empty space in front of him, knowing the bomber was out there. Understanding now why the door was open.

A trap. A trap to lure Whitmore in. Because when the man came home, he'd see his door open, and go inside to investigate. And then… boom.

But that meant the bomber was laying in wait. That he'd seen them arrive, seen them approach the house, seen them go inside. And perhaps it was curiosity or something else that kept him from blowing them up, but either way, he'd stilled his hand and watched as they found his device and disarmed it.

And as Church stared into the darkness, he began cursing himself.

He'd been so worried that the bomber was targeting him, he'd never stopped to consider whether or not the bomber even knew he existed.

If this guy was who Church thought he was, then maybe he hadn't even been thinking about him. Maybe he hadn't even known that Church was still alive, and hadn't put him on his kill list at all.

But now—if he was out there and had seen Church go in. Was seeing him right now. Was looking right at him…

Church came to terms with a cold, frightening truth.

If he wasn't on that kill list before, he was pretty sure, by his own hand, that he was on it now.

TWENTY-ONE

TWENTY-FIVE YEARS AGO

THEY ROLLED OUT AT SPEED, on course for Pristina.

DD was driving and Gaz turned round in the seat the moment they were outside the farm to look at Church and Grandad. They were sat in the back, kitted up and ready for what lay ahead. They'd had all of twenty minutes' notice to get their shit together and get rolling, but they were well practised at that, and gearing up was muscle memory now. Gaz, fresh off the phone with NATO, had been told that they needed to hit an HVT and they needed to do it now.

'Right-o, lads,' he said, looking from Church to Grandad and back. 'Here's the long and short of it: we're headed for Serbian Central Command. We've got to get inside and we need to extract vital intel for NATO. That's the mission and that's what's got to be done. All right?'

'Intel?' Grandad asked back, folding his arms over the stock of his M16 and leaning forward in the seat a little. 'I thought that's why we had Markovich? I thought that was the whole idea, that Markovich had to get us the blueprints of the building so that NATO could drop a fucking bomb on it and end this whole war?'

Gaz sighed a little, his frustration clear. 'Yeah, you weren't the only one. Turns out, though, that what Markovich delivered ain't good enough. But they do think that it will allow us to pull a rabbit out of a fucking hat, apparently. And while an air strike would definitely be easier, NATO say that it's going to destroy evidence. Evidence that they need to swing the votes for an air campaign, evidence they need to prosecute after this is all over. They want to get planes in the air—B52s —but they can't do that without something ironclad. And when there's blowback from the European courts, they need to be able to hold up a piece of paper that says we were well within our fucking rights and we knew what we were doing—because right now, well, they'd be shooting in the dark. And that's where we come in.'

'They need evidence of the ethnic cleansings,' Church said.

'Exactly,' Gaz replied. 'Anything and everything we can get. Hard drives, paper files, whatever it is, shove it in a fucking bag and bring it home.'

Grandad looked less sold. 'So what, we just stroll in the front door, say, hey, please let us in to the file room. We'll just be a sec'.'

'What do you fucking think?' Gaz said. 'Look, I

know it's not pretty, but it's what's on the fucking table. All right? If you don't like it,' he said, pointing at the door next to Grandad, 'feel free to open that and jump out. Just remember to tuck and roll when you land, because we ain't slowing down. Or, you can untape your bollocks and get with the fucking programme.'

Grandad raised his eyebrows as though the crass language wasn't necessary, but he didn't protest any more.

When Gaz saw that, he went on. 'We're going to go in two teams. Markovich's plans show that there's a radio tower built on top of the building that broadcasts all of the orders going out to the units stationed across Kosovo. Me and DD are going to hit their telephone relay first, cripple their ability to call for help, and then destroy the radio tower, and make sure that they're not sending out any messages any time soon. Really throw a wrench into their fucking war plans. And while we do that, you two,' he said, looking between Church and Grandad, 'are going to slip inside, secure the hard drives and the files, and then slip back out again. DD and I will make enough stink that everybody's going to come running, and then you go in the back. Yeah, nice and easy.'

'Nice and easy,' Grandad parroted back, almost tutting.

Church didn't think he quite had the balls to do it right in Gaz's face.

He understood, though. This plan wasn't just brazen, it was borderline stupid. But it sounded like they didn't have much choice, and Gaz didn't need to remind him any more that this was what they'd signed up for.

The countryside fell to the darkness as they drove, the hour growing late as they hammered across Kosovo towards Pristina.

As they neared the city, it became apparent that the region's capital was in the vice grip of the Serbian Army. DD and Gaz had planned the route meticulously and took them on back roads, across rough country to get to the city, avoiding the police and military checkpoints set up and controlled by the Serbs. If they got stopped at any of those—four British soldiers in unmarked tactical gear, armed like they were, headed towards the city, armed to the back teeth with plastic explosive and automatic rifles—it would only mean one thing. And Church knew they would no doubt be shot on sight. But the route was planned to avoid that, and they managed to sneak inside the city limits, parking the truck on a quiet suburban side street about a mile from Central Command.

They left the car and went on foot from there, sticking to alleyways and deserted streets. They had no doubt that if anybody did see them, nobody would call it in. Although Pristina was under Serbian control, it was the capital city of Kosovo, and that meant that these people had mostly lived here in harmony with the ethnic Albanians for years. And seeing their fellow denizens driven out, rounded up in the streets like cattle and slaughtered, didn't sit well.

So whether or not they were sympathetic to the

KLA, seeing soldiers running the streets would likely make them draw their curtains, not make any phone calls. Or at least that's what they hoped.

They kept pace, spying military checkpoints in the distance and stopping every now and then to allow troop carriers and police cars roving the city to drive by, sprinting between cover until the hulking headquarters of the Yugoslavian Army's Third Army Corps—where all of the military operations carried out across Kosovo were being coordinated from—swam into view.

It was a huge complex. A hulking building surrounded by barbed-wire-topped fences, fortified with sandbags and military 4x4s parked around the entrances.

They stared out at it from a darkened alleyway across the road, and it was Grandad who said what they were all thinking.

'Bloody hell,' he muttered. 'How the fuck are we supposed to get in there?'

Gaz didn't answer right away, and it was the first time Church considered the fact that he didn't have a solid plan here and was flying by the seat of his pants.

Their captain closed his eyes, as though formulating a solution in his mind, visualising the layout of the building, and then, after a minute of silence, he spoke.

'On the west side,' Gaz said, 'the building abuts right up to the street. The administrative wing. Here,' he said, slipping his backpack off and handing it to Church. 'There's a hook and line inside. You'll make your way to the roof and then slip in to the offices via the windows accessible from that first level. DD and I are going the other side. There's an adjoining building that houses the telephone relay and from the roof there we can get across to command and up to the tower.' He held his watch up. 'Sync watches, lads—we're going to blow this thing in exactly thirty minutes. Everyone ready?'

They did as they were told, raising their watches and setting the timer dials to thirty.

'Sync,' Gaz said, and they clicked the buttons to set the countdown hand. 'Good luck, lads.' He nodded to them in turn.

Church stared at the tiny green glowing numbers on his watch face and slid it around to the inside of his wrist. It was common practice during an OP and something that had now become second nature to him. It meant that you could see the time when you were holding the barrel of your rifle, but also that any glow or reflection coming off the face wouldn't be seen by enemy combatants. He thought about it consciously for the first time, watching as the three other men did the same thing—all of them trained in the same way, in the same place, by the same people, to do the same things. Impossible things. Things that no other soldiers could do.

Things like this, Church thought, as Gaz and DD ran back down the alleyway and disappeared around the corner.

Grandad remained still despite Gaz's orders, staring up at the complex, his eyes roving left to right, counting the armed soldiers. Church had done the same when they arrived, but stopped when he got to two dozen—

and that was just what was in view, let alone how many were inside.

'This isn't stupidity—it's suicide,' Grandad muttered under his breath.

Church reached out and squeezed him on the shoulder, hard, to bring him back in line, to bring him back to reality.

'I think that self-preservation instinct is getting too strong, old man,' Church said. 'Dreaming of a caravan in the West Country, whiling away your twilight years in a deck chair, all of a sudden?'

'Fuck off,' Grandad growled, shrugging his hand off. 'When you've been doing this as long as I have, you can see it. You can see it when something is an accident waiting to happen. And this is exactly that. Whatever happens tonight, something is going to go wrong.'

'Well, aren't you a ray of sunshine tonight?' Church sighed. 'If you want to stay here, I can do this on my own.'

'Like fuck you can,' Grandad said. 'The only reason I'm here is to make sure you don't catch a bullet before we even get inside.'

'Well then,' Church said. 'You better keep up.'

And with that, he moved from the alleyway, stuck close to the buildings, and ran parallel to the outer fence of the complex all the way to the end of the street until it cut right. A hundred metres down he saw what Gaz had been talking about. The barbed wire marking the perimeter ended at the corner of the building that faced directly onto the street—a concrete wall that rose up some twenty-odd feet to a flat roof. There was a heavy concrete lip at the top, and though it was primitive, the folding grapple hook and rope Gaz had furnished them with would do the job.

It was after ten at night now, and though the war was in full swing, Church hoped that anybody on the administrative side of the building would still be keeping regular hours—would be long gone for the day. Though they were exposed on the street regardless, and he didn't want to waste any more time.

He pulled the hook from the bag and backed up, sizing up the ledge above him.

It wasn't a big throw, and the shape of the hook meant that as it was dragged towards the edge, it would catch on anything resembling a corner. They were designed that way.

Church swung it around, the steel pulsing through the air as it built momentum, and then launched it, listening to it whistle softly as it arced into the darkness, falling onto the flat roof with the crunch of the chipped stone there.

He dragged it gently until he finally got it to hook up, and then kept the line taut, keeping weight on it. If it slackened and then you gave it a jerk, it would fly over the lip and they'd be back to square one.

He offered the line to Grandad first.

'Nah,' he said. 'You go. You think I got any chance of pulling your huge arse onto that fucking roof?'

He knelt then and slapped his thigh as though to give Church the signal to use it for a boost. He didn't complain and took the chance. Every pull on that rope would be a big expenditure of energy, and even one or two less could mean the difference between life or death for what came after. He planted his heels on the wall and scrambled upwards, putting his boots on the sill of a ground floor window, then on the centre of the frame, jumping upwards almost and taking in as much line as he could before the rope groaned under his weight and swung him free of the wall.

He hauled himself skywards, kicking off from the surface until he reached the lip and pulled himself over, already sweating. He turned, making sure the hook was secure, and then put his belly on the ledge, looking down for Grandad. He was still strong, but a twenty-foot straight climb up a rope in full gear with an M16 hanging off your back was no easy task.

As the old man drew closer, Church stretched down and offered his hand. Grandad took it, thankfully, and Church pulled him upwards, the man scrambling up the side of the wall until he managed to reach the top and pulled himself over.

He rolled onto the stones, catching his breath.

'Fucking hell,' he said. 'I haven't done that in years.'

'Next time we'll take the stairs,' Church told him.

Grandad laughed a little and slapped him on the shoulder, getting to his feet. 'Come on. Let's get this over with. We don't want to be caught inside with our pants down when Gaz's welcome gift goes off.'

Church knew he was right and got to his feet, reeling

in the rope and stashing it in his backpack before they headed forward.

In front of them was a row of large, wood-framed windows—all of them dark, all of them leading to what Church suspected were offices.

They selected the one closest to them.

Grandad already had the pry bar out by the time they approached.

Church slowed him down, pointing to a window to their right instead—one that looked to be left ajar.

'That makes life easier,' Grandad whispered to him as they changed course and headed for that one instead.

Church hooked his fingers underneath it and slid the huge sash window up, stepping over the low sill into the room, his rifle raised and pointed at the door he could see ahead.

The office was large and drab. The high ceiling was without mouldings or cornices, the walls white except for lifeless prints of the Serbian countryside the civil servant working here no doubt thought he was saving.

There were filing cabinets, a leather sofa at the far end of the room, and to Church's left, two chairs set before a desk, and—

He froze as he took stock of the room, seeing something glowing in the darkness.

He turned quickly, fixing his rifle on it—seeing that it was the lit ember at the end of a cigarette.

And that it belonged to—and was firmly lodged between the lips of—a man sitting behind the sprawling wooden desk that dominated the left-hand side of the room. Grandad came in after him and saw that he had his rifle trained on something, bringing his weapon up instinctively, the pair of them zeroing in on the paper pusher in front of them.

He was a guy in his fifties with a bald head and tufts of hair above his ears. He had thin glasses on, a tired suit, the shirt and tie pulled loose at his neck, a tangle of chest hair sticking out the top. He was sitting in almost complete darkness, save for the dim green-shaded desk lamp to his right, illuminating a mostly spent bottle of vodka and an ashtray full of stubbed-out cigarettes. Here this late, he was desperate not to go home—or perhaps he just didn't have a home to go back to anymore. The war had been hard on both sides, and the KLA had not spared the Serbs, or the city. Pristina had seen its fair share of destruction.

The man stared at the two soldiers in front of him and instinctively began raising his hands, knowing that if they were coming in through the window with guns raised, they weren't friendly.

Whether he was just drunk or brazen, Church didn't know, but he took a long drag on the cigarette in his mouth regardless and then lowered one of his raised hands to take the cigarette out. He blew a long stream of smoke into the air and then returned the cigarette to his lips once more before finally raising his hand again.

The question of what came next flashed in Church's mind. Their rifles had suppressors attached, but that barely dimmed the noise.

And if there was one person here, there could be others.

Any kind of gunshot, silenced or not, could be heard, could be recognised, could be reported.

Which left only one option.

This person—whoever he was—was a witness. And that was the exact opposite of what they needed right now.

Church risked a glance at Grandad, who was staring at the guy, unflinching.

'Go on,' Grandad said, feeling his gaze, knowing the question, offering the answer. 'Sort it.'

Church's mouth went a little dry at his words.

They were definite—not open for interpretation.

He lowered his M16 slowly and let it hang from the neck strap, approaching the desk and the man behind it.

He turned on his chair to look at Church but didn't lower his hands, didn't dare make a sound either—accepting his fate or knowing that voicing anything would make it worse. Church motioned him up and didn't give him the chance to comply before he pulled him to his feet and turned him round, locking his left arm around the man's neck.

The bureaucrat didn't struggle, didn't protest even, as Church drew the combat knife from his belt and searched for Grandad's eyes in the darkness once more.

The old man gave him a solitary nod, and putting any doubt out of his mind, Church took the blade and plunged it into the man's sternum. He lifted his left hand over the worker's mouth and held it firm, twisting the knife to sever the aorta cleanly, pulling the blade free, listening as the blood pumped and gushed from his heart.

It was a brutal way to do it, but one of the most efficient.

The aorta delivered blood from the heart to the entirety of the body below it, and cutting through it meant that all of the blood being pumped downwards would come rushing out. The sudden drop in pressure caused a loss of consciousness in seconds as the brain lost all flow. And shortly after, death. Not painlessly, but, he hoped, close to it.

The man struggled for a second or two, made a flailed, feeble attempt at getting away, but Church held onto him, angling his body away so that he stayed clean of his blood. He listened to it splash down onto his leather chair, onto his desk, onto the floor—and then, in just a few seconds, he went limp, sagging in Church's arms.

He guided the Serb back into his chair and sat him there, looking down to see the cigarette that had tumbled from his lips sitting on the carpet, its ember still lit, blue smoke still curling upwards...

And then the spreading pool of blood reached it and extinguished it.

Church let out a soft breath and looked away.

Grandad was already moving towards the door.

'Come on,' he said, not another word of acknowledgement coming from him.

Church's eyes lingered on the man he had just

executed for only a moment. And then he went after Grandad.

He peeked the corridor and, seeing it empty, stepped out into what felt like blinding light. On the wall a few feet down was a map of fire exits—but the floor plans they contained were more than useful.

'One floor up,' Grandad said, whispering, tapping his finger to it. 'Here.'

Church looked to where he was pointing, seeing that there were a group of large rooms clustered together. Meeting rooms, Church thought. Had to be.

Grandad set off at speed, keen to get this done, and Church wasn't complaining about that.

They found the stairwell and entered, keeping their rifles up, moving cautiously but quickly.

On the next floor, they paused at the door, and Grandad stopped to listen.

When they heard nothing, he peeked it and they stepped into the corridor, making their way down until they reached the rooms Grandad had pointed to.

They opened the doors one by one, checking them off—and then Grandad let out a little sigh of what might have been victory. Or maybe just relief.

'Bingo,' he muttered, motioning Church over and opening the door wide.

Inside was a huge meeting room, a massive oval wooden table with twenty-odd chairs positioned around it.

In the centre were a ring of telephones with notepads set up in front of each.

There was no one here now, but it was clear that this was where it all happened. All the big decisions.

Serbian flags were set up in the corners of the room on brass poles, and all across the back was a bank of computers and radios so that any decisions made could be immediately sent out to the troops.

It was a situation room like any other. And Church hoped that meant they were practically home free.

'Let's get this done,' Grandad said, closing and locking the door behind them, moving swiftly around the table.

Church went the other side, the two of them flanking it, reaching the bank of computers at the same time. Church brought his backpack down off his shoulder once more and began digging inside for the small toolkit that he had there—the screwdriver to undo the screws and access the innards of the computers.

But he never even found it before Grandad pulled the first hulking desktop off the table and set it down on the floor, the back facing up towards him. He grabbed his knife from his belt and rammed it into the corner of the case, twisting and prying the thing open until the thin fasteners gave way.

The case split like an oyster shell and he wasted no time in removing the hard drive, ripping it out before reaching for the next tower.

Church abandoned the screwdriver now and did the same thing.

There were six computers. Six hard drives to get, and time was of the essence.

A quick check of the watch said they were less than ten minutes from Gaz's firework show—they'd taken longer than Church realised. And when it did go off, they needed to already be on the way out.

It took a few minutes to secure the hard drives, but that wasn't all they needed. There was a bank of filing cabinets to their right, and the only reason they'd be here was if they contained the kind of information Church and Grandad were instructed to retrieve.

The old man approached quickly, raising his knife, aiming for the seam above the first drawer.

The skeleton key proved useful once more, and once they were inside, they began sifting through the files and the papers contained within. It was all in Serbian, and they couldn't understand a thing.

But somehow they had to choose what to take and what not to—there were four cabinets' worth, and there was no way they could carry it all. Nowhere close.

Grandad was walking his fingers along the tops of the files and paused on one of them, lifting it up and showing it to Church.

'I don't know what the fuck any of this says,' he said, looking at the printed pages inside. 'But—' he went on, closing it and pointing to the big red stamp on the front— *строго поверљиво* —'that kind of thing usually means important, right?'

Church stared at the words, the heavy scarlet ink. Classified. Top secret. Something that meant they needed it.

He nodded and went on looking, as Grandad stuffed

it in his pack, pulling anything that had the same kind of marking—anything that looked like it may have been important. He sifted through the documents at speed, scanning photographs and transcripts, lists of names, anything resembling a field report or orders, missives, emails and letters—anything that looked redacted or like it might be incriminating.

He made snap decisions, guessing mostly, pushed file after file into his pack, knowing that each folder, each page made it heavier, would make it harder to run, would make it harder to get this done. To get out. But there was so much here. How much could they take? How much should they take? What would they miss if they didn't take it all?

Church didn't have time to decide.

He hadn't realised, but the clock had counted down.

He was trying to make sense of an aerial map printed in grainy black and white when the first shock-wave rippled through the building.

Church swayed on his feet, the whole place shaking, and a moment later, a deep siren began to wail all around them.

Church checked his watch. There were still four minutes to go.

'He's early,' Grandad said, looking at his own. 'Must have run into some trouble.'

Church glanced over at the old man. 'Let's call it. If it's not enough, I don't know what else we can do,' he said, flapping his rucksack down and securing it on his shoulder.

Grandad nodded. 'Let's go,' he said, the pair of them taking off towards the door, lifting their rifles once more.

Church was immediately aware of the weight of his bag—the energy and effort of each step, how much it fucked with his movement, how much it was throwing off his balance.

Grandad peeked the corridor again and, satisfied that no soldiers were running towards them, he stepped in and made a break for the stairwell.

The siren was louder here, the fire alarm ringing in full force.

Church stopped for just a second to look into one of the offices they passed on the way, seeing through the window facing out over the courtyard of the complex, towards the other end of the building.

Bright yellow flames were billowing from the roof, silhouetting the radio tower there, crawling up its metal legs, the iron already bowing, the tower beginning to topple. Church's eyes lingered a second longer before Grandad whistled to him and dragged him back to the matter at hand: getting the fuck out of there. Which was getting more and more difficult by the second.

If attacking Serbian Central Command didn't attract every soldier in a ten-mile radius, Church didn't know what would.

'Double time,' Grandad ordered him, bursting into the stairwell and hammering down towards the ground floor.

The plan was to get out the same way they had got

in—but as they headed down, the last sound they wanted to hear echoed from below.

The ground floor stairwell door flung itself open and shouts of panic and anger rang up to them. Heavy boot steps of Serbian soldiers. The clacking of rifles. All pounding up the stairs.

Grandad stopped Church in his tracks and looked back at him, motioning for him to pull up the face mask hanging around his neck. He did so, covering his features, knowing that that only meant one thing—that they weren't getting out of this cleanly anymore.

They were going to have to shoot their way out.

Grandad pulled a stun grenade from his belt and showed it to Church, pulling the pin without warning and dropping it into the centre of the stairwell, turning away and covering his ears as it detonated.

The boom was loud, threatening to burst Church's eardrums even though it had gone off twenty-odd feet below. The sound amplified in the bare concrete space —an echo chamber.

The men who'd taken the brunt of it yelled and clamoured, disoriented for a few seconds. In unison, Church and Grandad leant over the rail and aimed downwards, letting off a stream of fire towards the soldiers below. The sound of bullets crunching into flesh and bone sang their sinister tune and the two men pushed forward, swirling down the stairs like a wave— Grandad leading—and Church hoped, with some kind of plan for how they were going to get out of this.

As they rounded the last corner, two men were still

gathering themselves back up, two already down. Church and Grandad lined them up, reuniting them with their comrades without hesitation.

They hadn't even settled onto the floor, leaving bloody streaks on the concrete behind them, before Church and Grandad were through the door and running down the length of another long corridor. But Church realised after a few steps—not towards the outer wall, but towards the inner courtyard.

'Where are we going?' Church called out, checking his six, knowing that they were plunging deeper into the belly of the beast.

'Car park,' Granddad said between heavy breaths. 'We'll never make it out on foot, not back to the Landy at least.'

Church trusted him—it was all he could do—and followed as he cut right and then left down different hallways.

Church had no idea whether he knew where he was going—and he certainly didn't—but he guessed this wasn't the first hairy situation the old man had pulled himself out of, and all he could do was cover his back.

As they reached the exit, the car park visible through a glass pane on the door, Granddad shouldered through it and out into the cold night air, thick with smoke.

Flames were still billowing upwards from the top of the building, a jagged brushstroke of smoke rising into the sky above.

Church saw a dozen soldiers all running that way, leaving their posts, charging into the building.

Gunfire was echoing in the distance, and Church hoped that Gaz and DD could handle their shit.

As much as he wanted to go after them—as much as Church wanted to follow the fire, to assist, to make sure his brothers got out alive—that wasn't the mission. Their mission was to extract the intelligence and deliver it to NATO. Their mission was to help end this war.

Gaz and DD were giving them the distraction they'd promised, and Church knew that not taking advantage of soldiers running the other way would be the stupidest thing they could do.

He and Granddad tore themselves away from the smoke and flame and angled themselves towards the cars parked along the nearest wall, hiding behind their bonnets, crouching, making themselves as small targets as possible as Granddad selected the right vehicle.

Most of them were newer model German saloons, expensive bureaucratic cars that were almost impossible to hotwire and steal without setting off alarms or immobilising the engine altogether. But at the far end—there at the far end—was the exact thing that Church and Granddad were hoping to see.

A Lada Niva.

A compact sort of hatchback on steroids that was about as simple as cars could be. The kind of car that leaked when it rained, overheated in the sun, and just stopped working altogether in the winter.

But right now, it was their best chance to escape, because it could be broken into and started in all of about thirty seconds—the wires for the starter motor hanging invitingly below the steering column, basically begging to be stolen.

'Give us some cover,' Granddad ordered as he made for it.

Church emerged behind him and took a knee at the back corner of the Lada, hoping that none of the soldiers would turn around, that they'd keep looking up at the flames, they'd keep charging into the building.

Granddad put his elbow through the driver's side window and Church tensed, moving his sights across the men whose backs were to him, hoping that their shouts, the fire alarm, the gunfire, the crackle and roar of the flames above would drown out any sound.

Granddad was already inside and reached across, opening the passenger door for Church before they were noticed—and only as he climbed in did he hear the first shout of alarm.

Church tucked his M16 between his knees and drew his sidearm, twisting in the seat and putting his arm through the open door, firing on the soldiers that were now turning towards them, pointing, gesticulating, raising their guns.

The whinny and grumble of the engine firing to life filled Church with hope, and Granddad rammed it into reverse, hurling them backwards with a squeal of tyres and the whine of a woefully underpowered engine.

They spun into a J-turn, Church's side swinging towards the soldiers.

He kept firing, chasing them into cover with bullets, counting them in his head as he emptied the magazine.

And then Granddad was spinning the front wheels, dragging them forward towards the exit, towards the wooden barrier blocking the way.

As the Serbian soldiers got to their feet behind and began shooting back, peppering the back of the car, shattering the rear window, they smashed through the barricade and streaked into Pristina, drenched by night, racing towards the edge of the city and, Church hoped, the end of the war.

TWENTY-TWO

PRESENT DAY

THEY SEARCHED THE AREA, but there was no sign of the bomber or anyone else.

Church stood in the doorway for what felt like a long time, staring out into the darkness, looking for the man he knew was staring back, looking for Darko Vida.

But as much as he wanted him to emerge, to face him, to end all of this right here, right now… he didn't. He slunk away into the darkness and disappeared—not pulling the trigger, not conducting himself with honour. Though that was no surprise to Church.

After they'd done their sweep of the grounds and made sure that they were alone and that there was truly no sign of Whitmore either, they returned to the house for a second time, and this time combed through it more carefully, coming to the conclusion that Whitmore hadn't been taken under duress. His computer had been stripped of hard drives, his laptop gone. Clothes had been removed from the wardrobe, and there were no suitcases to be found. Which meant that they packed and left before Darko had even got there.

But that wasn't hard to believe. Before Fletcher had been able to make the connection that everybody being targeted was a ranking NATO official during Operation Allied Force, Whitmore would have made that jump immediately, as soon as he saw the names of the first victims. He would have known that it was his friends, his colleagues who were being killed, would have understood right away the danger posed to him and his family and that, like Church, his past had finally come calling. Hell, he was probably out of the country the same day that the bomb went off in Birmingham.

How long had they been vacated from the house? A week? More? Church couldn't say, but all he knew was that both he and Darko were too late.

As he and Mitch shipped out, driving south once more away from Whitmore's house, Church came to the conclusion that things had gone too far now for him to handle alone.

If he had given himself away to Darko, then that meant that if they weren't already, Nanna and the girls were now in the crosshairs. And as much of an axe Darko would have to grind with the NATO officials for not helping his people the way that they should have, the way that they promised, his grudge with Church would be far more personal. And while a simple explosion was good enough to wipe out the men that had bombed his country, what fate would lay in store for Church and his family?

He and Darko had locked horns more than once—and that was putting it mildly. No. If Darko had gone to these lengths to deal with the men who signed off on Allied Force, Church was struggling to imagine what kind of payback he would want to inflict on him.

And that left only one option. It was time to loop Hallberg in. Interpol might have been a step behind Anastasia Fletcher in their investigation, but that didn't mean that they couldn't still help track Darko down—and more importantly, keep him away from Church's family.

Light was beginning to creep into the sky when Church took his phone from his pocket and, with a deep breath, called Hallberg.

She answered quickly, awake despite the early hour, and met him with the two words that he thought were more than fair.

'What's wrong?' she said, skipping the introductions completely.

Church let out a little sigh, preparing himself. 'I just left the home of Gordon Whitmore,' Church said.

Hallberg paused for a moment. 'Who's that?' she asked.

'He was a ranking official in NATO during Operation Allied Force—the bombing campaign that ended the Kosovo War,' Church replied. 'And the bomber's next target.'

Hallberg made a sort of grumbling noise under her breath. 'And do I want to know how you know that?'

'I'm sure you do,' Church said. 'And I'd be glad to tell you.'

There was a silence on the other end of the line. Church read it as stunned.

'That's out of character for you,' Hallberg said, not bothering to mind her words or her tone. 'You fall down and hit your head?'

'I know,' Church said. 'And I'm sorry. I was holding myself to some sort of misplaced loyalty,' he replied. 'But things have gone too far now. Whitmore had already gone to ground by the time both we and the bomber got there. Which meant we were able to get our hands on one of his devices.'

'One of his devices,' she replied. 'He was there? Close by?'

'I don't know,' Church said back. 'I think so. I could feel him, but he was gone by the time we swept the ground.'

'And you didn't think to loop me in? Call Interpol and let them know the man they've been running all over Europe trying to hunt down was within reach?' Hallberg all but snapped.

Church was silent. He didn't have an answer for that other than simply saying, no, he didn't think to do that. He wanted Darko for himself.

'You have to come in,' Hallberg said then. 'We have to debrief—you have to tell me everything.'

'I know,' Church said, laying his head back and rubbing his tired eyes. 'We're already on the way.'

Hallberg came to them.

When they arrived back at Mitch's farm, she was already there, standing outside the house waiting for them.

She had a stern look on her face and was clearly strung out from the endless days spent working on this investigation. The frustration was coming off her in waves as Church approached, her hard expression telling him just how annoyed she was that he'd been withholding what was now going to prove to be vital information. How much of her time had she wasted? How much energy? How many lives would be lost because they were days behind where they should have been? Church didn't need any help feeling guilty. He was putting enough of that on himself already. Any lives that Darko claimed, he felt were as much on his shoulders as on anyone else's.

'Let's go inside,' Church said, motioning towards the door.

Hallberg scowled at him, and then at Mitch, who sucked air between his teeth, making a vague effort to hide his rifle behind his back. Though the pair of them, dressed in their tactical gear, couldn't hide what they'd been doing.

'I'll put the kettle on,' Mitch said, sliding past Hallberg and into the farmhouse.

When they were alone, Hallberg put her hands on her hips and stared up at Church, shaking her head at him.

'You're unbelievable,' she said. 'You know that?'

Church made a vague effort to smile. 'I assume you don't mean that as a compliment?'

She just scoffed and then turned her back on him, still shaking her head as she headed in towards the kitchen. Church followed slowly, leaning his rifle against the wall on the inside of the door and slipping off his flak vest, hoping that if he looked more like a civilian, Hallberg might be more amenable to hearing the human side of his story. He went through into the kitchen and sat at the table as Mitch busied himself filling the kettle and putting together the cups, leaving the two of them to talk it out.

'You want to just get right into it?' Hallberg asked. 'Or do you want to waste any more of my time?'

Church bristled a little but knew that that was more than called for.

'The man you're looking for,' Church said, 'his name is Darko Vida.'

Hallberg sat bolt upright, as though not expecting a name or anything quite so concrete to come out of his mouth.

'Darko Vida,' she repeated back slowly.

Church nodded. 'Yeah. He was the leader of a Kosovo Liberation Army faction during the war. Myself and a small team of operators were inserted into their ranks to help combat the Serbian onslaught in Kosovo.

We arrived early in 1999 with a mandate to help arrest the Serbians' march across Kosovo and protect as many fleeing Kosovans as we could. But while we were there,' Church went on, watching Hallberg hang on his every word, 'we had word that a ranking official in the Serbian army was looking to defect, was looking to flip on his own and stop the ethnic cleansing. It was his intelligence that put Operation Allied Force into full swing and what effectively ended the war. But your bomber, Darko Vida, was a true ethnic-Albanian, Kosovan patriot. He hated the Serbians for what they did and would have lived and died for Kosovo a thousand times over fighting them. And the only thing worse than winning that war was winning it with the help of a Serbian defector. He would rather have watched that country burn than accept help from a Serb.'

Hallberg watched him quietly, waiting for him to go on.

'Operation Allied Force killed nearly five hundred Serbian civilians, but it was a justified evil to put a stop to the ethnic cleansings. Still, nobody's hands were clean in that war. What both sides did… none of it was justified. The Serbs struck first—killed, raped, burned Kosovo village by village. Executed farmers and civilians en masse and tossed them into mass graves. And when the KLA had the chance to hit back… they didn't hesitate. And they didn't hold back.'

Hallberg shifted in her seat a little. 'I… I didn't know.'

'No one does,' Church said. 'History has a way of

sanitising war. But I can tell you, there was nothing clean about that conflict. Nothing at all.'

Hallberg's brow creased, and she shook her head a little.

'I'm not sure I understand,' she said. 'With Darko. If… if NATO helped the KLA win the war, then why does this Darko Vida want them dead? Surely you want to send them a fruit basket rather than a block of C4?'

'Operation Allied Force didn't start until late in March of 1999, but the cleansings began long before that. A year of fighting. Of cleansing. Of killing. NATO were well aware of what was going on, but they didn't step in to help. They left the Kosovans to fend for themselves. Thousands died because of it. Thousands died because they stood by and did nothing, and then when they finally did step in, it was only with the help of a Serb.' Church thought on those words. On the whole war. He could remember it still like it was yesterday. Even when he didn't want to. Especially when he didn't want to. 'I'm not saying it makes complete sense,' he went on, 'but if you met Darko you'd know that it didn't need to. Once he decided something, that was it. His hatred for the Serbs seared a hole right into his soul. The people that knew him…' Church said, thinking of Marsella, 'they told me that he wasn't like that before the war, but seeing his country razed, his people massacred, it changed him. It shook something loose in him. It broke him, and I can attest to that fact.'

'But why now?' Hallberg asked.

'That I don't know,' Church replied. 'But… I don't

think that matters. What matters is that we know who he is, we know who he's after, and that means we can stop him.'

Hallberg took that in.

'Okay,' she said slowly, sticking out her bottom lip as though piecing it all together in her head.

Mitch returned to the table with cups in hand and put them down in front of Church and Hallberg, leaning back against the counter with his own, not interrupting, just listening.

'I don't disbelieve anything you've said,' Hallberg told Church, leaning forward and resting her arms on the table either side of her steaming tea. 'But I can't just take this information and run it up the flagpole without some kind of official statement to back it up. You're going to have to go on record, Church. I'm sorry. I know you probably don't want to, but—'

'I will,' Church replied, cutting her off. 'I'll do it. Nobody else needs to die because of me.'

Hallberg pressed her lips together and met his eye, seeing, hearing the confliction in him.

'Alright. Thank you,' she said quietly, smiling for the first time now.

Church felt a flicker of warmth in his breast looking at her, and felt for the first time that he was doing the right thing, that he'd made a good decision.

He thought back then, to Kosovo, to all the people. Who died. Who didn't need to. The people that he killed. The people that Darko killed. The ones he didn't save. The ones he couldn't. The ones who died when

Allied Force started. The ones who died because it didn't come quick enough. He could understand it—the need for revenge. The fury that Darko was feeling—but that didn't change the fact that he needed to be stopped.

And Church knew that he would be the one to do it. That he had to. That somehow that's how it had to go, and that's how it would be.

'There is one more thing,' Church said.

'What's that?' Hallberg asked.

'Last night,' he said, 'at Whitmore's. I think Darko saw me.'

Hallberg stared at him.

'I don't know if he knew that I was still alive or if he planned on targeting me, but after seeing me...'

'I understand.' Hallberg nodded. 'You're worried about Nanna, about the girls?'

'I am,' Church said firmly.

'Say no more,' Hallberg replied. 'I'll reach out to the Met, make sure somebody's posted outside their house. That they're watched until we get a bead on Darko, until we know where he is and what he's doing. They'll be safe,' she assured him.

'I appreciate that,' Church said, unsure if he believed her, but knowing that now he was in her hands in all senses, he had to trust her.

And though he made it his business not to trust anybody, he thought if there was anybody that should be an exception to that rule...

That it was probably the woman sitting in front of him.

TWENTY-THREE

TWENTY-FIVE YEARS AGO

THEY LIMPED BACK INTO CAMP, weary and wondering if, after all this, the plan would finally come to fruition—if what they gathered would be enough to really put an end to this.

How many men had died last night to protect the information Church had extracted?

And how many lives would that ultimately save?

They'd linked back up with Gaz and DD, dumped the car that he and Granddad had stolen somewhere outside Pristina on the side of the road, and then made for the hills as a four.

Gaz was headed straight back out to rendezvous with his NATO contact to hand off the intel, and Granddad was going with him. DD—still not 100%—needed the rest, and Gaz was happy to give it to him.

And Church... well, being trapped in a car with Gaz

for another few hours wasn't something that either of them really wanted just then.

They'd been at loggerheads over the Markovich situation and it showed no sign of calming anytime soon.

So without needing to explain, when Gaz pulled into the camp, only two of them got out. And then, with a little salute from Granddad, Gaz turned the car around and trundled back onto the road, disappearing in a cloud of morning dust.

Church stretched his shoulders and cracked his back, squinting up at another rising sun, wondering how many nights he'd spent doing this kind of shit and how many nights of the same lay ahead.

Granddad had lasted more than 20 years in the service, but he was one of the few, and a life sentence was rarely that long for troopers. For one reason or another.

DD didn't bother to say good night before he limped off towards the tent, clutching at his ribs. Church was impressed that he was even on his feet, let alone back working, and though he was sure that Gaz had done his utmost to keep him out of the fray, judging by the way he was cradling his body, that hadn't been entirely possible.

Church stood alone, looking across the empty farm-yard, a few chickens strutting their way across, pecking for grubs and insects between the stones.

Behind him a gentle breeze struck up, cool but not unpleasant against his skin, sticky with dried sweat and the dust of the trip, the sound of the wheat in the fields around them rustling softly. He kept moving his eyes around, hopeful that she'd be there, but knowing that she wouldn't.

But then she was.

He froze, staring at Marsella.

She was standing next to the well, filling up the bucket of water they used to fill the troughs for the animals in the paddock beside the house. She had one hand on the lever, the other on the top of the bucket, and she was frozen in place, staring up at him.

He kept looking at her, expecting that she was going to turn away, but she didn't.

Instead, she stood and dried her hands off on the front of her tattered blue dress.

She began walking towards him, her expression stern, and he wondered if she was about to tell him off again.

If she was, he didn't think that he could take it.

As she got near, he lifted his hands to beg for mercy, but instead of speaking, she threw her arms around his neck and squeezed so tightly that it was difficult for him to breathe.

She held on, her breath shaking a little.

He could feel it warm on his neck and couldn't help but lace his own arms around her back and hold her, his eyes closing as he pulled her close.

Finally she let go and he put her down, though she kept her hands around his face, staring up into his eyes.

'What was that for?' he asked cautiously.

She shook her head, as though not able to find the words right away. 'I... I wasn't sure if you were coming back. I thought maybe you'd gone. For good.'

Church looked over her head then at the main house, wondering if anyone was watching from inside. If Darko was there, that was something he was keen to avoid, especially without Gaz to pull him off the man if he started any shit.

Church took Marsella by the hand and led her to a spot out of sight behind the steel barn. She waited for him to speak, and he thought that there was only one thing that he could say.

'I'm sorry,' he began, shaking his head.

'No, I'm sorry,' she cut him off. 'I'm sorry for how we left things. I was angry. Not at... not at you, but at myself. What Darko did, what I let him do, it's... I'm not trying to make excuses for him, but before the war, he wasn't like this. He wasn't. Now he's just... he's just so angry.' Church held her shaking hand.

'I was just trying to protect you.'

'I know,' she replied. 'And I get it. It's just... things are hard. Everything's hard. This place, being here, seeing what the war has done to us—'

'You don't have to say anything else,' Church replied. 'I understand.'

With that he began to turn away, glad that she'd seen fit to forgive him, to understand what he tried to do, but tentative not to push things too far too quickly.

She was going through a lot, and hell, he was too.

Perhaps this wasn't the time for them. Or for this.

His involvement with her could only jeopardise the mission—could only put risk on the relationship between them and the KLA.

It was stupid and that wasn't something that he could afford to be right now.

But as he tried to walk away, he felt her reach out and take his hand. He turned back to look at her, searching her pale blue eyes for her intention, but before she made him guess, she took a step towards him and reached up, guiding his face downwards towards her, kissing him before either of them could say anything else. And then she let him go and, still holding his hand, began to lead him away from the farm altogether.

He glanced back at it before asking a question he hoped that he already knew the answer to. 'Where are we going?'

'Somewhere private.'

That was all she said as they continued to walk over the road leading to the farm and into the wheat field surrounding the buildings. It was a stretch of open land, hundreds of metres to the nearest tree line, and as they began edging towards it, cutting through the hip-height wheat, he couldn't help but wonder if there was some secret spot that she knew. Though they were just halfway there when she slowed and looked over at the farm buildings, small in the distance now.

'Here,' she said.

Church looked around them, the stalks of wheat waving gently in the morning sun, glowing golden, the chittering of grasshoppers filling the morning air, the distant songs of birds drifting on the breeze and the faint rustling of the grain, all creating a din of white noise that seemed to extinguish all hints of the war.

She stepped closer and tugged at his shirt, pulling him towards her. He felt her weight as she began to settle backwards, pulling him towards the ground. They settled down, crunching the wheat beneath them, flattening it into a cocoon, and she lay on her back on a bed of crushed, dry hay, long-since dead from a summer and winter with no harvest—an endless sea of grass that placed them on another world.

She lay on her back and looked up at him, slowly reaching to her collar, beginning to unbutton her dress. Church felt his heart beat a little harder as he watched from his knees, staring down at her.

'Are you sure this is a good idea?' he asked.

She just nodded, stopping with her own buttons, the curve of her breasts exposed, her skin soft and milk-white. As though he were going too slow, she began searching for the hem of his shirt, and though he knew that she was wrong, that this was a bad idea, he didn't think he'd ever wanted anything more in his life. And if this was the wrong choice and he had it to do a thousand times, he'd choose the same thing. Every time.

They made love for hours in that field—quiet, sad love that was slow and powerful.

She raked at his skin with her nails. She bit at his shoulder with her teeth, sinking them into his flesh so hard that it hurt as much as the bite of the bullet had weeks before.

She cried, and when he asked if she was alright, all she could do was nod and smile, and when he tried to stop, she would shake her head and tell him no, that this was what she wanted.

'Please,' she would say, 'I need this.' And without another word, he gave in, loving her as tenderly and as desperately as he'd ever loved a woman before.

The sun was high in the sky by the time she pulled her head from his chest and brushed her hair behind her ear, saying the words that he dreaded would come.

'I should get back,' she said. 'Someone will notice that I'm gone.'

Church allowed her to sit upright and watched as she took the dress from the ground, a makeshift blanket for them, and clothed herself.

As he stared up into the sky, only outclassed by the colour of her eyes, he thought about Markovich's words —how from this angle, staring at this untouched blue canvas, you could imagine, believe even, that there was no war going on at all.

But there was, and it wasn't over yet.

When they dressed, they walked back towards the farm, Church wondering if he should take her by the hand.

But they weren't at her sides.

She was holding them in front of her, wringing them gently, almost in a trance, no doubt thinking about what was to come next, wondering whether someone would find out, whether Darko would find out—and when he did, what would happen then.

As they reached the farmyard, Church spied Gaz's vehicle. They'd come back at some point and he'd not even heard the engine, but there was no missing the congregation in the farmyard.

Gaz, Grandad, and DD were standing there, talking to Darko and Ismet, their men formed up behind them, their exchange clearly heated even before Church was able to discern what it was about.

Darko looked up, seeing Marsella and Church, his right arm still bandaged at the wrist from where Church had broken it, and immediately surged towards them. Something flashed in his left hand and Church looked down just in time to see a long metal bar in his grasp.

He weaved around Marsella, who reached out to stop him, but he was too fast for her, sidestepping before she could get hold of him, and without any warning he swung it at Church.

The weapon whistled through the air and the only thing Church could do was throw his hands up to block it. It rebounded off his forearms, nearly shattering them. The pain was immediate and terrible, but better than if it had struck him in the skull as Darko had intended. He probably would have cracked it.

Church danced backwards, any joy that had been lingering from his time with Marsella now evaporated—replaced with a cold rage of battle.

Darko came in again, over the top this time with the bar, looking to cave his head in fully, but he was swinging with his left and was slow, lumbering, and Church swept to the side, taking the bar from the air and getting behind Darko. He pulled it up to his neck and leaned back, driving it higher, forcing it under his jaw and taking him clean off the ground.

He could twist it quickly, snap the man's neck and be done with him here and now.

And though Darko was fighting him, pulling down on the bar with everything he had, it wasn't enough. His life was in Church's hands, and though he wanted to kill the man, he couldn't help but look for Marsella, needing her approval if he was going to.

But instead of seeing her, it was a wall of Darko's men, their rifles raised and pointed at him. Gaz was standing by, not ready to leap in this time—waiting to see if Church could make the right decision on his own, and if not, willing to let him suffer the consequences of his own actions.

He found Marsella finally, standing at the side of it all, her hands clutched gently to her mouth.

They locked eyes and Church knew that what they'd done would have far-reaching consequences—that it would jeopardise the mission and everything they'd accomplished here.

And yet he still didn't regret it.

Not one bit.

TWENTY-FOUR

PRESENT DAY

THE SUN WAS UP, weak and cool with the meagre heat of winter's morning, as Hallberg stepped from the farm and into the courtyard.

She squinted up at it, lifting her chin to the light before closing her eyes. She stayed there for a moment, languishing in the stillness, the birdsong, the isolation, and the peace of the place. It was what Church loved about it the most. It was why it had felt the closest thing to home in years.

It was almost as though here, tucked away behind the veil of trees, you could pretend everything in the outside world wasn't happening. Hell, if you closed your eyes and you wished hard enough, you could almost pretend that the outside world didn't exist at all.

And yet, despite the moment of respite, they both

knew that it did. And that it demanded a lot of them both.

Hallberg turned and gave Church a nod, starting towards her car. She made it a step before Church reached out and took her gently by the elbow.

She looked down at his hand, huge around her arm, and then up into his eyes.

'I'm sorry,' he said. 'About holding back, about not telling you about Kosovo.'

She didn't reply, and he didn't expect her to, didn't expect her to tell him that he was forgiven, or that it was all right. They both knew that if he'd come clean right away from the start, that perhaps lives could have been saved.

'The important thing now,' she said, 'is that we find Darko. And believe it or not, Interpol did connect some of the same dots that your source did—I'm guessing Anastasia Fletcher?' she asked, searching his face for any tell.

He tried to keep his expression stony, tried to protect her as best he could, but she only seemed to take his lack of denial as confirmation.

'We knew that the bomber was targeting former NATO officials,' she went on. 'But we hadn't made the link to Kosovo. But now that you've given us that, it'll be a big help. And once we run Darko Vida's face through facial rec, splash his picture on every wanted list and police board on the continent, the net will close quickly. And even if he does slip through, we can put together a list of the officials involved in Allied Force and maybe, if we're lucky, still get out ahead of Darko. Set a trap for him.'

'Even if you do catch up with him,' Church said, 'he won't come willingly. Not without a fight.'

'No,' Hallberg said. 'Doesn't sound like the type.' She let out a soft sigh. 'But that's the job, that's what we do.'

'How many will die?' Church asked her.

She didn't have an answer for that.

'One is too many,' he said then.

'It is,' she replied, almost hesitantly.

'So send me instead.'

'You?' Hallberg asked, unsure exactly what he meant.

'Let me get to Darko. Let me kill him. Spare anybody else's life.'

She considered that for a few seconds, and then shook her head, tugging her arm out of his grasp finally.

'No,' she said. 'You've done enough. Giving us his name, giving us Kosovo. That's enough for now. But...' she said, the gears turning in her head. 'You know, there is something else you can do.'

'Name it,' Church said.

'We were following up on the list of current and previous high-ranking NATO officials, and one name we came across led us straight into a brick wall.'

'What do you mean?'

'The day after the second bomb went off, a guy

called Gerhard Steiner dropped off the face of the earth. Went into hiding—clearly fearing for his life.'

'And you want me to find him?' Church said.

'No,' Hallberg said. 'We already did. It's getting to him that's the problem.'

'I don't understand?'

'He's still got friends in high places and he's holed up in the mountains in Austria, surrounded by armed guards, local police, PMCs. We sent someone to the gate, but they got turned away practically at gunpoint. The situation escalated and the local police sided with him, told us that he was safe, that he didn't know anything, and then escorted us off the premises.'

'Okay,' Church said tentatively. 'And you think this guy is somebody Darko will target?'

'I think this guy is someone that can give us the list of people he will. That's what we want from him. Thousands of people worked for NATO over the years and who knows how many were involved during the Kosovo war. But this guy was a decision-maker, a top dog, and no doubt if he made the leap as soon as Darko started knocking off names, then he knows who else is going to be on his target list.'

'So you want me to get to him,' Church said. 'And... make him talk?'

She measured his words. 'I'd suggest asking nicely first, but if he doesn't seem amenable, then yeah,' she said. 'Press. Just a little.'

Church nodded, understanding.

They were looking to save this person's life, not take it. But there were ways that he could be persuasive without leaving permanent scars, and Church was well versed in those methods—almost as well versed as he was in the other sort.

'This guy's cagey,' Hallberg said. 'And he's scared to death, judging by the way his security are stacked up around the property. They're on orders to shoot first and ask questions later, so if they see you rolling up to the front gate, I'd expect a bullet rather than a red carpet.'

'Noted,' Church replied. 'But don't worry. I have my methods.'

'I'm sure you do,' she said. 'But we also have ours. I'm not leaving you to your own devices here. We can get you close.'

'Yeah?' Church asked cautiously, reading something in her voice. 'How close?'

'10,000 feet.'

Church lifted his eyebrows.

'SAS does stand for Special "Air" Service, doesn't it?' Hallberg said, holding back a grin.

'Yeah,' Church replied. 'It's just... been a while, that's all.'

She laughed a little. 'Nah. I'm sure it's like riding a bike. Don't worry.' She reached up and clapped him on his bull-like shoulder. 'I'll send you the details,' she said before stepping away towards the car. When she reached it, she opened the door and turned back. 'And Church?'

'Yeah,' he replied, folding his arms.

'Get this done without killing anybody,' she said,

'and you can consider yourself officially back in my good books.'

Church was the one who laughed now. 'Don't kid yourself,' he said, feeling himself grin for the first time in what seemed like an age. 'I never left them.'

TWENTY-FIVE

TWENTY-FIVE YEARS AGO

THE LAST THING Church expected was for it to all end in a civil discussion.

And yet here they were, he and Gaz on one side of the table, Darko, Marsella, and Ismet on the other. The old man was in the middle, Darko on the left, looking as mean and pissed off as ever, Marsella on the right, staring at the table with a glazed look, wondering how, as a grown woman, it had all come down to this.

'I'm going to make this plain and simple,' Gaz said. 'If you can't control Darko, then we're going to pull our support. I'm going to advise NATO that the KLA aren't deserving of our help and we're going to walk out of here and you're never going to see us again.'

Marsella looked up at Church then, as though fearing that that might well be the case—that Darko couldn't be controlled, not for love or anything else.

Ismet stroked his beard, considering it.

Gaz went on, as if to reinforce the point. 'I can't have your men attacking my guys all hours of the day and night with no provocation and no warning. Jesus, if Church didn't have half a brain in his head, Darko would've killed him out there, and you know it.'

Ismet stopped stroking his beard and looked up at Gaz, nodding slowly. 'Yes,' he said. 'But it was not unprovoked, was it?' He turned his attention then to Church before letting his eyes cast all the way around to his daughter. She kept her head bowed, her eyes on the table.

Church couldn't help feeling responsible for it. If he'd just refused her advance, as he should have, then they could've avoided all this.

And yet, even now, he still didn't regret what happened—and he hoped, despite Marsella's expression, she didn't either, though he wasn't about to speak for her or think for her, either.

'What are your intentions?' Ismet said then, without warning, fixing his eyes on Church once more.

Church stiffened a little at the question, looking back at him. 'What do you mean?' Church replied.

'Your intentions,' Ismet insisted. 'With my daughter. Do you intend to marry her?'

Church blinked, sideswiped by the question. 'Marry her?' he asked back, hoping that Ismet's command of English had suddenly left him and he was confusing that word. He looked at Marsella then, who was looking back at him—not with any kind of expectation, but almost with dread at what he was going to say. Because right here, right now, there seemed to be no correct answer to that question for either of them.

'I ask,' Ismet said, reaching to his chest and pinching the crucifix hanging there, 'because if you don't, then I wonder if you expect us to stand idly by while you defile her and then be happy about it afterwards.'

Marsella did speak up now. 'He's not defiling me,' she practically spat, but Ismet lifted a hand and hushed her before she could go any further.

'If your intentions are pure,' he went on, 'then there is no problem. Are they?' he asked Church directly now.

He could also feel Gaz's eyes on him, Darko's, Marsella's—everyone waiting for an answer that he wasn't prepared or even able to give. If he said no, then he'd be jeopardising the mission, the relationship between the KLA and the SAS, and whatever kind of fragile agreement they had in place. And if he said yes, he'd be lying. He'd be committing to something that he'd never even considered.

What he had with Marsella—whatever it was—was in some sort of infancy. But even beyond that, neither of them knew what they were. They'd barely spoken. They'd shared a moment of intimacy in the middle of a war—a distraction that they both desperately needed, some kind of comfort, some kind of belief that there was something good out there in the world for them, whatever form that took.

Ismet settled back into the chair now and let out a

long breath. 'Darko may have been hasty, perhaps even overzealous in his protection of his sister—but that is what it is. He was protecting his family. He was protecting his country from people who are not from here, who do not understand our ways or our culture. In the same way that the Serbs have come into our home and violated everything sacred to us... you have too,' Ismet said, ratcheting the pressure down on Church. 'So I ask you again—once your mission is complete here, then what?'

This time silence fell, and Church knew that there was no getting out of it with silence, no refusal to answer.

But he said the only thing that he could—the thing that wasn't an answer at all.

'I don't know,' he replied, hating himself with every word.

Marsella looked away, averting her eyes so that Church didn't see what was lingering in them.

Shame? Hurt? Anger? He couldn't tell—and he didn't think he would ever have the chance to again.

'Then it is settled,' Ismet said with a certain finality. 'You and my daughter are to have no contact going forward. You will not speak. You will not see each other. You will not interact. And Darko will have no reason to fight you.' He looked around the table. 'Are we clear?'

And though no one answered, the lack of protest proved that everyone was.

Ismet pushed himself to a tired stance then—an old

man, hunched back and exhausted from the war going on both outside his walls and inside them.

He extended a hand across the table to Gaz, but not to Church—not to the man who had, as he said, just defiled his daughter.

Gaz reached out and shook it, giving the old man a firm nod, and then dragged Church to a stance too, and pushed him towards the door.

He resisted, looking for Marsella, searching for one look from her to tell him that it was okay in some fashion—that she understood, she accepted, that she forgave him.

But she wouldn't look at him.

She continued to stare at the wall, her back turned, and then Gaz was too strong and they were suddenly outside.

He shoved him into the courtyard and gave him what Church knew he would.

'You fucking idiot,' he snarled. 'How could you be so goddamn stupid, huh, Church?'

Church turned and turned his palms outwards, almost shrugging but not wanting to antagonise his captain any further. All he could do was offer his guilt.

Gaz shook his head. 'Look, I fucking get it, right? Middle of a war, piece of tail—yeah, you're not the first man, you won't be the last. But Jesus Christ, Church, now? With all this going on? Seriously?'

Again, all Church could do was stand there and take it.

He had no answer for Gaz, and even if he did, he didn't think it would be good enough.

'At least—at least tell me you're going to do what Ismet says and just stay away from his fucking daughter. Just for a bit longer, yeah? We're almost done, aren't we, Church?'

'Are we?' Church asked back. 'Are we almost done? What about Markovich? He came through for us and we got the intel we needed for NATO. Are they going to hold up their end of the deal?'

Gaz stared at him, flexing his jaw. 'I'm going to tell you what I told you the last time you asked that. It's not our mission, Church,' he said, shaking his head and walking away. 'And it's not our concern.'

TWENTY-SIX

PRESENT DAY

HALLBERG'S QUIP about 10,000 feet had been totally wrong when it came to Austria.

Many mountains themselves exceeded that height, with the tallest—the Grossglockner—rising to over 12,000 alone, which meant that they were currently cruising at around 16,000 feet above sea level and around 11,000 above their target DZ.

Mitch and Church were sitting in the back of a Pilatus PC-6 Porter—a single prop plane designed to carry up to ten jumpers.

Though other than the pilot, an ex-German Air Force captain who now flew private charters, they were alone. They were flying by night, the plane jostling around in the high mountain winds. It wasn't quite a storm, but this high in the mountains and at this time of year, there was no such thing as calm weather, and any breeze that came rattling up the valley would build and gather into a torrent before shooting upwards off one of the ridges below, creating inverted waterfalls of air and a whole lot of turbulence.

They rattled and bounced along and though Church and Mitch were both used to this, had both experienced far rougher flights in their tenure in the Forces, it still wasn't a pleasant experience, and the thought of jumping into the sub-zero wind in the dark with no test jumps or recent practice under their belt would be daunting for anyone.

Hallberg had said that it was like riding a bike, and she wasn't wrong. Church still remembered how to do it: breathe slow, keep an eye on the altimeter, pull the cord before you hit the ground. Pretty simple stuff. But either way, *relaxed* wasn't a word he'd have used to describe how he was feeling. Just then, the plane plunged a few dozen feet, the engine whining as it pulled itself back up to level, Church and Mitch's stomachs falling out of their arses in unison.

Mitch reached out and grabbed onto Church's shoulder strap, steadying himself on the seat.

'Jesus Christ,' he muttered. 'Fucking hated this shit twenty years ago and I still hate it now.'

'Maybe the SBS would have been a better fit for you,' Church smiled in the darkness, laying his head back against the headrest.

Mitch tutted to himself. 'I'm not really a strong swimmer.'

Church stuck out his bottom lip. 'Maybe you should

have pursued a career in macramé or knitting instead, then?'

'Yeah, very funny,' Mitch said, feigning a laugh. 'Maybe you should pursue a career in shutting the fuck up.'

Church let his smile persist, but said nothing more. Little distractions like that were a welcome respite in times like this.

Church lifted his watch in the darkness and checked the time. The pilot said when they began their climb up to the mountains, there would be about forty minutes until they hit the DZ and they were already forty-one.

They'd been flying into a headwind, fighting their way over the mountains, but still, they had to be getting close. And then, as though the pilot had heard Church's thoughts, he opened the little door between the cockpit and the cabin and turned around in his seat, yelling down the length of the fuselage.

'Two minutes!' he called, his voice swallowed by the engine noise. He reached between the seats and pressed a button, switching the red jump light on above the door.

'Showtime,' Church muttered, standing up and dragging Mitch to his feet too. 'You know it's not too late to back out of this,' he said. 'I can do it alone. You stay here, head home.'

'And let you die?' Mitch said, getting himself to his feet. 'Fat chance.'

'Is that why you're here, is it? To keep me from popping my clogs?'

'Well, if you do, then who's going to clean the gutters at the farm?'

Church put his hand on his breast as though to cover an arrow wound to the heart. 'Is that all I am to you?' he asked. 'Gutter cleaner?'

Mitch laughed. 'When you don't pay rent, yeah. Basically.'

Grinning, Church moved towards the door and glanced up at the pilot, giving him a nod. The man pulled the hatch back across, sealing himself off from the rest of the plane, and then Church reached for the door lever, twisting it and pulling it aside. The plane was cruising at about 120 knots, and the wind rush was instantaneous. It sucked the meagre warmth from the cabin instantly and filled it instead with a biting wind.

It swirled inside, ruffling Church's sleeves and tugging at his beard, nipping at his cheeks and the end of his nose. He gritted his teeth against the temperature change and let out a steadying breath, waiting for the green light to jump. He checked his watch again. Two minutes late. It wouldn't make a difference.

And then he lifted his right wrist and turned it inwards so that he could see the altimeter there. He pressed the button on the side of the screen, bringing it to life, and then twisted the outer dial until the number displayed read 6000 feet. He locked it in, scheduling the alarm for him to open his chute, and nodded to Mitch, making sure he'd done the same. There was time for one more breath before the light above his head turned green and Church knew there was nothing else to wait for.

His carbine was strapped tightly to his ribs. His pistol secured in his thigh holster. His belt adorned with several pouches containing the essentials. He reached out and squeezed Mitch's shoulder before pulling up his face mask, tucking the back under his black beanie, the front under his goggles.

And then he jumped. One step forward into nothingness.

Best not to think about it.

That's how he'd always done these things, and how he always would.

He folded his arms over his chest and plunged into the darkness, steadying his breathing and his heart before he opened his arms and legs and began his dive, spread-eagle, towards the earth. It wouldn't be a long free fall, and he watched as the numbers counted down on the inside of his wrist, plunging from fifteen to fourteen to thirteen, and then suddenly at ten already. He kept his breathing slow, kept his focus sharp, not seeing anything except whipping cloud and snow below him.

It swirled in an endless, grainy grey sea, a bottomless fog that he knew had a very abrupt cut-off point if he left it too late. He knew Mitch was somewhere above him, but it wasn't time to think of anyone else right now. It was just time to make sure that he was watching his altitude, pulling a chute when he needed it and landing where he was supposed to. As the altimeter clicked down to seven, he began drawing a deep breath, began tensing his muscles, began reaching up to his chest to search for the rip cord, and the moment it hit six he gave it a firm pull, locking his muscles against the sudden jolt.

The top of his pack opened and the chute deployed upwards, baggy at first and buffeting in the wind before it caught the air and opened fully, the straps digging into the inside of his thighs, into his ribs and shoulders. He kept his neck tight against the jerk and exhaled as the straps took his weight, listening as just above him, Mitch's chute did the same thing, opening with an audible slap in the darkness.

As he glanced upwards, there was no sign of him, the cloud thick.

Church guided himself down in circles, keeping them as tight as he dared without putting himself into a spiral.

They were landing on an open powder field about a click up the valley from Steiner's lodge, and it was there that they were going to dump their chutes and start down on foot towards the target, landing far enough away not to attract any attention, able to make their approach under the cover of darkness through the trees that surrounded the man's home away from home.

Church broke through the bottom layer of cloud just a thousand feet above the ground now, and saw the layer of snow below him open and vast, glowing white in the darkness.

He glanced up again, this time seeing Mitch tight on his tail, and afforded a small breath of relief.

Though they'd done this dozens, probably hundreds of times, Church still knew that it was easy for things to go wrong. That one bad pack of the chute could mean the difference between life and death. But he was touching down and so was Mitch, and that meant the hard part hopefully was over.

Church pulled up, drawing on the handles that pulled the edges of his chute in, and lifted his heels, bringing himself into a slow glide, feeling the soles of his boots grazing along the soft snow. High above, the wind had been swirling, but down here there was no more than a gentle breeze, the tiny flakes of ice rattling along the layer of soft snow, a few flakes drifting around beneath the thick layer of cloud.

And then he was down, sinking up to his knees in the early winter snow, twisting and reeling the chute towards him on muscle memory, folding it into a ball and pressing it into the holes left by his legs.

He shrugged off his pack entirely as Mitch touched down beside him, giving him a nod as the two men readied themselves with practised precision.

Instinctively, they crouched, pulling their guns to attention, watching the tree line below, making sure that they hadn't been seen, that they weren't going to be engaged; staying that way for a few seconds until they were sure that they were alone.

Mitch broke the silence first, standing up and stretching his back.

'Fucking hell, that doesn't get easier as you get older, does it?' he said.

'Did you remember to breathe in before you pulled the rip cord?' Church asked him.

'Did I remember to breathe in before I pulled the rip cord?' he practically spat. 'You know I've done more jumps than you, right?'

'Yeah,' Church said. 'But you're also older and I wasn't sure if dementia had started setting in yet.'

'Older?' Mitch practically squawked. 'It's five years, mate.'

'Really?' Church said, raising his eyebrows. 'I always thought it was about twenty. At least.'

'Sod off,' Mitch clapped back.

'I'm just saying,' Church replied, shrugging and stepping out of the wells he'd left in the snow, making his way down towards the tree line. 'There is such a thing as moisturiser, you know.' He strode off before Mitch could strangle him, jogging to stay out of reach.

They made their way down through the snow and into the trees, the pair of them wearing light grey cargo trousers, lightweight hard shell jackets to give them some cover and protection against the snow. They moved quickly but carefully, staying single file, their rifles equipped with suppressors and night vision scopes. Though a suppressor didn't do much to dull the noise of a gunshot, it would all but hide the flash and make it impossible to pick them out in the darkness if they didn't need to engage the small army that Gerhard Steiner had hired to protect him.

But that was the last resort.

Their intention was to slip in unnoticed, and Church was keen on making sure that's what happened.

When they reached the lower tree line, Church

signalled for them to stop and they looked down from their elevated position over what had been, in the spring and summer, Gerhard's sprawling lawn. Church had seen pictures and satellite flyovers of the place. A single lodge with attached carport surrounded by open grass-land—around fifty metres on every side to the trees.

The area of forest where the house was had been clear-cut to build the house itself, which was about as sustainable as construction got, Church thought, the whole place made of wood cut down from the place that it was standing. But as impressive as the house was, that wasn't what they were scouting.

Despite the snow, Church picked out no less than four men doing the rounds, patrolling the perimeter of the grounds.

There was what looked to be a single small guard house at the gate leading to the access road, and Church figured there would be at least two more there. On the other side of that he could see two cars parked on the road facing outwards—no doubt with another four men inside, ready to deal with anyone oncoming. Which made ten in total.

Hallberg said it was a dozen. And depending on how accurate her intel was, it meant that there was at least one, if not two men with Gerhard inside the property.

The man was divorced, no children, which meant he was alone in there, save for his security detail—which made things easier. Nothing put a damper on torturing a man like a screaming wife and children. Church grimaced at that thought and returned his attention to the four men patrolling—two of them walking in a clock-wise loop, two of them counter-clockwise. They were doing their best to keep pace, to keep equidistant, but it meant that there was a small window after two passed when their backs would be to each other and Church and Mitch would have an opportunity to sneak through. It wouldn't be easy—the tracks in the snow visible—but with a little bit of careful planning they could make it work.

Church motioned for Mitch to follow him, and they began trundling down off the rise towards Steiner's home, angling themselves so that they were approaching from the back, picking a line between what, in the summer months, would have been raised vegetable beds, hoping that it would give them some cover.

As they approached, Church lowered himself to the ground and Mitch did the same, and they snuck forward between the planters, pausing at the corner, shrouded in darkness, the snow falling lightly on their backs, and waited for the guards to pass.

They moved by no more than ten feet from them, finally giving Church a good look at their capabilities. Hallberg had said local police and PMCs and Church believed that, but they weren't heavily armed—equipped only with pistols, wrapped up in jeans and heavy jackets. Not an elite fighting force by any means, and no doubt begrudged to be walking around in the early hours of the morning, in the snow, in the dead of winter, waiting for an attack they probably thought wasn't even coming.

Which meant, with any luck, they wouldn't be expecting or looking for fresh tracks in the snow.

It seemed clear that whatever kind of assault they were expecting was going to come from the front, and that wasn't surprising. The only way you could get down from above was in the way that Mitch and Church had, and from the other side it was a steep climb through a snow-drenched woodland from the valley floor—an almost impossible feat for anybody.

Which meant that the only feasible option was coming up the road.

As the two guards passed, they muttered a few grumpy words to each other in German. Church slowly lifted his hand, signalling to Mitch to be ready to move.

The moment the two men had gone by, they moved from their position, pausing a few feet short of the trail the men were leaving, hopping over the mound of untouched snow and landing in the well-worn track, bounding in a single step towards the house and landing in the fresh snow once more, leaving the patrol's circuit unbroken.

Mitch followed, the two of them moving quickly now, covering the last twenty feet to the house without hesitation, stepping up onto the porch and pressing themselves against the back door. Mitch covered Church while he fumbled his lock-picking set from a pouch on his belt with cold hands and unfurled it, feeling for the different picks and torsion tools blindly in the dark.

'Any time today,' Mitch whispered, pulling his rifle

to his shoulder and making sure the guards hadn't heard them and turned around.

'Who put two pence in you tonight?' Church muttered back, finding the pick he wanted and turning to the door.

'Excuse me for missing my warm fire and a cup of tea,' Mitch said. 'This isn't really how I expected to be spending my Saturday night, to be honest.'

'It's Wednesday,' Church growled in reply, slipping the pick into the lock and then manoeuvring the torsion tool in behind it.

'Either way,' Mitch said. 'That isn't how I wanted to spend my retirement.'

'Well, you didn't have to come,' Church said to him.

'Yeah, I've got enough lives on my conscience,' Mitch replied. 'Just open the fucking door, will you? We can bicker like an old married couple later.'

Church twisted the torsion tool and the lock came free, the door swinging silently inwards. He glanced over his shoulder.

'You're definitely the wife,' he said, flashing Mitch a quick smirk before he snuck inside.

Mitch backed in after him, Church guiding him over the threshold with a hand on his shoulder, and once they were both safely in Steiner's kitchen, Church eased the door to the jamb and twisted the knob before he shut it, making sure that the click of the bolt didn't give them away.

They both remained there in the warmth of Steiner's kitchen, listening for any sounds of movement, but except for the clock ticking on the wall—an old-fashioned cuckoo thing that Church hoped wouldn't be making any announcements any time soon—the house was silent.

Church motioned for Mitch to move up, and he nodded, neither of them needing to say that it was time to go silent.

They crept towards the kitchen door and Church formed up next to it, taking the handle with his left hand, letting his rifle hang from his shoulder strap as he eased his pistol from his thigh holster, bringing the muzzle up to the frame before he opened the door. He cracked it just an inch and stared through the gap before pushing it slightly wider.

There were two men in the room that Church could see. A guard standing by the window, staring out through a split in the curtains with a pair of binoculars to his eyes, and Steiner himself sitting asleep in an armchair in front of the log fire, a glass of whisky in his hand on the arm and an open, half-drunk bottle to his left on the side table.

A few logs crackled in the huge stone hearth, stuffed heads of deer and goat adorning the walls, their horns casting gnarled shadows across the ceiling. The room was warm and smelled like wood smoke, and though as Church looked around he felt a pang of envy for the kind of quiet life that Gerhard Steiner was leading, he pushed that down, knowing that they had a job to do.

He pointed Mitch towards Steiner and then began his approach towards the guard, sneaking up behind him, holstering his pistol halfway there to keep his hands free. And when he was within striking distance, he did just that, leaping to his feet and lunging across the ten feet of space between them, throwing his hands around the unsuspecting man—one arm under his left armpit, the other over his shoulder and around his throat, pinning his chin above his elbow, Church's bicep against his carotid artery. He pulled sharply upward on the man's arm and clamped down on his neck in one swift moment, pinning him in place, almost lifting him clear off the floor as Church leaned back, starving his brain of oxygen, his lungs of air. He wouldn't scream, and he wouldn't stay conscious—not for long anyway.

The man struggled, kicking his heels at the floor, reaching with his free arm towards his belt, scrabbling for the radio there. But before he managed to get it free, he began to go limp, and only once he'd stopped struggling altogether did Church lay him slowly on the ground and slip a cable tie from the back of his belt. Securing the man's hands behind his back, he pulled two squares of black cloth from the same pouch as the zip ties, tying one around his eyes, the other firmly around his mouth, gagging and blinding him. He didn't need to see what was about to happen next, and once Church was confident the man would be no trouble when he woke up, only then did he turn back to Steiner, who, now awake, was sitting in the armchair with his hands up next to his head, his eyes firmly fixed on the barrel of Mitch's rifle, levelled at the spot between his eyes.

As Church approached, Steiner looked over at him before looking back at the gun.

'Are you going to kill me?' he asked, his English accented with an Austrian twang.

'Hopefully not,' Church replied. 'We need your help.'

'I have a phone, you know,' Steiner remarked, curling one of his hands into a loose fist and pointing at the device next to the open bottle of whisky on the table.

'Yeah, and if you'd bothered to pick up, we could have avoided all this nastiness,' Church replied smoothly, folding his arms. 'We're here about the bomber—the one killing all your friends.'

'So you're not...' he started.

'About to blow this place up? No,' Church said. 'But that doesn't mean that if you don't help, you're not going to come out of this without some bumps and bruises. Maybe a few fingernails short of a full set.' He didn't waste any time crouching so that he was at eye level with Steiner, leaving Mitch to keep him covered with his weapon. 'The bomber is a former member of the KLA looking to settle a score,' Church said without hesitation. 'He's targeting NATO officials who had a hand in making Operation Allied Force happen, though I suspect you already know that. Hence...' He trailed off, glancing over towards the bound and gagged guard near the window.

Steiner resisted the urge to roll his eyes at the ineffi-ciency of the men he'd hired to protect him, but didn't voice that opinion.

'And you think this is something I can help with?' he said then. 'Helping you find out who this man is?'

'No,' Church replied. 'We already know who he is. What I need from you is a list of names. Everyone who gave the green light for Allied Force. That's who the bomber is hunting. That's who we need to get to first.'

'Those names are privileged information. Beyond privileged!' Steiner puffed a little.

'I'm sure they are. But I still need them.'

'And if I refuse?'

Church didn't look away from the man, but instead reached to his thigh and pulled his combat knife free, letting it hang loosely, obviously, in his grip—the carbon steel blade glinting in the firelight as he turned it side to side.

'You know you're threatening a senior official of NATO, you do realise that?'

Church smiled easily at the man. 'I think you're mistaking me for somebody who gives a fuck,' he said. Church stood then, and sighed. 'Look, it's late, we're all tired,' he said. 'I'm sure you are too. Drinking yourself to sleep with worry, wondering if the bomber's going to come through that door and shove eight ounces of Semtex up your arse at any given moment...'

He let that mental image settle in before he went on.

'So I'll let you choose how this is going to go down.' Church brought the knife up then, and drove it with one swift, hard motion into the side table, releasing it so that it stood upright, buried half an inch into the wood.

The whisky bottle jumped and sloshed, and Steiner stared down at the knife, the blade shivering under the force of the impact.

He gulped audibly and then slowly looked up at Church.

'I suggest you choose fast,' he said, his gaze unflinching. 'We're on the clock.'

TWENTY-SEVEN

TWENTY-FIVE YEARS AGO

CHURCH WOVE through the Kosovan countryside, guiding the battered 4x4 around mortar craters and over-turned vehicles, burned-out husks of military jeeps on the side of the road, abandoned civilian vehicles that had done all they could to get families to where they needed to go and run out of petrol, blown out a tyre or just given up.

He felt like he knew this route well now—the route to Gurtesh, Markovich's village.

He'd reached out, demanding to meet, and again it fell to Church to go and lie to the man.

He ground his teeth as he drove, thinking about the exchange with Ismet and Darko a few days earlier.

He wanted to catch Marsella in a quiet moment, to apologise, to try to explain, but despite his willingness to go back on his word with Ismet, it seemed she wasn't.

He'd not only not been able to speak to her, he'd not seen her at all.

With that thought in his mind, he came up on the village and this time bypassed the pull-off that he'd used before to leave the car, driving the vehicle straight in instead. He pulled to the edge of the square and got out, walking on to the uneven cobbles, pausing at the fountain—any thoughts of what this place looked like before, of any kind of peace that had once been here or might return, gone from his mind.

The first hint he got that he was not alone was the subtle click of a pistol being aimed at him.

He turned around to see Markovich there, striding towards him with a weapon raised, pointed right at his head. Church had his own pistol strapped to his hip, but had left his rifle in the car, and as he stared down the barrel of Markovich's gun, he was slightly regretting that now.

'Hands,' Markovich told him, a terrible look fastened to his face. It looked as though he hadn't slept in days, his face lined and drawn, his eyes sunken—a different version of the man Church had come to know.

Church just looked back at him.

'Hands,' Markovich demanded again. 'Lift them.'

'Why?' Church replied.

'Just fucking do it,' Markovich spat.

Church measured Markovich.

'Either you're here to demand that we follow through with what we promised,' Church said, 'in which case you can't kill me. Or you've decided to flip

back to the Serbian army and you think delivering me—
one lone SAS trooper—to them is going to do something to persuade them that your betrayals can be
forgiven. Which I'm going to tell you: it's not. For a
couple of reasons. One, because I'm not worth shit and
I don't know anything worth telling them. And two,
because I'd rather you fucking shoot me than go
anywhere with you in chains. So which is it, Dragan?'
Church asked. 'You still want my help or do you want
my life?'

Markovich stood there for a few more seconds and
then lowered the gun.

'Shit,' he said, shaking his head. 'I just— I just—'

'I know,' Church said sombrely. 'You want to force
me to make good on our promises. And believe me, I
want to make good on them too.'

'Do you?' Markovich asked, sighing, looking up
with an expectant look. 'After what happened in
Pristina, at the HQ, the Serbs are looking for a head to
make roll. Just a matter of time until they find me.
When will my family be safe?' He was practically
pleading. 'We're packed and ready to go. We just need
you to tell us where.'

'Soon,' was all Church could say back, the word
sour and poisonous in his mouth. 'NATO are putting the
intel they gathered—they got from HQ—to good use.
They're planning something,' Church said, hoping that
that much wasn't a lie.

'An attack?' Markovich said.

Church resisted the urge to shrug. 'I don't know. But

it's something big. They won't tell us what. But they told us to be ready for it.'

'Something that will end the war?' Markovich demanded of him.

'I hope so,' Church said, his voice strained. 'You've just got to hold on. Just a little more time.'

'I don't have more time,' Markovich said, laughing incredulously at that. 'You promised me they'd be safe. You promised. Tell me. Just tell me…' He stepped forward, pistol shaking in his hand. 'Did you lie to me? Was there ever a plan to get them out? I need to know. Because if not, then… then… then I have to try myself. We have to run.'

Church could see in his face that he meant those words—that he would do anything to save his family. And though he barely knew this man, he respected him. Liked him, even. Could see that he was a man of honour. That maybe he'd done bad things, made bad calls, been forced to kill—but inside, he knew right from wrong, and he was trying to abide by that.

Or perhaps, Church thought bitterly, I'm just projecting what I hope is true about myself.

'I am promising you now,' he said then, finding some resolve in himself. 'If they don't come for your family, I will. I will get you out of the country.'

'How can you?' Markovich asked, stepping towards him, shaking his head.

'I'll figure out a way,' Church assured him.

But that wasn't enough, and Markovich sagged a

couple of inches, his shoulders rounding, his head falling.

'If that's all the reassurance I have,' he said, 'then I fear I might as well bury my wife and daughter now. I gave everything for this. Everything,' he said, looking up at the man in front of him. 'Everything, Church. Do you understand?'

'And I'll make sure it wasn't in vain.' Slowly, Church extended a hand towards him, offering not just his word, but himself as bond.

But this time, Markovich didn't take it.

He just stared down at it, realising now that it was no more than a poisoned chalice.

TWENTY-EIGHT

PRESENT DAY

Steiner put up a little resistance at first. But once he realised that no one was coming to save him, he quickly acquiesced to Church's request and started reeling off names faster than Church could write them down.

'There was Klaus Meyer,' he said. 'Lars Jonessen. Thomas Zielinski.'

Church looked up at him. 'Zielinski?' he asked, getting the pronunciation right.

Steiner nodded. 'From Poland. Z–I–E–L–I–N–S–K–I—I think.'

Church nodded, noting it down in the little notebook that he'd been carrying in one of the pockets on his trousers.

'Then Helena Sorensen. Petros Antinou…'

But as he kept reeling off names, Church's attention drifted a little. He looked over at Mitch, who was standing at the window now, peeking out through the same gap in the curtains that the guard had been.

He'd regained consciousness and was lying still, listening to what was going on, unable to speak or move in any way. But Church wasn't paying him any mind. He'd have no way to identify them.

And though Steiner had seen their faces, once they left here there would be nothing to actually report other than breaking and entering. But how was that going to stick in light of everything else?

'Mitchy,' Church called out softly to him across the room.

Mitch turned back from the window and looked over at him, his expression stern.

'What's wrong?' Church asked.

'There's nobody out there,' Mitch replied.

Church looked at him, reading his expression. At first he thought that was a good thing—they were safe for now. But as he read the apprehension in Mitch's face, he realised exactly what he meant.

'No one at all?'

Mitch shook his head, returning to the window once more. 'No. The guards were doing laps. But now...' He trailed off. 'There's no sign of them.'

Church felt a little prickle on the back of his neck and stowed his notebook reflexively, unholstering his pistol and walking towards the window.

Mitch backed up to allow him access, and Church touched his nose to the glass between the curtains, looking left and right across the open space before

Steiner's house. Despite the darkness, the snow had a way of casting a dim glow such that you could see further than you normally would. And Mitch was right. Even from here, Church could see the trail that the guards had been cutting in as they walked the perimeter.

But now there was no sign of them. There should have been four of them out there walking in opposite directions and yet… there was no one.

'What's going on?' Steiner asked from his position in his chair, sipping on a fresh glass of whisky.

Church hadn't seen the need to bind him, and had even allowed him to refill his drink before giving the list. The man was harmless and not liable to be a flight risk—and even if he was, it wasn't like he could outrun either Church or Mitch. He was in his seventies and far heavier than he should have been if he wanted to see eighty.

Church glanced over at Steiner but said nothing back, instead motioning to Mitch to cover him.

Mitch nodded, understanding without the verbal command, and headed back to Steiner, standing beside him and drawing his own pistol, keeping it loose at his side. Church crept towards the door and reached for the handle with his left hand, lifting his rifle with his right.

He cracked it an inch and poked the muzzle through the gap, drawing the night vision optic to his eye. He stared out into the darkness, the snow burning white in his scope.

Nothing was moving.

He'd hoped that perhaps his eyes weren't as good as

he thought they were, and that he was missing the obvious patrols of the guards—but they were nowhere to be seen.

Church risked opening the door a few inches more, just wide enough that he could get half of his body through it, could see a wider portion of the grounds. Could get a full look at what was going on out there.

'They're out there, right?' Steiner asked loudly, taking a big glug of whisky.

Church scowled, eye pressed into the optic, and turned back his shoulder, nudging the door slightly wider as he was about to tell Steiner to keep quiet.

But that momentary opening was all that was needed.

Church felt the graze of the bullet first as it unzipped the air next to his face, flying through the narrow gap in the door, barely missing his head—close enough to slash the skin on his cheek.

The pain and the report of the rifle came at the same moment, and Church dove backwards instinctively, hitting the ground with his elbows and kicking the door shut with his heel, throwing his hand to his face, the blood already pouring down over his jaw.

He swore, screwing his eyes shut against the pain and scrambled to his knees, looking up towards Mitch, ready to order him to get to cover, to get an eye on the shooter—the one who'd nearly taken his head off.

Darko, was all he could think. Darko had taken a shot at him. Had tried to kill him—and he'd missed!

But that instantaneous feeling of relief, that feeling

of good fortune, evaporated as quickly as it had bloomed, as he realised that despite the snow and the darkness and the wind…

Darko hadn't missed his shot at all.

He'd not even been aiming for Church.

As he lifted his eyes towards Mitch, all he saw was Steiner's face contorted in shock and pain, his hands clamped to his belly, blood spilling through his fingers.

Mitch was already tending to him, pressing down on the wound with the heels of his hands, swearing as he tried to staunch the bleeding from the gut shot.

Church stared at it and then touched his fingers to his face gingerly, feeling the depth of the wound there. Large calibre rifle round, he thought—it had to be. Straight into Steiner's stomach. Who knew what it had hit. Intestine, liver, pancreas, spine. Hell, there was no good place to get shot, but the belly was one of the worst.

There was no way they could treat that here. Steiner would need an operating room and a damn good surgeon to have any hope of surviving, and Church didn't even know where the nearest hospital was.

He moved forward, getting to his knees and then to his feet, coming towards Mitch, reaching for his phone, ready to call for help. The mission was scrubbed. Now all that mattered was making sure that Steiner made it through this. And that Darko didn't.

Church would call Hallberg, tell her what was going on, and she'd get every agent she could here. Police, armed response, counter-terrorism. Vans. Trucks. Heli-

copters. Right now, Darko was within reach, and regardless of what happened to Steiner, they weren't going to
let him slip away.

But before Church could even dial the number,
another sound reached his ears.

A hollow pop and whistle echoing in the distance
outside.

A sound he knew well—but at first didn't recognise.

He stood there, stopped in his tracks. Perfectly still,
a feeling of dread writhing in his gut.

Holy fuck.

The realisation dawned suddenly and he lunged
forward, grabbing Mitch by the arm, dragging it from
Steiner. The man groaned, twisting in the chair as the
pressure was released from his wound and blood spurted
over his knees.

'What are you doing?' Mitch all but yelled, his
hands soaked red.

'We've got to go!' Church replied, hauling him
towards the door.

'He needs help!' Mitch protested, fighting him.
'He'll fucking die if we don't keep pressure on it!'

'In about five fucking seconds, it's not going to
fucking matter,' Church snapped at him, wheeling him
around with all of his strength, overpowering the man
and shoving him towards the door. There was no time to
get out the back. This was their only chance.

He wrenched it open and, taking Mitch by the collar
now, hurled him across the wooden porch and down into
the snow, tearing after him as quickly as he could.

He looked up then, searching for it as he ran, hunting for the thing he knew was coming—the top-attack missile that had been fired from an FGM-148 Javelin, a fire-and-forget guidance system that sent an explosive payload high into the air before it came hurtling down towards earth from above, designed to destroy armoured targets like tanks or fortified enemy positions where the armour was weakest—on top.

Church had seen them. Had heard them. Had fired them.

It was a sound not easily forgotten. And the thing that produced it would make short work of Steiner's log home—and short work of anyone who was inside.

Mitch hadn't heard it, but Church had. And he knew, as Mitch stumbled in the snow in front of him and Church grabbed him up, almost throwing him to keep him moving, that they weren't far enough away.

And as the little flash of white fire from the tail of the rocket cut through the darkness above, all Church could do was rake in a final, freezing-cold breath and brace himself for the impact.

The missile screamed down.

The shockwave came first, blowing him off his feet.

The heat, the pain, the noise came just after.

He was clear of the ground and careening through the air, tumbling, flipping, shards of wooden shrapnel hissing through the air on all sides, the fire biting his skin, the explosion threatening to burst his eardrums and shatter his teeth.

He landed hard. Bounced and twisted. Gouging

craters in the snow as he came rolling to a wet and smouldering stop.

He sucked in a shallow, violent breath and tried to fill his lungs. Pain. Pain everywhere. Hurt, he thought. Lacerations? Broken bones? Questions his brain asked him. He instinctively moved his fingers. Moved his toes, his feet, making sure his back wasn't broken, that he wasn't paralysed, and ran a mental check over his entire body.

He was still in one piece—just about.

But a second later and it would have been a different story. His ballistic vest, the layers of clothes he was wearing to ward off the cold, they were probably the difference between the pain he was feeling and his skin being burned clean off.

It was hard to breathe, his lungs not wanting to work, his diaphragm seemingly not within his control.

He tried to get his elbows under him, his knees, knowing that Darko was still out there—that he was no doubt coming for him. But as hard as he tried, he couldn't.

He didn't have the strength.

His body was not his own.

He didn't know where he was, how far he'd been flung, where Mitch was... hell, if Mitch was even alive.

He could hear nothing except the ringing in his ears, could feel nothing except pain in every corner of his body.

He was clinging on to consciousness with every shred of will he had left, focusing on his breathing, begging his body to work. To do something. Before it was too late.

His heart beat fast in his ears, everything in his brain telling him to give in. All he could do was try to breathe through it, wait for it to pass, but then there was something else.

Something in the periphery of his meagre consciousness.

He became aware that he was no longer alone.

Footsteps cut through the ringing in his ears, slow crunching in the snow.

They approached methodically, circling him.

Moving up from his feet.

Towards his head.

He lifted his face out of the slush stained scarlet with his own blood and stared up into the night sky, illuminated now by the column of fire billowing from what remained of Steiner's home.

A figure stood beside him, cut out by the flames. Tall. Gnarled. A phantom in the night.

Church tried to speak, tried to form the word 'Darko'.

He tried to say it, but no sound came out.

Slowly, the figure stooped, resting its hands on his knees, sagging forward, forcing itself into an awkward, stiff crouch—almost inhuman in its movements, as though all sense of humanity had left it long ago.

Church fought back the blackness, kept himself in the moment, knowing if he fought it, if he resisted it for long enough, that maybe, just maybe, he could reach for his pistol, his knife—something. That he could gather the strength he needed to end Darko here and now, before he killed him, before he went after his family, before he hurt anyone else.

'Solomon Church,' came the gravelly voice from above.

Church froze, trying everything he could to focus his eyes.

'It's been a long time,' the voice said.

Church racked his mind, trying to fix the sound of that voice to his memory of Darko. But something was jarring somehow. It didn't fit. It didn't feel right. Didn't sound right.

And yet the voice wasn't unfamiliar.

He knew it—knew the man that it had belonged to.

The figure stooped further, leaning down, placing a hand in the snow next to Church's head, as though hell-bent on meeting his eye. And when he got low enough, that's exactly what he did. And Church realised, all at once, agonisingly, how wrong he'd been.

The man staring at him wasn't Darko Vida at all.

He was a man that he thought had died in Kosovo twenty-five years ago. A man that he was sure he was responsible for killing.

Colonel Dragan Markovich.

Markovich looked into Church's eyes, peeling back the layers of his soul with a stare so hollow and empty, Church shivered under its weight.

'I read that you had died,' Markovich said slowly, as though revelling in this moment. 'So can you imagine how much unbridled *delight* I felt when I saw you that night outside Whitmore's house?' He smiled with crooked yellow teeth, his face not the same one Church had come to know decades ago. He'd been a handsome man then, but now he was scarred. Weathered. As though he'd died and been brought back to life as some unhuman monster.

And Church thought that was exactly what had happened.

'I had so, so wanted to kill you for what you did,' Markovich said with a sigh. 'And now I get to do just that.' He reached out and ran a rough, uneven knuckle along Church's brow, as though making sure Church was real. As though reminding Church that *he* himself was.

Church recoiled from the man, hating his body for not being under his control, hating himself for not having the strength to get up and strangle the life out of Markovich once and for all.

'But first,' he said, his fingers stopping on Church's cheek, 'you must know the pain that I have felt.' He withdrew his hand slowly and held it up to the firelight bleeding over his shoulders. Not a hint of shake in it. It shone red with Church's blood, glinting in the reflection of hell.

'Solomon Church,' Markovich said with a satisfied sigh, taking his eyes from the blood. He eased himself slowly to his feet and turned away, stepping slowly into the darkness, the shadows swallowing him by the second, his footsteps slow, unhurried. Savouring every moment.

'You think you know loss,' he said, his voice fading with every word. 'You know nothing yet.'

He laughed.

'But you will.'

And then... he was gone.

TWENTY-NINE

TWENTY-FIVE YEARS AGO

IT WAS dark when the sat phone started ringing.

It was balanced on top of Church's pack, twelve inches from his head.

He woke the moment it started vibrating, the little green screen lighting up in the dead of night, casting a dim glow around the tent.

Reflexively, he rolled over and reached for it, expecting the call even in his sleep. The way he'd left things with Markovich, he knew it was only a matter of time before he called—perhaps to say that he'd reconsidered, or more likely, to say that things had gotten worse.

When the call came, Church still didn't know what he would do, was still wrestling with himself, but either way he answered it and pulled it to his ear, knowing only one person would be ringing at this time.

'Markovich,' he said without hesitation. 'What's wrong?'

'My wife was stopped today at the supermarket and questioned about my movements,' he said without any kind of greeting.

Church heard a sort of restrained tension in his voice. He wasn't frantic, but he had every right to be.

'She was asked by the Serbian military police whether she'd noticed anything strange about my behaviour—any late-night phone calls, unscheduled meetings at the house, whether she'd seen me talking to anybody she didn't recognise, anyone with a strange accent or that didn't look local.'

Church listened, his fist wrapped so tightly around the phone he almost crushed it in his grip.

'Does she know what you're doing?' Church had to ask. 'Does she know…' He trailed off, a little unsure how to word the next part.

'That I'm betraying my country,' Markovich whispered bluntly.

Church imagined him standing at the window to his living room, peeking through the blinds, looking for an unmarked military car parked outside his house, watching him, monitoring his phone lines, everything he was doing.

Church didn't respond to that—only waited for Markovich to answer his own questions.

'She knows,' he said. 'And she knows it's not a betrayal. She wants this war to end as much as I do, and neither of us feels that this is our own country any more

—not after what it's done to its own people. But that doesn't change the fact,' he said. 'She lied for me today. But if they're asking her, it's because they believe that I am the mole. And regardless of what she said, they're not going to let it lie. So I'll ask you the question that I asked you today, and I hope knowing that will change your answer: when are we getting out?'

Church could feel his pulse throbbing in his temple, could feel the slow, almost pained boom of his heart in his chest.

'Soon,' was all he could say. His eyes squeezed shut. 'I'm working on it.'

'That's not good enough,' Markovich said tiredly. 'I'll pack up my family tonight. We'll go to Gurtesh and wait for you. You can pick us up there. You promised to get us out, and now it's time to make good on that promise.'

'No,' Church said suddenly, trying to keep his voice hushed, trying not to wake the other men. 'You can't. It's not safe. And we're not ready yet.'

When he had relayed what had happened with Gaz at their last meeting, Gaz had given him strict orders not open to any interpretation: hold fast. Wait for further information from NATO. Wait until they gave the green light. Wait until they were ready to get Markovich out. And it wasn't something that he felt like he could argue, despite desperately wanting to.

'We'll tell you when the time comes,' Church said.

'When?' Markovich demanded. 'It's always tomorrow. Tomorrow, tomorrow, tomorrow. Tomorrow I could be in front of a firing squad.'

'I'm working on it,' Church pleaded with him, pinching the bridge of his nose hard enough that it hurt.

'No,' Markovich said. 'It's time to admit it.' His voice was grave now. 'You lied to me, didn't you? We were never getting out.' He scoffed, and before Church could respond to that and lie to him again, he hung up.

Slowly, Church lowered the phone and stared at the screen, seeing the glint of Gaz's eye across the tent from him, lying on his side on his bunk, staring at Church.

He let out a soft sigh. 'I'm sorry,' he said. 'That's the way it goes sometimes.' And then, quietly, he whispered the words Church was growing to despise. 'It's the job.'

And with that, he slowly rolled over and showed his back to Church, who sat there in the dark of the tent, the light of the phone dying in front of him, returning them all to the blackness.

THIRTY

PRESENT DAY

CHURCH FELT hands on him and rolled over, swinging with a heavy, slow swat.

Mitch reeled backwards, catching a blow to the shoulder, and stumbled, falling into the snow. He got up with some difficulty, cradling his left side, and staggered towards Church a second time.

'It's me, it's me, Sol, it's me—it's Mitch,' he said, collapsing next to his friend, hand on his chest, shaking him back to life.

Church's eyes came into focus. The air was thick with smoke, and the sirens were already beginning to wail in the distance. He looked around, groaning as he rolled onto his side, but there was no sign of Markovich.

He was gone, swallowed by the night.

Church planted his hand in the snow, his knuckles covered in blood, his skin grazed and cut from the explosion. He grimaced and forced his arm to bear weight, pushing himself to a painful, difficult knee. He coughed and spat something black into the snow, feeling Mitch pulling him upright.

'We've got to go, Sol. We've got to go now,' he said, trying his best to drag Church to a stance.

With one eye open, Church looked around, taking stock of the area. Steiner's house was nothing but a ruin, one wall still standing, the rest collapsed inwards—a pyre of logs still in flames.

'Jesus Christ,' Church muttered, looking at it. He hoped Steiner had gone quickly, at least.

The sirens wailed louder in the distance, the first hint of blue light splashing through the trees beyond the gate. Fire engines, ambulances, police... who could say which?

But either way, it would be best if they were gone by the time they arrived. Mitch hauled Church up, hooking his great arm over his shoulders and bore his weight, starting him forward towards the tree line. The progress was slow at first, but with each step Church regained some semblance of strength.

Miraculously, he didn't think anything was broken, but it felt like he'd been run over—a feeling that he actually had a frame of reference for. 2011 had been a difficult year for him and one he was not keen to revisit, and he'd all but forgotten what that sensation was like until now.

They gathered pace, pushing forward towards the forest and the steep bank leading down to the valley floor. Impossible to climb up in order to get to Steiner's lodge, but getting down was another story. The rendezvous point was a kilometre away as the crow flew, on a forestry access road directly east of Steiner's house. And as they began the trudge towards it, Mitch dragged his phone from his pocket and typed a few words into a text message, sending it to the pre-programmed number that would trigger their exfil to say that they were en route. He stowed his phone and hiked Church higher on his shoulders.

'Jesus Christ, you're heavy,' he said. 'You're going to have to get on fucking Weight Watchers or something when we get back. I can't keep dragging your big arse around like this.'

Church laughed and it hurt, the sound turning into a strangled groan as they trudged through the snow, reaching the trees just as the first police cars arrived at the gate, ducking into the shadows just as headlights sprayed across Steiner's lodge and the mess of dead bodies left in Markovich's wake.

The ground grew steeper before them and they started sloshing and sliding through the forest, battered and half dead but still moving, Church spurred on by the knowledge that if he fell here and didn't get up, there would be no one to stand between Dragan Markovich and his family. There was no ambiguity in Markovich's words—he was going for Nanna and the girls, and he was going to make it hurt.

Church felt like he was looking through a pinhole as

they moved, his teeth gritted so hard he thought they would split.

But then they arrived at the road, panting hard, and collapsed onto it, waiting for their pickup. Church closed his eyes and breathed through the agony, listening to the distant cries of sirens high above and waiting for the hum of an engine that would tell them their ride was here—knowing that for each minute that passed, that was one more minute ahead that Markovich was, and one minute less to save Nanna and the girls.

Church didn't recall much of what happened next, just a blur of vehicle interiors. The rendezvous car, which took them to an airfield to transfer into a private plane flown by the same German pilot that had dropped them over Steiner's. He flew them back to the UK, touching down at a private airfield, and from there, the back of Hallberg's SUV, which took him directly to a private hospital, where he was sat on a table, cut out of his shirt, held in place by Hallberg and Mitch while a doctor stuck her needle in him. He struggled and pulled away from them—not because he was desperate to avoid the pain, but because he was desperate to get to Nanna.

'They're fine!' Hallberg kept assuring him through gritted teeth, straining against his bulk, her arms firm around his neck, practically hanging off his back to keep him seated. 'There are six people stationed around her flat. Markovich is not getting to them. Not tonight,' she said. 'You need to rest!'

'He needs to stay still,' the doctor, a woman in her

fifties with curly hair, said sternly. 'If he doesn't, he's going to rip these stitches before I even get them in.'

'So stick some fucking glue in it instead,' Church growled, meeting her eye with a fierce enough look to stop her dead in her tracks.

She looked at Hallberg for confirmation, and she shook her head.

'Do it right,' she said. 'He's not leaving here until I know he's okay.'

In any other situation, Church might have been near moved by Hallberg's words, by the sentiment, by her desire to make sure that he was all right. But tonight, he barely heard her at all—barely felt it as the hooked needle sank into his flesh, as the doctor pulled chunks of wood from his skin. Barely saw the light as she looked into his pupils to make sure that nothing was ruptured, as she took his blood pressure and heart rate, as she assessed him for concussion and internal bleeding. He was a wolf in a snare, and he'd have chewed his own leg off to get out just then. But finally, when they were finished, Hallberg agreed to take him to Nanna.

He called en route and she picked up groggily. It was six in the morning and he'd woken her, but he didn't care about that. Didn't even think about it.

'Nan—' he said, breathless, a flood of warmth rushing through him as he heard her voice. 'Are you all right?'

'Am I all right?' she groaned. 'It's six in the fucking morning, Solomon. Are *you* all right?'

He let out a long, rattling sigh. 'The girls—they're asleep?'

'Are you deaf as well? It's six in the morning, of course they're asleep,' Nanna said seriously. 'What is it? Why are you calling? What's wrong?'

'Nothing,' Solomon said. 'Just go back to sleep. I'll be there soon.'

There was silence for a moment, and then Nanna seemed perfectly alert. 'You're coming here? What's going on?'

Church looked over at Hallberg, who was giving him an *I told you so* look—the one he should have been expecting since she told him, emphatically, multiple times, not to call Nanna. Not to wake her. That she was getting regular updates from the officers stationed outside Nanna's house. That all was quiet there. That they were perfectly safe.

But he insisted, and now she was worried.

'Everything's fine,' Church said. 'I just... I need to see you, is all.'

'You're worrying me, Solomon. I know when something's wrong,' she said. 'Tell me what's going on. Right now.'

Church ran his tongue over his teeth, feeling one of his top left molars a little loose from the tumble he'd taken, and he squeezed on it until it hurt—until it narrowed his mind, until it gave him clarity.

'I'll explain everything,' he said. 'When I get there. I promise.'

'Everything?'

He let out a sobering breath. 'Everything.'

He hung up then, and Hallberg drove on, seemingly knowing that her look was enough. That telling him he shouldn't have called her—shouldn't have worried her —would achieve nothing. Instead, she did something far kinder and reached over, putting her hand on his trembling arm.

'They'll be OK,' she said. 'I promise you that.'

'I don't think you can,' Church said, staring almost absently through the windscreen. 'I don't think anyone can.'

They wove into London just before rush hour got into full swing and arrived at the house a little after seven.

Church spotted two unmarked police cars, one right outside Nanna's house, one a little down the street to get an early view of anybody approaching by road.

Where the third car was—and the fifth and sixth officers—Church didn't know. But he trusted Hallberg. And if there was one thing she wasn't, it was a liar.

He got out of the car, dressed in a grey T-shirt that Hallberg had brought him, little spots of blood seeping through the fabric where the untidy stitches had begun to bleed.

Church climbed the stairs gingerly, still in pain, doing his best to mask it as Nanna opened the door to receive him. She was in a robe and pyjamas, and stood in the doorway as though barring his entrance.

'Tell me what's going on. Right now,' she demanded, wrapping her hands around herself.

Church took her by the shoulders and turned her around, steering her into the hallway, kicking the door shut behind him.

He never liked laying his hands on a woman, and especially not his sister. There was too much of that in their childhood for either of them. But he wasn't thinking clearly. She tried to shrug him off, tried to elbow him, but he kept moving her, kept pushing her, until she dug her heels in, elbowing him in the gut.

'Stop!' she yelled.

The point of her elbow caught one of the sets of stitches and he winced, doubling forward, the pain instant and blinding.

When he looked down and saw it begin to bleed more profusely, and as he straightened he realised at least one of the stitches—if not more—had pulled. He pressed his hand to the cut, trying to staunch the bleeding, and though any other sister might have tended to him, might have apologised, Nanna stood her ground, dead-eyeing him.

'You tell me what's going on right fucking now, Solomon,' she said. 'You don't get to push me into my own home. It doesn't matter what's happening out there.' She threw a hand towards the door and Church looked after it.

He blinked, as though regaining himself all at once in the presence of his sister, and stared at her, lifting his gaze—then to the two figures hovering on the top step of the stairs. Lowri and Mia stared down at him, wide-eyed, frightened.

They rarely heard their mother shout, and even more rarely saw Church rattled. Nanna looked up at her daughters and cleared her throat, putting on one of those fake mum smiles that she hoped would tell them everything was OK—but would only succeed in letting them know just how wrong things were.

'Go back to your rooms. Get ready for school,' she said, her voice light and somehow shrill, strained.

They looked at each other, and then returned their stare to their mother and Church.

'Now, girls,' Nanna said firmly. And that was all it took.

They knew there was no arguing with her, and went without another word of protest—their bedroom doors creaking open and then shut, but not hitting the frame, not latching with a click. Left open an inch, Church was sure, so that their ears could be pressed to the gap, so they could hear—could understand—what was going on.

They were older now. But not old enough, Church thought. Not for this. Not for what he was about to say.

'Kitchen,' Nanna said, her voice low and as sharp as the blade Church had driven into Steiner's coffee table the night before.

He did as he was told, moving through into the kitchen, still cupping at bleeding ribs.

Nanna was without remorse as she followed him through, ordering him to sit on one of the bar stools at the kitchen island.

'Coffee,' she said—not even a question. 'I figure

you need it. You *must* be drunk to storm in like this and frighten the hell out of the girls.'

'I'm not drinking again,' Solomon assured her.

'Well then, you'd better have a damn good reason for coming in here like this, because you're not just scaring them. You're scaring me too.'

Church leaned forward, resting his elbows on the polished marble of the kitchen island, and put his face in his hands, running his fingers slowly through his hair, pushing the ash and grime backwards on his scalp.

'I was wrong,' he said, not sure how to start, but knowing that silence was not an option.

'Wrong about what, Solomon?' Nanna said, leaning forward, bracing herself on her hands.

'Wrong about everything,' Church replied. 'The bomber,' he said. 'It's not who I thought he was. Not the man that I thought he was.'

'I don't understand,' Nanna said. 'If he's not who you thought, then who is he?'

Church let out a shaking breath. 'His name is Dragan Markovich.' He looked up to meet his sister's eyes, searching for her approval, for her kinship before he said the next part. 'And I killed his family.'

Nanna stepped back a little and stood straight, swallowing as she steeled herself, knowing that he'd had a long career of serving his country—and perhaps not always in the most honourable ways. War was hell. She knew that.

'What—' she started, stumbling over the words. She

cleared her throat, as though something was stuck in it. 'What do you mean, "you killed his family"?'

'I thought I killed him as well,' Church went on.

She tried to tease apart his words, tried to glean some kind of understanding, but couldn't. 'Tell me what happened... How? How did you...? Why did you...? When did you...?'

'I tried to save them,' was all Church could say, doing his best to make sense of his own thoughts in his head, to organise them into something that might explain what had happened. He'd done everything he could to lock it away, and yet he'd never taken the time to make sense of it. Never tried to interrogate it or process it. And opening that box now, looking inside, all he saw was a festering mess of guilt and shame. 'I tried to save them, but I couldn't. I've lived with it for twenty-five years and now...'

'And now what, Solomon? You're not making sense,' she said, the kettle beginning to whistle behind her.

'He's back,' Church said. 'He's back to take from me what I took from him.'

Her eyes widened a little, realisation dawning.

'He's coming for you, Nan. Maybe the girls too. And it's all my fault.' He sagged forward again into his hands, his head too heavy for his frame to bear. His eyes burned under his palms, his throat hot, like Markovich was twisting a red-hot iron into his gullet.

He heard Nanna move in the darkness of his periphery. Expected her to be running to the girls after his confession. Expected her to be already moving—to pack up, to run from Markovich, from Church, from everything he'd done, from the man he really was, from the monster he'd always pretended not to be.

But he didn't hear her footsteps drift away and fade.

They crept closer and closer, and before he could find the strength and the courage to open his eyes, to look for her, he felt her hand on his shoulder, running across his back, enveloping him slowly. And then she began tugging at him, pulling him towards her, into her breast, into an embrace that he didn't know that he needed—but one that he never wanted to leave.

'It's OK, Solomon,' she said after what seemed like an age of silence. 'You're a good man. And I know that you did everything you could have.'

He wanted to say something back. Anything. Everything. There was so much that he wanted to tell her, that he needed to tell someone. So much he felt like she deserved to know about who he was and who he'd been. But his throat was aching as badly as any other part of him, and he knew that if he removed his eyes from his hands, that tears would come spilling out.

But of all the things he wanted to tell her, one thing reigned supreme.

That she was wrong. That that wasn't the truth. That he wasn't a good man. That he didn't do everything he could have. That he could have done more.

And somehow, he couldn't help but wonder if this was what he deserved.

And then the realisation came as suddenly as Markovich's bullet had the night before.

It was.

It *was* what he deserved. He had no right to be sitting there. No right to be held and to be told that it was all OK.

Markovich's family didn't deserve to die.

But neither did his.

There was only one person in that house that death should come for—and when all was said and done, Church promised himself that at the end of this, Nanna and the girls would live.

And if that meant that he had to die, then good.

THIRTY-ONE

TWENTY-FIVE YEARS AGO

THE BOMBERS BEGAN to rumble overhead around dawn.

US-supplied B-52s and B-1B Lancers were carrying heavy payloads of laser-guided missiles and cluster bombs towards Pristina and further north into Serbia, aiming for Belgrade.

Church held his breath, staring up at them from the mouth of the tent as they streaked above, high in the clouds—little, near-invisible black dots that would rain hellfire down on whoever was unlucky enough to be standing underneath.

Word had come from NATO just the night before that the bombings would start in earnest through the night, and that by the time the sun rose, Serbia would be flame and rubble.

Gaz passed the information along to Ismet and Darko, and they'd taken to celebrating, drinking every last drop of alcohol they'd stockpiled and raided over the last few months. Music blared from the house continually, and their shouts and laughter pierced the night.

But now that the sun was rising, their celebrations were being drowned out by the sound of jet engines, and Church wasn't sure if that was a mercy or something even worse.

Gaz made his way back across the farmyard from the latrine tent they'd set up, buttoning his trousers as he walked. Church stared at him, waiting for the man to look up, and when he finally did, he stepped out to meet him.

'What's happening with Markovich?' he all but demanded, holding his hands up to stop Gaz.

'How the fuck am I supposed to know?' Gaz asked, trying to move past.

'There's been no calls to the sat phone. Did NATO get in touch with him directly? Did they get him out like they promised?'

Gaz could only shake his head.

'You really think that I'm looped in to every single thing they're planning? We are bottom of the totem pole, Church, and not exactly in a position to ask for further information or make any demands of them. You want to know so much, fucking call them,' he said, tired of this conversation, which it seemed like they'd had a thousand times in the last few days. 'Hell, the number of my NATO contact is in that phone you've been holding on to. If you want to hear the answer to that question, then go right to the source, make a phone call, and end this fucking tantrum, right? But whatever you do, just stop fucking asking me, okay?'

He strode past then and back into the tent, maybe keen to snatch another few minutes of sleep if it was possible. None of them had managed to get their heads down with everything going on inside the house.

Church grumbled, unhappy with the result of the confrontation, and pulled the sat phone out of his pocket.

He'd called Markovich a half dozen times in the last few hours but there'd been no answer. He hoped that he'd made a break for the border on his own and that at least he might make it before he was stopped by either the Serbian army or by the KLA.

Church wasn't sure which was worse or what fate would be more brutal. If the Serbs caught him, they'd put him in prison, torture him for the information, then hang him. If it was the KLA, well… it would probably be the same story, but bloodier.

Church thumbed through the numbers saved in the phone then and dialled the second one, waiting for it to connect. It rang and rang and rang for what seemed like an age, and then, when the person at the other end realised he wasn't going to quit, they finally answered.

'Hello?' came a woman's voice, tired and strained. 'I told you not to call this number,' she said. 'I'll call you when I need something—'

'It's not the captain,' Church interrupted her.

She fell silent immediately.

'My name is Solomon Church,' he said, 'and I need to speak to somebody about Dragan Markovich.'

'Is Captain West...?' she began speaking.

'Dead?' Church answered for her. 'No, he's not.'

'So then why are you calling?' the woman asked him.

'As I said, I need to speak to someone about Dragan Markovich.'

'Dragan Markovich?' the woman replied.

'Don't play dumb,' Church snapped, practically at the ragged edge.

The woman fell quiet again.

'I'm the one that's been meeting with him out here, and though I don't expect you to realise what it's like in the middle of a war zone—what with being tucked up in a cosy office somewhere—out here, shit is hitting the fan. I've been dangling his family's safety over his head to get information for you for the last month. So tell me —are you making good on your promise to him? Are you getting him out of the city?'

'The city?' the woman asked back.

'Pristina,' Church snapped.

She was silent for a while, and then perhaps it was her humanity that made her speak again.

'I don't know what's happening with Markovich or his asylum,' she said. 'It hasn't been mentioned. Not to me. And I'm the one who's been in direct contact with him,' she added, her voice hushed as though afraid somebody might overhear.

'So where does that leave him and his family?' Church urged her.

She let out a quiet sigh. 'I don't know,' she said. 'But if he's still in Pristina, well… I'd say in a few hours, there's not going to be much of it left to escape.'

'You're hitting the city this morning,' Church confirmed.

'I can't give you specifics,' she replied. 'But if he's planning to try to make an escape of some kind on his own, then he should do it soon.'

'How soon?' Church pressed her.

He heard her swallow on the other side of the line, her words catching in her throat.

'Very,' she said, and with that she hung up the phone.

THIRTY-TWO

PRESENT DAY

THERE WAS a knock at the door, and Church peeled himself from Nanna's embrace, putting his hand on her arm, moving her gently to the side to stare down the corridor towards it.

He rose from the bar seat and ran his knuckles roughly across the bridge of his nose, sniffing back all the things that had almost come spilling out—tears included. 'Wait here,' he said, eyes fixed on the door.

He strode towards it, his hand resting on the grip of his pistol on his thigh but not drawing it. Nanna stayed where she was while Church approached, glancing back to take stock of her position before he placed his hand on the handle and cracked it an inch, seeing Hallberg and Mitch standing on the top step.

He stared out past them, making sure the Met officers were still in place, then opened the door a little more. When he turned round, Nanna was standing right at his shoulder, close enough that he jumped a little.

'I told you to wait in the kitchen,' he said.

'This is my house, Solomon,' she replied, putting her hand on the edge of the door. 'Get out of the way.'

He let go, and Nanna pulled it wide, the four of them stood there on the threshold. Nanna looked Mitch up and down—his face cut from the explosion, his stance awkward, leaning over one side to cradle his ribs.

'Jesus Christ,' she said, looking at him. 'What has Sol got you involved in this time?'

'He volunteered,' Church said quickly.

She turned her gaze to him. 'Then you should have done a better job keeping him safe.'

'I *did* keep him safe! I saved his fucking life,' Church snapped at her. 'They dropped a damn missile on us.'

'A missile?' Nanna blinked. 'A *fucking missile*?'

Church was about to open his mouth and retort when Hallberg cleared her throat loudly and stepped forward between them. She pushed her hand towards Nanna, shouldering Church backwards.

'Hello. We haven't met,' she said. 'I'm Julia Hallberg. I'm heading up the Interpol operation to apprehend the bomber.' She spoke astutely, without hesitation. 'I'm sure all this is coming as a shock to you, but I want you to know you're perfectly safe and this investigation is well in hand. We know who he is, and we're homing in on his position by the minute. His name is Darko Vida, and—'

But before she could get any further, Nanna shook her head, ignoring the handshake altogether.

'No, it's not. It's Markovich. Dragon Markovich. Or something.'

'Dragan,' Church corrected her, stepping around Hallberg.

He looked at the pair of them in turn—Hallberg almost bowled over by this new piece of information. 'I'm sorry I didn't tell you sooner,' he said to her. 'I was...' His stare drifted to his sister. 'Preoccupied.'

Church could see Hallberg visibly seething at the fact he had withheld vital intelligence—the identity of the bomber—for hours. But she didn't lose her composure. Instead, she put on her best PR smile and finally withdrew her offer of a handshake, looking at Church.

'A word?' she said—her voice light, but sharp enough that both Mitch and Nanna gathered Church was in for a stern talking-to.

Nanna motioned Mitch into the house. 'Come on, you,' she said. 'Kettle's just boiled.'

Mitch gave Church a final look, one that said *you're on your own this time*, and then slid past, following Nanna into the kitchen.

'Talk. Now,' Hallberg ordered him.

The second they were out of the hallway, Church gathered himself a little, wondering where to start. 'We dropped in and approached Steiner's house as planned,' he said. 'Got inside nice and clean, got Steiner talking, got most of a list of names, and then...' He trailed off.

'And then what?' she said. 'Because all I'm hearing

from my end is that by the time the police arrived, the place was a burning wreck and there were twelve dead bodies strewn about the property. You're telling me that wasn't you and Mitch?'

'What? No,' Church said, surprised she even had to ask. 'It was Markovich. Dragan Markovich. The bomber.'

'Not Darko Vida?'

'No.'

'You were certain.'

'And now I'm certain it's Dragan Markovich,' he said firmly. 'He shot Steiner through the doorway and then dropped a fucking Javelin on the house.'

'What's a Javelin?' Hallberg asked, folding her arms.

'It's a type of top-attack, shoulder-fired missile,' Church said. 'It arcs high into the air and then drops down from above, hitting fortified targets where the armour is the weakest. Tanks, bunkers—that kind of thing. Turned Steiner's house into kindling—and him with it.'

She hung her head and swore under her breath. 'They hadn't found him yet,' Hallberg replied. 'I was hoping he might have got out.'

'They haven't found him because there's nothing left to find,' Church said. 'A Javelin can punch through three inches of steel. Steiner was sixty percent whisky—probably combusted the second the missile hit.'

Hallberg glared at him. 'Is that supposed to be funny?'

Church shook his head. 'Just the truth. We barely got out of there alive ourselves. The blast tossed us like rag dolls and when I came to... Markovich was there. Standing over me.'

'And who is this Dragan Markovich? Because you seem to be pretty familiar with the guy.'

'He's an ex-Serbian military colonel,' Church told her. 'He was the one feeding intelligence to NATO. He made Operation Allied Force happen in exchange for his family's safety.'

'So why is he targeting NATO now?'

'Because they reneged on their deal,' he said. 'They never got Markovich and his family out. They just dropped a fucking bomb on his house and killed them. And I thought they killed him too.'

'Jesus Christ,' Hallberg said under her breath, shaking her head. 'What a fucking mess this is.' She ran her hand through her hair and let out a long, tired sigh. They'd all been awake all night, and the realisation had dawned that she'd been looking in the wrong places for the last few days. More time wasted. More time for Markovich to get out ahead—and plan his next attack.

Church, sensing the lull in the conversation, took the opportunity to steer it in the direction he wanted.

'Markovich told me that he's coming for Nanna and the girls,' Church said. 'Promised me he'd kill them before he came for me too. I want them moved to a safe house. Today.'

But before Hallberg could reply, there were footsteps behind them.

Church turned to see Nanna standing halfway down the corridor, two cups of coffee in her hands. She stared through the steam at them.

'We're not going anywhere,' she said. 'You think I haven't noticed the unmarked police cars outside the house? Outside the girls' school when I drop them off? You've had people watching us for days, and we've been fine. We're as safe as we can be right here, Solomon. We're not going anywhere.'

'The hell you're not,' Church replied, turning to her. 'We have to get you out of here. We have to get you somewhere Markovich can't find you.'

'Well, it sounds like he's pretty good at finding people, no matter where they are,' Nanna snapped, still holding the coffee. 'You know Mia's only just stopped waking up every night with nightmares after what happened at Mitch's farm? Do you know how many times she cried out and I'd have to go in there and hold her, rock her back to sleep, tell her she's fine, she's not in that fucking cellar anymore? That no one's coming to kill her. That they're safe? I'm not doing that to her again, Solomon. I'm not taking her somewhere else. I'm not making myself a liar. If you can protect us there, we can be protected here. This is the most surveilled city in the world, and there's a half-dozen police officers out there watching us. There's no way he's getting close to us without anyone seeing him.'

Church stared at his sister, knowing her once more to be the same immovable object she always was. And regardless of whether or not he considered himself an unstoppable force, he knew she wouldn't budge an inch. If that's what she decided, then that's what it would be. And there was nothing he could do to convince her.

He spied Mitch then, in the doorway over her shoulder, and let his eyes drift to his brother's. They lingered there, and after a few seconds, Mitch nodded—one solitary dip of the head that said it all.

Church felt better suddenly and let out a soft breath. 'Fine,' he said. 'You want to stay here, you can stay here. But Mitch is going to stay with you. That's non-negotiable.'

Nanna's jaw flexed, her grip tightening around the cups. They must have been red-hot by now in her hands, but she seemed unfazed by it. 'Okay,' she said. 'At least if he's here, I know you won't be getting him into any more trouble.'

A flicker of a smile passed across Church's face at that.

'And what are you going to do?' Nanna asked him then, lifting her chin almost defiantly.

Church considered that for a moment, but he knew there was only one answer.

'I'm going to take the fight to Markovich. Put his face on every screen in the country. You said this is the most surveilled city in the world, right?' He glanced at Hallberg. 'Then let's give those cameras something to goddamn look for.'

THIRTY-THREE

TWENTY-FIVE YEARS AGO

BY THE TENTH phone call in a row, it seemed that Markovich had begun to understand the urgency of Church's call.

He picked up the phone.

'What?' came the flat reply.

'Don't talk, just listen,' Church said. 'I just got word from NATO. There are bombers already in the sky. They're hitting targets all over Kosovo—Pristina included. Are you still in the city?'

'Of course I'm still in the city,' Markovich replied hurriedly, the words almost garbled he said them so fast.

'Okay. Get your family. It's time to go. Right now.'

'NATO are getting me out,' Markovich said, the smallest tinge of hope in his voice.

'No,' Church said. 'I am. Meet me in Gurtesh as soon as you can. We're headed for the border.'

'The border?'

'Macedonia. They're inside NATO, and if we're stopped, we can tell them what's happening.'

Markovich scoffed. 'The Macedonian border? We will be arrested—if we're not shot first!'

'That's the plan,' Church said. 'Get you into custody inside a NATO country. You'll be given a fair trial and then we can sort all this out.'

'You want to put me behind bars? My family? That's the grand plan?' Any hope there had been had now waned.

'I think it's just about the only plan we've got,' Church said, clamping his eyes shut, realising how stupid it sounded now that he'd said it out loud.

'And what about you?' Markovich said. 'How do NATO feel about you disobeying orders? I assume they told you to stand by and let me die, did they? Hell, my address is probably on the bombing list.'

There was a good chance that that was the truth. Church thought that when he'd taken the list of high-ranking officials and their addresses from high command in Pristina, *Dragan Markovich, Colonel*, would have been on there—and no doubt would have been one of their primary targets in the city.

And he doubted that they'd made any effort to remove him from that list after they handed it over.

If they dropped a bomb on his home and wiped him from existence, there'd be no record of his transgressions or his involvement with NATO at all. Probably their preferred outcome.

And one that Church was determined not to let come to pass.

'It doesn't matter what happens to me,' Church replied.

Then, finding a certain soberness in the moment, he turned his eyes to the once-blank blue canvas that Markovich had talked about, and, seeing the silhouettes of the bombers high above—their trails of death across the sky as they carved a path towards the city—there was no ignoring the war was well and truly here now.

'Alright,' Markovich said after what seemed like too long. 'We'll leave as soon as we can. I just... I hope it's not too late already.'

'I do too,' Church said. 'And Markovich? I'm sorry about everything.'

Markovich seemed to consider that for a few seconds but said nothing back. He simply hung up the phone, leaving Church standing there, drowning in the distant roar of the bombers sailing overhead.

THIRTY-FOUR

PRESENT DAY

Church stood behind Anastasia Fletcher, watching over her shoulder as she put the finishing touches on the article.

A huge photo of Dragan Markovich's face perched beneath the title, which read: *The Kosovo War: A Genocide Not Easily Forgotten.*

The first line was just as punchy:

A string of bombings have rocked Europe over the last few weeks and while rumours have swirled this is the work of a terrorist cell, the reality is much more chilling—and much more human. Dragan Markovich, a former Serbian military colonel, is solely responsible for the death and destruction caused and is waging his own personal war in recompense for what NATO did—and didn't do—in March of 1999.

Church let out a solemn breath. 'It's good,' he said, nodding.

'It's a cannon,' she said. 'And when it hits, it's going to blow a hole right in NATO's side. We do this, Church, it's going to piss a lot of people off.'

He huffed sardonically. 'Yeah, they can get in fucking line. Send it.'

Fletcher hesitated a little and then looked over her left shoulder, waiting for the final confirmation. When Hallberg gave it, she pressed the button and winged the article to a load of news websites, a hundred journalists, twenty-five news channels, thirty blogs and even a few dozen podcasts.

Church had to confirm what the last one was, but Fletcher assured him that if you wanted to get something out there fast—and have people actually listen—podcasts were the way to do it. Church had to take her word for it. He'd been dead for the last ten years and a lot of life had seemingly passed him by.

Before he could tell Fletcher that she'd done a good job, she looked up at him.

'Thank you for that,' she said. 'I know it couldn't have been easy, that you didn't want to tell your story. But you did the right thing. You did a good thing.'

'It's not my story,' Church said back. 'It's Markovich's. And what happened in Kosovo… people need to know. The truth's been buried for too long. I'm just sorry I didn't come forward sooner.'

At that, he felt Hallberg's presence fade from the room, and when he turned his head, she was disappearing through the doorway of Fletcher's office and into her apartment.

Church followed her, and by the time he reached the corridor, she was already through the front door. He jogged to catch up, pulling it closed behind him and calling out, stopping her in her tracks.

She slowed and looked back.

Scowling at him as he approached, she shook her head and then turned away, attempting to leave again, and Church had to reach out and take her by the arm to stop her.

She rounded on him, throwing him off. 'You know how much of a spotlight this puts on me, right?' she said.

Church did, but he didn't think saying yes would actually be helpful. 'I'm sorry,' he said. 'It's my family. I had to do it.'

She narrowed her eyes at him. 'I know it's your family, Sol, but this? Is this really how you want to do this? You just want to splash his name across every news station? You really want to poke the bear now? We could've found him,' she said, stepping forward and lifting her hands, taking two fistfuls of his shirt. '*I* could've found him. I just needed time. You didn't need to… you didn't need to put yourself in his crosshairs, just to draw him out!'

Church lifted his hands and put them on her shoulders, holding them there until she released his shirt, leaving two crumpled bunches in the fabric.

Church stared down into her eyes, and she stared

back at him, searching his face for any willingness to walk this back, to rush in there and tell Fletcher to email those people and say that she'd made a mistake, to make a retraction, to let Hallberg take care of this. To let her take care of *him*.

'Thank you,' he said after a few seconds. 'But this is my fight. It's always been my fight. This'll force Markovich's hand one way or another, force him to try and hit them sooner, to go after Nanna and the girls sooner. And when he does, I'll be waiting. I'll be ready.'

'Ready to have a shootout in the middle of London,' Hallberg grumbled, lowering her eyes to the floor. 'It'd be my head if they knew I was sanctioning this.'

'They could draw and quarter me and I'd never roll over on you,' Church said.

She sighed and then reached up, smoothing the creases she'd left in his shirt with the palms of her hands. 'I know you wouldn't.'

Church swallowed a little, feeling her fingers running across his chest. 'I need to do this,' he told her.

'And what if he gets you killed? What if Markovich gets what he wants?' Hallberg asked him.

'So long as I take him down with me, it'll be worth it.'

She paused, her hands still, her fingers hovering at the points of his collarbones. 'You really believe that?'

'I do. And deep down, I knew it was always coming…' Church said. 'One way or another.'

THIRTY-FIVE

TWENTY-FIVE YEARS AGO

Night had begun to fall over Gurtesh, and Church had lost all sight of the individual planes.

It was now only the engine noise echoing through the sky that told him the campaign was still going on—and would for some time yet. Days, weeks, months even. It depended how long Serbia held out before they agreed to withdraw forces from Kosovo, before they relinquished their grip on the region, and before they admitted defeat.

He couldn't help but wonder how many would die—how many innocents would die—before that time came.

He'd been waiting all day and there was no sign of Markovich, but now he heard the squeal and whine of brakes and looked up to see headlights turning into the square.

An SUV by the look of it.

He put his hand to his hip around the grip of his pistol there, just in case it wasn't Markovich.

And as the car drew closer and pulled up, showing its side to him, he realised it wasn't.

But despite that, he released the pistol and pushed himself to a stance off the broken fountain. The driver's door opened and Gaz stepped out, with Grandad and DD disembarking a moment later.

Church hadn't asked permission before he'd taken a 4x4 and headed out to Gurtesh to meet Markovich, and when he'd done it, he hadn't really given a shit about what the consequences might be.

Court martial, investigation, stripped of his rank, prison time even—none of it mattered.

All that mattered was keeping his promise. But now, with Gaz standing here in front of him—not looking fierce or angry but just sorry—he realised that he'd been too late.

'What's going on?' Church asked, glancing around, their faces all sombre.

Gaz stopped a few feet short of him and hooked his thumbs into the front of his belt, looking up at Church.

'It's too late,' he said. 'It's over. Done.'

Church stared back at him and blinked. 'What do you mean, it's over?'

'NATO levelled Markovich's district an hour ago. He's dead. Sat flyover showed direct strike on his house.'

'On his house?' Church repeated back, not quite understanding the words. 'I... I don't understand.' Church came forward.

'There's nothing to understand,' Gaz said coolly. 'That officer list that you provided to NATO—Markovich's name was on it. And the things he's done... The ethnic cleansings that happened under his watch and command. The mass murder. The torture. The rape. The Korçevans would never stand for it, and neither would NATO. Regardless of what he gave us, there's no way in hell they'd let someone like him walk free. Not here or anywhere else. Trust me,' he said, reaching over Church's shoulder. 'It's better this way.'

'Better?' Church spat, pulling back out of Gaz's reach, leaving his hand hanging in the air. 'We promised a man his freedom for his help.' He cut the air with his hand. 'He was a colonel, not on the front fucking lines. Who did he kill with his own hands? We promised him the freedom, the safety of his family—his wife, his daughter—and then we turned around and just left them to burn? How is that better than what Markovich did?' He towered over Gaz now, staring down at him, not realising he'd come forward, not realising that his hands had locked into fists at his side.

Reflexively, Gaz looked up at him, unflinching.

'Stand down, soldier,' he said, voice cold. At his sides, both Grandad and DD came forward a little, ready to pounce on Church if he did something stupid.

But as much as Church hated the man standing in front of him now, it wasn't fury he felt—it was disgust.

'Do you even care?' he asked him.

Gaz swallowed, holding his chin up high. 'It doesn't matter if I care,' he said. 'And I don't have to tell you why.'

THIRTY-SIX

PRESENT DAY

CHURCH'S BACK WAS HURTING.

He'd been sitting on a little camp chair for the best part of ten hours, hunched over beneath a suspended tarp on top of a building across the green from Nanna's house.

A tripod was set up with a long monocular and rangefinder trained on her front door. It read 220 metres, and Church had zeroed the rifle set up next to it to that exact distance—meaning there would be no bullet drop.

If his scope was trained on Markovich as he walked up Nanna's front steps and he pulled that trigger, the bullet would strike exactly where he was aiming. And with the calibre of the Accuracy International L115A3 bolt-action rifle—provided to him courtesy of Mitch—sat on its mount, wind shouldn't be a factor either. No, getting struck from this distance with a .338 Lapua Magnum would only mean one thing: the fate that Church was sorry he'd spared Markovich from twenty-five years ago, and the same fate he was determined to give him again.

His phone buzzed in his pocket and Church sat a little straighter, arching his back and stretching it.

There'd been no sign of Markovich as of yet, and though the three unmarked cars were still positioned around Nanna's house, Church didn't think that would deter the man, and nor did he trust it to be enough to stop him. No, the trap had been set, and all he needed now was for Markovich to walk into it.

And when he did, he could end this all right now.

Keeping his eyes fixed on Nanna's house in the distance—the kind of trained focus that only came with years of elite military service—he reached into his pocket and drew out his phone. He didn't look at the screen before he answered, knowing that only a few people could be calling. He flipped it open with his thumb and held it to his ear.

'Yeah,' he said, barely a whisper. The key to staking out a place and remaining hidden was not to move, not to make sound, not to draw attention. Whether it was from your target or simply passers-by, no one could know he was here—and that's how he intended to keep it.

'Church,' came Fletcher's voice over the line. 'I've been getting a flood of emails since we put out that article,' she said. 'People asking for my sources, people wanting to know more, people warning me of what this could bring.'

'I told you,' Church replied, 'that it was going to piss a lot of people off. A cannon, I think you described it as?'

'Yeah. Well, whether or not it's knocked NATO off balance, I can't say, but I think it may well have reached your other intended audience.'

Church drew a little breath but tried not to react, tried not to get ahead of himself. If Markovich had reached out to Fletcher, it could be a diversion. He could be trying to draw Church away from the real target, pull his attention from Nanna and the girls and direct it somewhere else.

'It's a message from someone claiming to be Markovich,' Fletcher said.

'Probably bullshit,' Church interjected, determined to stay on mission.

'It's got a video attachment,' she said. Church listened to the frustration in her voice. 'I'd say I'd send it over,' she replied, 'but I don't think you can tie videos to the legs of pigeons these days, can you?'

'Ha ha,' Church said sarcastically. 'Play it for me. Hold your phone close to the speaker.'

Fletcher sighed emphatically and muttered under her breath. He could hear her voice a little garbled in the microphone, like she was pinning the phone between her shoulder and her cheek. 'You seriously need to get a smartphone or a laptop or something,' she said, tapping away on her own computer in the background.

'Not a chance,' Church replied, eyes still fixed across the green on Nanna's house.

There was a crackling of static and then another voice played through the phone, second-hand, coming out of one speaker and into the mic. But despite that, Church recognised it instantly—and it took him back to the ruins of Steiner's lodge and then back further. Twenty-five years further, to Kosovo.

It was Markovich. He had no doubt of it.

'I read your story, Solomon, it said. *An interesting read, to be sure... but I think it leaves out some key details, of course. But I appreciate your weak attempt at placation, at humanising me. At trying to make me see the humanity in what I'm doing. Make me reconsider the weight, the cost of my actions.'*

He laughed softly.

'By now, you should know that I cannot be swayed by anything you say. Before you waste any more of your energy, the truth is this: your family will die. You will know that pain. I promised you that, and it's a promise I intend to keep. But I also know you—more so after Kosovo. You were at the top of my list, and I made it my life to know the man I was going to kill first. And because of that, because of what I know about you, I know that despite my promise, you will not make that easy for me.

'I have seen your Hannah, your Lowri, your Mia in their beautiful home. I have watched them. I have imagined their deaths, revelled in them. Such a wonderful

family... but not easy to get to, especially with those policemen you have waiting outside.'

Church's blood pulsed harder in his neck and his eyes swept the green, the surrounding streets. He'd been here. Recently. Was he close now?

'But I have time. I can wait, Markovich went on. *I'm a patient man. I have learned that over the years. But I suspect that you are too. So wherever you are—wherever you're waiting with your rifle, I suspect, pinned to your shoulder, your eye trained in your scope... you will be waiting a long time.*

'So I will grant you this: man to man. One chance. Throw yourself at my feet. Accept your fate. And if you show true remorse... I will spare your family.

'You, however, cannot be allowed to live. That die has already been cast.

'So you must choose, Solomon Church. Your life, or that of your family. And perhaps this time... you might keep your word. If you wish to spare your sister and your nieces the end you know I'll give them, if you wish to die with honour like the man you told me you were all those years ago, you will find me at home.

'That is, if you have the courage to face the fate that has always awaited you...'

The voice faded and the static stopped, replaced by a long, rattling sigh let out by Fletcher.

'It's a trap,' she said. 'Obviously. You go to him, he'll kill you, and then he's going to kill them anyway. He just wants you out of the way.'

'I know,' Church replied.

'You know? Good,' she said, letting out another sigh, this one in relief. 'So you're not considering it then?'

'No, I'm not considering it,' he said, sitting upright, closing his eyes, finally taking them off Nanna's house. 'I'm not considering it because I'm doing it.'

There was silence for a few seconds.

'You heard what I just said, right?' Fletcher practically scoffed.

'I did,' Church replied. 'Thank you, Fletcher, for everything.' He pushed to his feet then. 'But this is on me now, and I have to finish it.'

'He'll kill you, Church,' she said as directly as possible, as though to make him finally hear, finally understand.

Church arched his back and drew his hands into tight, trembling fists.

'That's what I'm counting on.'

THIRTY-SEVEN

TWENTY-FIVE YEARS AGO

'ENGLISH!' came the booming voice of Darko across the farmyard.

Church, Gaz, Granddad, and DD all looked at each other from their cots.

There were no more orders coming down from on high now, and with the NATO bombing still under way for almost a week, they were just waiting for what they expected would be a pull-out order.

Until that happened, they were to stay put. But judging by Darko's tone and volume, the seeming peace and quiet they'd been enjoying—or at least enduring—for the last few days had now suddenly come to an end.

They rose together and, with Gaz at the vanguard, stepped through the flaps of the tent and into the sunlight, where Darko was standing at the head of what remained of his band of men.

Gaz put his hands on his hips and let out a long, loud sigh. 'What is it now, Darko?' he called across the yard, running his eyes over the dozen or so men in front of him, all strapped with their M70s, a mean look on their faces.

'You lied to us. You think we're stupid?' Darko called out.

Gaz looked left and right at Granddad and Church before turning his eyes back to Darko. 'You really want me to answer that?'

None of his men laughed, and Gaz didn't expect them to, Church thought. It was a fair question.

'You want to cut to the chase?' Gaz said. 'You're interrupting my reading time.'

Darko took a big step forward, lifting his shattered right wrist and massaging it through the plaster.

'The Serbs,' he said, the word clearly like poison in his mouth. 'You're working with them.'

Gaz stilled for just a second, but his poker face didn't slip. 'The fuck are you talking about?' he snapped back.

'We heard,' he said. 'That someone has been behind the back of the KLA, has been working in tandem with the Serbian army.'

'Is it now?' Gaz said. 'And where did this filthy little rumour come from?'

'We have eyes and ears everywhere,' Darko said back. 'Other KLA factions all across Kosovo. You think we don't talk, but we do,' he said, wiggling a finger. 'We know you're not the only group out here helping us.' He emphasised the word to show that he meant it in its loosest possible term. 'But you are the only group who sneaks off in the middle of the night, who makes phone calls when you think no one is listening, and who always seem to know where and when to strike the enemy. So we have to ask ourselves—where do you get this information from? Except directly from the source.'

Gaz let out another emphatic sigh. 'So your reckoning is that we're working with the Serbs to kill the Serbs, is that it? They just, what? Took one look at you and your lot and thought, oh, this is completely futile fighting in this war, we best just off ourselves instead—make the whole thing easier. Is that right?'

Darko bristled and took a step forward, pointing with his mangled hand. 'You treat us like we are shit on the bottom of your fancy English boots—'

'Made in Germany,' Gaz said with a shrug. 'But go on.'

'—And now you come here and you play dumb with me, you insult my people.' Darko spat on the ground between them to illustrate his anger.

Gaz looked down at the chunk of phlegm and then back up at the man. 'Well, pissed off as you might be, I'm a little tired of this conversation, and I don't like being accused of things I know fuck all about. Alright? We act on the intel we're given. And yeah, maybe NATO are working with some Serbian defector or something, but that's their prerogative, isn't it? Because they know if they don't do that, if they don't get their hands dirty, that it's your lot who are going to be swallowing Serbian bullets and ultimately paying the price. So choose your poison. You either fucking die because you don't know what the fuck you're doing—or live because somebody else does. Now if you'll excuse me.'

And with that, he turned his back on Darko and began striding back towards the tent, only stopping when the clack and rattle of the fleet of M70s echoed behind him. He stopped and turned around to look down the barrels of a dozen assault rifles.

'Oh, that's a stupid fucking thing to do,' he said, curling a smile. 'Is that really a fight you want to pick?'

Darko stayed silent, just staring at Gaz.

'Look around you, son,' Gaz said. 'The war is over. So just fuck off back inside, drink your vodka, and wait until that white flag is raised. Hell, this place has seen enough bloodshed—surely you don't want to add to it.'

Darko's lips twisted into a snarl, but he didn't respond.

Church suspected in his mind there was some sort of dignity at risk, that he was determined somehow to save face, and thought the only way he could do that was by executing the men that had given everything to protect his country.

'This is settled,' Gaz said. 'We're done.' He cut his hand through the air to illustrate the finality of his remark. 'And don't you worry—another day or two and I'm sure we'll be out of your hair and you can have this beautiful country all to yourselves, alright?'

Church felt himself stiffen at those last words. A day or two before they pulled out? But he didn't get to question Gaz on it as his captain motioned for them all to return to the tent.

Church fell into line and did so, backing away with each step, Darko's men lowering their rifles once they were inside.

Gaz let out a long, rattling breath and flexed his hands. He'd been playing it cool for Darko—who'd been more right than he knew.

'Jesus Christ, boys... that was close,' Gaz muttered. 'I thought for a minute there they were just going to shoot us.'

'I think we all did,' Granddad replied.

Gaz cast around them, nodding his thanks for having his back. 'And with that... lads, I think it's getting to be that time. Bags packed, is it? I get on the horn and make that phone call. I think we finally overstayed our welcome here.'

As the men murmured their agreement, Church found his eyes and attention drifting away, back towards the sliver of light coming into the tent, the thin band of farmyard he could see between the flaps. He moved his head back and forth so that he could see more of it, and kept going until he saw what he was looking for.

Not Darko. Not his men. No—suddenly he didn't care about them at all.

What he did care about was Marsella. And when he finally spotted her standing at the corner of the farmyard, looking on at the exchange that had just happened, he felt a deep pang in his chest, knowing that soon... he would never see her again.

THIRTY-EIGHT

PRESENT DAY

THE WIND WHIPPED across the runway, cold and slicing.

Church shivered a little and turned his head, looking down the long length of tarmac, the sun just beginning to set over the Kosovan countryside. It'd been a long time since he'd been here, and he'd hoped that he'd never have to come back. And yet here he was—not just back in this place, but in that time too. As though the last 25 years hadn't happened. He was picking up right where he left off.

He'd left Kosovo with so much unfinished, and now here he was to finish it. Finally.

He pushed that thought out of his head—the thought of his own impending death—and hoisted his duffel bag full of kit into the passenger seat of the battered Toyota Hilux that Hallberg had secured for him. He heard her light footsteps on the asphalt behind him and turned to face her. She was wearing cargo pants and black boots, a canvas jacket over a white T-shirt—the kind of outfit that someone with no combat experience thought people wore into combat.

On any other day, he might have found it charming —endearing even. But today there was no humour in him. No warmth.

Just a dark void.

A void that could only be sated by blood. His or someone else's.

She reached into her pocket and drew something out, holding her hand towards him. He extended his own, and she dropped a little black earbud into his palm. He looked up, feeling her eyes searching for his.

'Do you really want to do this?' she asked him, voice a little strained, her eyes flitting back and forth across his face as though searching for the hint of doubt. Or maybe she was just trying to memorise it, in case she never saw it again.

'If you keep asking me that,' Church replied, 'I'm going to start thinking you care about me.'

'I do care, Solomon,' she said, stepping forward then. 'And you don't need to do this. We know where Markovich is. We can go in there, we can arrest him, we can end this,' she pleaded.

'No,' Church said, shaking his head and closing his eyes so he didn't have to look at her. 'There's only one way this ends—and that's with me and him.'

'I don't understand,' Hallberg said, turning away

from him, putting her head in her hands. 'He could kill you.'

Church sighed, a little tired of this conversation—the same conversation they'd been having the entire plane ride here. 'I don't expect you to understand,' he said. 'The things I did—I need to answer for them, one way or another.'

She scoffed then, unabashedly, and turned back to him, the fear in her expression gone, replaced by anger. 'You're putting your life in the hands of some higher power all of a sudden? If you're meant to die, you'll die? Is that it?' she spat.

'It's nothing as complex as that,' Church told her, mustering a sad smile. 'The man's family is dead because of me. He deserves to look me in the eye, deserves to know that I'm sorry—that I wish I'd done more.'

'And then you're just going to kill him?' Hallberg asked, almost laughing at the ridiculousness of it. 'Where's the sense in that?'

'Sometimes,' Church said, 'honour doesn't make sense.'

He reached out slowly and put his hand on the top of her arm, leaning in gently, pressing his lips to her forehead.

She became very still under his touch, holding her breath until he drew away, meeting her eyes one last time.

'I should get going. It'll be dark soon.'

She stood there in silence, at a loss for words, and

watched as he closed the passenger door and walked around to the driver's seat. He climbed in, rolling down the passenger window to get a better look at her as he started the engine.

'I liked working with you,' he said.

She swallowed but said nothing back. Maybe she didn't know what to say. Maybe she couldn't say anything at all.

Church stared out at the runway ahead, afraid if he kept looking at her, he might start to reconsider. Without waiting any longer, he put the car into first and drove away. Church stole a glance in the mirror, watching as Hallberg shrank in the rear-view, fading into the gathering darkness.

He thought of Markovich, the sun setting behind as he drove east towards Gertesch, a thin veil of anxiety draping itself across his shoulders, his hands a little sweaty on the wheel. He wasn't sure if he thought about anything more on the way there, falling into a kind of trance-like state as he meandered through the countryside, following the route hewn in the granite of his mind on autopilot. It had been two and a half decades since he'd driven it, and yet his body still knew every twist and turn. And though the road was now empty, he could still picture it as it was then.

Overturned cars, burnt out. Tanks. The places where he'd seen people's belongings—their lives—strewn in the ditches at the side of the road. Bodies burnt and mangled, gunned down as they fled or fought. They whirled in his head, a blurry maelstrom dredged up from the abyss of his mind, blending together with newer and older memories from different parts of the world, different corners of war that he'd found himself in over the years.

When he saw the sign for the village, he came crashing back to reality and unfastened his hands from the wheel, realising that he'd been gripping so tightly that it had left indents in the ancient foam.

He pulled in short of the buildings—the same layby that he and Granddad had parked in before—thinking of the old man for the first time in years. He wondered if he was still alive, and if so, how old he'd be now. In his seventies? Just a shadow of his former self, Church thought. God, I'm old too. Too old for this. Old enough, perhaps, for the end.

The question hung over him as he killed the engine and climbed out, walking around the nose of the truck to the passenger seat.

Opening the duffel bag, he pulled out a Kevlar vest and slotted it over his shoulders, fastening it tightly around the sides. He took out his C8 carbine and checked the magazine, making sure it was loaded before snapping it into place and chambering a round. He put his Glock in his thigh holster, slotted his combat knife into his belt, made sure that everything was where it was supposed to be—loaded, greased, ready for a fight that he wasn't sure he had the strength to endure.

And yet his feet carried him without hesitation towards whatever came next, guiding him between the buildings and down the main street.

During the war, Gurtesh had been almost completely levelled, leaving behind ruined husks of buildings, the inhabitants driven across the border to Albania or back into the bosom of Serbia. This was a place where Serbs and Albanians had once lived together in harmony, but it was cleaved in two, the inhabitants driven apart—the bombed-out husks the only reminder that they'd ever lived as one.

After the war, the people never returned here, never rebuilt. It was too much effort, or too few remained. Perhaps it was too painful. Whatever the reason, the streets were silent. Dead. And yet, they still felt familiar.

And as Church walked, the only thing that had changed between now and the night he'd come here looking for Markovich, ready to extract him 25 years ago, was that nature had tried to reclaim this place. Hip-height grasses covered the streets, sticking between the cobblestones.

Trees had sprouted up inside the dilapidated walls of the broken buildings, and the fountain that he and Markovich had sat on was almost completely engulfed by vines and creeping plants. Church walked slowly towards it, checking the alleyways and doors around him for any sign of movement, any sign of life, training his rifle on the same darkened space that Markovich had popped out from all those years ago and held him at gunpoint.

He hadn't shot back then.

He would now.

But Markovich was not here.

There was no sign of him.

And as Church reached the fountain, he wondered if it had been a misdirect after all.

If Markovich had questioned his honour and sacrificed his own—had tricked him, drawn him away from Nanna and the girls to clear the field so that he could attack. And yet somehow he didn't think that was true, didn't think that was who Markovich was.

He stopped and looked around, the air cool. Though Church didn't feel it against his bare arms, his mind was elsewhere. His eyes drifted around the village square until they came to rest on a house to his right. He looked at it, remembering then what Markovich had said—that he was from here, that he had a home here that had been destroyed.

He'd pointed it out to Church, and it was the one Church was now looking at. That's what he'd said: 'You'll find me in my home.' Is that what he meant? Not just Gurtesh, but his family home. Church moved forward cautiously, stepping quiet, keeping his head on a swivel as he made it to the rotten front door. He looked down, noticing that it had been pushed open recently, carving a path through the dirt that had built up on the threshold. It had been forced open, and there were even fresh footprints leading inside.

Markovich, he thought.

He had to be inside.

The air was close, musty, the smell of damp wood permeating the space. Church could barely see a thing and knew that the muzzle flash of the C8 would blind him in such tight quarters, so without missing a second, he pushed his rifle down under his arm and pulled out his pistol instead, walking forward, checking the living room to his right, finding it empty and missing a ceiling as well as the roof above, giving him a clear look into the night sky.

There were no clouds, a black canvas studded with stars.

What had Markovich said back then?

That when you looked up at something like that, you could almost imagine that there was no war going on at all.

He shook that thought from his head and kept moving forward, passing the door on his left, pausing and opening it just an inch to peek inside, seeing a set of stone steps leading down into blackness—a cellar carved right into the earth, the thick solid oak trusses that held up the ground floor stretching out ahead of him over the top of the narrow staircase.

He left the cellar behind and kept going, pushing on now into the kitchen. He stopped on the flagstones and looked around. The kitchen was all but gone—just an echo of counters left around, just holding on to their integrity, some of them collapsed under the weight of the solid tops, the sink fallen through to the floor, sitting lopsided and rusty on a pile of rotten wood. But above that there was a window, and through it Church could see the figure of a man—his back to him—standing, facing into the fields beyond the garden.

Church moved swiftly towards the back door, sights of his rifle trained on Markovich's heart.

He could do it now.

He could pull the trigger, put a bullet in his back and watch the man fall, watch the man die, put an end to it, make sure that Nanna, Lowri and Mia were safe once and for all.

But he couldn't. Not yet.

Instead, he stopped short of Markovich and slowly lowered his gun. He'd asked Church if he was a man of honour, and shooting somebody in the back was not something he was going to allow himself to do. No matter what.

He'd rather die with his head held high than beat Markovich like that.

If not for Nanna's soul, then for his own.

Markovich lifted his head a little but didn't turn, sensing Church's presence.

'Are you here to throw yourself at my mercy?' he asked, his hands clasped gently in front of him.

He turned then, and Church picked out the two graves behind him, the ones he'd been standing over, side by side. They both had wooden crosses planted in the earth, sticks tied together into makeshift grave markers. A tattered, discoloured teddy bear was sitting against the one on the right, legs splayed over the gentle rise of the mound of earth covering what Church guessed was the body of Markovich's daughter.

'You know,' Markovich said, pulling Church's attention back to him for a moment, 'I believed it. Believed you when you called and told me to come here.'

He smiled a little, only one corner of his mouth turning upwards, the other locked in place by the gnarled scar tissue covering most of his face. His cheek twitched awkwardly, monstrously, above it, but could not pull his mouth into the smile he was pursuing.

'We were in the cellar of our home in Pristina when the phone rang,' Markovich said. 'I told my wife, I told my daughter that they would be safe, that we were getting out. Finally. We gathered our things and we rushed up the stairs so fast...' He lifted a hand and made the motion of tiny legs, climbing stairs in front of him with his fingers. 'We could hear the planes overhead already, and we were halfway out the door when my daughter stopped me—"My bear! My bear!" she said.'

He threw his hands up, reaching for the sky. Reaching for that bear, or perhaps his daughter, his eyes fell back to earth and back to Church.

'She could not leave without her bear,' he said, moving to the side a little and stealing a glance at his daughter's grave. His eyes lingered on the stuffed animal for a few seconds before he dragged them across the ruins of his family home and set them on Church once more. 'She left him downstairs,' he said, his eyes dead and cold. 'I went back down to get him, found him on the floor, bent, picked him up, brushed the dust from his ears, and then—'

Markovich's hand leapt into the air suddenly and he began to bring it down, whistling as it dropped. Like a bomb. As it reached the ground, he made an explosion sound and clenched his fist so suddenly that Church almost jolted.

'The bomb hit the house directly,' he said. 'It collapsed on them, crushed them to death. I was thrown into darkness, and when I woke up, I was buried alive beneath the bodies of my wife and my child. I could still feel the bear in my grasp.' He held his fist up for Church to see. 'And my wife, my daughter... I could almost hear them. I could almost feel them. And after a day, two days, three, I could smell them.'

He grimaced at it, lips twisting downwards in disgust.

'I don't know how long I was down there, trapped, thinking, praying, wishing for death to be with them. But it would not come,' Markovich said, stepping forward then. 'I wondered why. Why do I live still? And eventually I heard digging, calls from firemen, police. "Here, here!" I said, my mouth dry, my body clutching at life like it was all it had left. "I am alive," I said as they called to me. And I knew then, as they took my hand and pulled me from my grave, still holding that bear... that I was still alive for one reason and one reason alone. To make the man who did this to me pay. To make them all pay. To make you, Solomon Church, pay.'

Flecks of spittle flew from his mouth, his eyes alight with the fury of ten thousand dead.

'And I will not stop until that is done.'

Church stared at the man in front of him, tears glistening in his eyes, and flexed his fingers around the stippled grip of his rifle.

'What then?' Church said. 'What happens after? After everyone is dead?'

Markovich shook his head and flicked tears onto the dry soil around him.

'It doesn't matter. If I rot in prison, so be it. If they kill me, so be it. My life ended the day that bomb dropped. I've been a dead man ever since.'

Church swallowed. 'You're doing this for your family.'

'I am,' Markovich said.

'And once you kill me, you're going to kill mine.'

'I am,' Markovich said.

Church moved his index finger from the stock of his C8 to the trigger, readying himself. 'Then you understand that I can't let that happen.'

'You can try,' Markovich said, a grim smile carving itself into one side of his face. 'You can try.'

THIRTY-NINE

TWENTY-FIVE YEARS AGO

THE FIELD WAVED gold around him.

Church lowered his hands, the brittle grain dragging gently across his knuckles, rustling as he waited, watched Marsella make the slow walk out towards him.

He had stepped between the tent flaps and into the farmyard, looking at her until she looked at him, not paying any mind to Darko or anyone else.

And when she finally looked up, he kept her gaze until he knew that she could tell what he wanted, and began the long walk out to the place where they'd made love just weeks before. But now, it seemed like a millennia ago.

She stared at him as she approached, stepping unhurriedly as though stringing out the walk, prolonging what she knew would be their end. But when she arrived, all too soon, she wasted no time in asking the question, keen to make this a quick, clean cut after everything and spare them both any more suffering.

'You're leaving, aren't you?' she asked.

Church looked at her, his voice catching in his throat. He nodded. 'The mission is over.'

She narrowed her eyes. 'The mission is accomplished, you mean?'

He shook his head at that. 'I wouldn't say that. It's just... finished,' he said tiredly.

She considered that and then nodded, reading his torn expression.

She didn't seem to need to know the details, or perhaps she just didn't want to.

'Is it true?' she asked.

'Is what true?'

'What Darko said. You were working with the Serbs.'

She didn't look anywhere near as angry as Darko had been. Maybe she accepted the war was nothing if not messy, and that anything that could be done to stop it, to end it quickly, to save lives, was excusable in some fashion—or at least justifiable.

'Just one man,' Church said back. Lying was futile now, it felt like. None of it seemed to matter anymore. 'He was a man who would do anything to save his family, that's all.'

Marsella thought about that for a long time before she spoke again. 'Was it right?' she said. 'How it happened?'

'There's no such thing as right,' Church replied, not wanting to talk about this.

He stepped forward and offered his hands to her.

She looked at them for a few seconds and then took them, almost reluctantly, squeezing his knuckles.

'I'm sorry we didn't meet under different circumstances,' Church told her. 'Somewhere else. Anywhere else.'

'I'm not,' Marsella replied. 'In another world, we would have been different people. Here...' She trailed off and looked out over the fields around them.

Church didn't quite understand what she meant by that, but somehow he accepted it anyway.

Sometimes there was a sort of perfection in imperfection, a sort of right in everything wrong, a sort of good in everything bad. Bittersweetness, he thought they called it.

But there was nothing sweet about that moment, nothing sweet about saying goodbye.

'Perhaps we'll see each other again?' Church asked.

She smiled and turned away, pulling her hands from his as she began the long walk back towards the farm, her former life, and whatever waited for her beyond the war.

'In another life,' she said, pausing briefly to look over her shoulder at him. 'Or perhaps in the next one.'

FORTY

It happened fast.

Markovich's hand leapt inside his jacket, the gun flashing in the darkness.

Church pulled up his rifle, the two men firing at the same time.

Church felt the bullet strike him mid-torso. A hard punch to the gut that booted the air from his lungs and sent him stumbling backwards.

He pinned the trigger, firing back at Markovich, who was already moving faster than Church thought he could.

He chased him with a spray of fire into cover, the man diving behind the tool shed at the corner of the garden.

Church, stuck in the open, knew he couldn't stay there. He backpedalled quickly, squeezing off bursts of three rounds into the corner of the building, hoping they were enough to punch through the ancient wood—but knowing they weren't.

He dropped back to the house and ducked in through the kitchen door, pressing himself to the stone wall just inside the frame, waiting for Markovich to come out. But he didn't.

Something beeped in the darkness of the kitchen, and Church spun his head around, looking for it, seeing something glowing green in his periphery, tucked underneath one of the old countertops.

A dim glow pooling on the floor.

He narrowed his eyes at it, unsure of what he was seeing.

And then he realised, throwing himself through the door and into the open, the explosive that Markovich had planted in the kitchen detonating at his trigger.

The force was instant, throwing Church off his feet, carrying him forward on the shockwave.

He landed hard in the earth, the bomb not big enough to tear down the house, but big enough to blow a hole through the kitchen wall and shower him with fragments of wood and rock.

There was a metallic ping in his periphery then, barely audible through the ringing in his ears, followed by a swooshing sound as something heavy arced through the air.

It bounced on the dirt in front of him and rolled towards Church, his eyes picking out the rounded shape in the moonlight, just a few inches from his head.

His eyes widened.

He knew exactly what it was.

An M67 round fragmentation grenade that would easily separate his skull from his body if it went off at this distance.

But they had a few seconds' trigger, and Church was fast—grabbing it reflexively and tossing it away from him, pinning his face to the dirt and covering his head with his forearms, curling up away from the imminent blast.

'No!' Markovich cried, charging forward blindly, insanely, as the grenade bounced over his family's graves. With complete disregard for his own safety, he dashed towards it, trying to kick it away before it went off—but the fuse was too short, the grenade too far away, and he barely made it halfway there before the thing exploded.

There was no fire—there never was with fragmentation grenades—just a concussive blast from the 180 grams of RDX mix at its core that would shatter and fragment the steel shell, sending two hundred shards of shrapnel in every direction, killing everything inside a three-metre radius.

Markovich didn't get that close, but he was close enough to get tossed sideways by the explosion and into the open. He flung his arms up just in time, arcing through the air, before he landed on his back, bouncing and rolling to a stop just a few feet from Church, the backs of his forearms shredded from the shrapnel.

Church could feel it too—the bite of the metal

shards across his shoulders, the tops of his arms. His head was swimming, his teeth vibrating in his jaw. He tried to open his eyes, tried to focus, just picking out Markovich rolling around, groaning, to his left. The pair of them dazed by it.

Church could hear the man—growling, grunting in pain as he tried to get himself upright.

Church watched, groping at his side for his rifle, but it was missing. He must have lost it when the bomb in the kitchen detonated. It was lying somewhere in the darkness around him, but he didn't know where, couldn't see it. Wasn't enough time to look.

He reached to his thigh now, pulling the Glock free, forcing his elbow under his chest, getting to his knee—but Markovich was faster, and by the time he tried to lift his gun, the man was already on his feet, swinging a brutal kick into Church's hand, sending the weapon flying over his shoulder.

Church slumped backwards out of the path of another kick—this one aimed at his head—and landed hard on his back, twisting sideways, his own weight pressing the shrapnel deeper into his skin as he scrambled to put space between them.

Markovich kept bearing down on him, and as Church made it to his feet, all he could do was fend off an onslaught of heavy blows. He threw up a guard and took a hard punch to the forearm, a second clipping his wrist and sailing past the side of his head, grazing him just above his ear. Pain lanced through his skull, focusing him suddenly, blowing away all remnants of the disorientation.

He could hear Markovich breathing heavily, slinging punches as hard and fast as he could, and Church knew that all he had to do was wait a few seconds. Keep dancing backwards until Markovich tired.

Regardless of his will, of his hatred, of the uncapped desire that he had to kill Church, he knew that he was just a man, and that he couldn't keep this up for long. And the moment there was a delay between the strikes —the moment that he had to stop to catch breath— Church opened his guard and picked his target, surging forward, throwing a heavy strike of his own. A jab right between Markovich's fists, catching him square in the nose.

The man reeled backwards and then dug his heels in, blood pouring over his snarling lips. He was charging forward again then, reaching out for Church.

He tried to block, expecting a punch, but Markovich was trying to grapple instead and took hold of his wrist, drawing him in close, locking up his other arm, Markovich pinning Church's elbow between his bicep and his ribs. Without warning, he threw his head forward, cracking Church just above the eyebrow with a vicious headbutt.

Blood immediately poured from the wound, running into Church's eye, all but blinding him. Church hefted the man backwards and then forwards, the two of them jostling for domination, the two of them fighting for their families; the death of one, the life of the other.

He was tiring now too, hurting all over. He had to end this, and he had to end it fast. His arms were trapped, and all he could do was throw a knee upwards as hard as he could, pulling his left wrist down—and Markovich with it—at the same time, so that the point of his patella connected with Markovich's gut.

The man doubled up over his leg, the grip on his arms releasing.

Church shoved him away and the man staggered backwards, gasping for air. Church did the same thing, running his arm across his forehead, the sting from a fresh, deep cut pulsating across his face.

He tried to open his eye and found that it was useless. All he could see were streaks of red studded with stars. And then Markovich was coming at him again, left arm cocked back to land a haymaker.

Church lifted his arms to block, but something glinted in Markovich's other hand as he did and Church was too slow to react, too slow to parry it—and the knife in Markovich's hand swung upwards in a steep, savage arc, burying itself in Church's side to the hilt.

It made a loud thud as the guard smacked against bone and muscle, the blade biting deeply into his flesh.

Church howled, twisting away so violently that the knife came clean out of Markovich's hand, still stuck in Church's body.

Markovich stumbled forward a little, almost being pulled off his feet as he lost his grip, and Church knew that he had to end this now, that he couldn't keep fighting for long. And on pure brute instinct he stepped in with his right foot and lifted his arm, crooking it tightly, driving his elbow upwards and over the top of Markovich's shoulder and into his cheek with everything he had—hard enough that he felt Markovich's cheekbone crunch under the impact.

He fell backwards, an agonised shriek escaping him, and fell, heels hooking up on the uneven ground.

He hit the floor and gasped, clutching at his face, leaving Church standing above him, swaying violently, his legs barely under him, his vision pulsing black at the edges, his breath ragged and laboured.

He staggered forward, teeth gritted, mouth filled with blood, and reached across his body, his fingers spidering over his stomach, onto his ribs, until he found the handle of the knife Markovich had driven through the strapping of his vest and into his flank.

He closed his fingers around the grip and pulled hard, yanking the blade free in a single movement, letting loose a terrible roar so loud it made his throat ache.

He felt the hot gush of blood down his side, soaking his trousers immediately, and held the knife before him, watching as his blood dripped slowly from the blade, pattering on the ground between his boots.

Over the top of it he could see Markovich's eyes, shining in the moonlight, the man still, one hand pressed to his face, the other at his side.

He stared up at Church and Church stared back before slowly, he lowered himself to a knee—Markovich fighting back no longer—just watching as

Church eased himself down painfully and held the knife aloft, thinking of Nanna and the girls, thinking of every reason he had to do this, ignoring every reason that he shouldn't.

And though he wanted to close his eyes and shy away from it, he forced himself to look. To look Markovich in the eyes as he brought the blade down, plunging it into his chest, right into his heart.

Markovich drew a short, sharp breath—his final breath—and smiled at Church.

His blood began to bubble between his lips, and with the last of his strength, the man lifted his right hand and Church's eyes drifted to his contingency plan—his final parting gift.

A black trigger device was in his grasp and Church wondered if he was going to push the button, realising after a second that he already had. That the thing he was holding was a dead man's switch.

And as the life drained from Markovich's eyes and from his body, his hand began to sag. And then it uncurled, letting off the trigger and sending the signal that would accomplish Markovich's mission, even if he himself failed.

Church forced himself to his feet, fingers dug into the wound on his side, blood spilling between his fingers.

A distant whining sound echoed across the field in front of him and he squinted, through his one good eye, into the darkness, watching as a shape began to emerge, tilting upwards. He didn't know what it was at first, but it quickly became apparent—the outlines of the vehicle-mounted missiles cut out against the glow of the wheat fields.

The first one fired, hissing and popping into the air, leaving a trail of white fire behind it as it screamed skywards. And then a second followed. Then a third.

They zipped upwards, arcing high into the air, and Church watched them, knowing that when they reached their zenith, they would turn their attention downwards and plunge to the earth with enough force to reduce what remained of Markovich's house to a smoking crater.

Church stared upwards, blood dripping from his head, his ribs, his arms, and drew the hardest breath he'd ever drawn, steeling himself for the end.

He thought of Hallberg then. Of Mitch. Of Nanna.

Her face burned in his mind, her voice echoing to him, telling him, suddenly, to run. To run like hell.

And then, like he always did, he listened to his sister, turned…

And gave it everything he had.

FORTY-ONE

PRESENT DAY

HALBERG WATCHED through the windscreen of the helicopter as, in the far distance, three tiny pricks of light flew high into the air.

She held her breath, wondering if her eyes had just played tricks on her, and looked on, praying she was wrong, as they began to descend, picking up speed as they plummeted towards the earth like comets. They landed in quick succession, and a ball of fire leapt out of the earth, reaching upwards in a column of brilliance that licked at the very heavens.

'Oh my God,' she said, staring at it, knowing that it was Markovich's house in Gurtesh, that it couldn't be anything else. That something had gone wrong. That he'd somehow made this happen, even though she had just listened to what she thought was Church killing the man.

And now there was nothing—nothing but static playing in her ears. She couldn't hear him anymore. And as she motioned for the helicopter pilot to fly forward, she knew it was because he was dead.

The Serbian pilot guided the police chopper in, and as they approached the village, Hallberg looked over her shoulder at Mitch, who was sitting wide-eyed in the cabin behind her, silent and solemn, understanding as clearly as she did what had just happened.

They touched down minutes later, the area lit by a hundred fires, a crater left in the backyard of Markovich's house, the house itself reduced to a pile of rock and smouldering splinters.

The moment the helicopter landed, Hallberg kicked the door open and ran forward, not knowing where to, what she hoped to find. And after a few steps she stumbled to a halt and sagged forward, hands on knees, looking around.

There was nothing left.

No one could have survived that.

There was no sign of Markovich either—his body incinerated by the blast?

She heard footsteps behind her and turned, seeing Mitch, stony-faced and tall, looking around, his head slowly turning through the destruction.

'What happened?' Hallberg asked him.

He swallowed, taking time to answer, as though deciding for himself.

'Some kind of missile,' he said, shaking his head. 'I don't know. Something fucking big.' There was a tremor in his voice, and that scared Hallberg most of all.

He swore and then grimaced, looking around but clearly believing the same thing as her. That no matter how tough Church was, there was no escaping this.

The minutes passed and slowly but surely, backup began to arrive. They'd been positioned ten kilometres out, waiting for Hallberg's go-ahead, waiting to come in and arrest Markovich if he killed Church. But now the mission had changed to one of recovery. Find Markovich's body—if anything remained of it—and if they could, that of Solomon Church too.

Hallberg moved numbly through it all, watching as the police began fanning out, sifting through rubble, lifting and rolling stones out of the way, pulling chunks of wood up almost haphazardly. It was impossible to know where to start.

Hallberg began drifting towards the back of the garden. She'd heard everything unfold through the earpiece she'd given Church.

She spotted it then—a tattered, discoloured teddy bear lying in the grass—and stooped to pick it up, wondering if it was the one from Markovich's story. If it could be, even.

'Here!' one of the policemen called then.

Hallberg clutched the bear, turning her head quickly, wondering if it was him. If it was Church.

She approached, breath held, and the policeman pulled a wooden board off the body.

She wasn't sure whether she wanted it to be or not.

But then she saw the body and let out a little sigh of relief. It was Markovich—one of his legs missing, his clothes burned and torn.

Mitch gravitated towards the man as well, standing shoulder to shoulder with Hallberg, looking down at him, at his face.

'My God,' he said. 'He's so scarred.'

They stared down his body, the knife still sticking out of his chest, and Hallberg could see out of the corner of her eye a little smile flicker across Mitch's face, as though he were impressed by Church's actions, even in death.

Hallberg turned away then, clutching the teddy to her chest. Mitch followed her.

'You heard everything, didn't you?' he asked.

Hallberg could only nod, words escaping her. Seeing Markovich like that... there was no way Church could have gotten away. The place was levelled. There was nowhere to run to, even if he'd tried.

'Did Church say anything before...?'

She shook her head.

'Nothing?' Mitch asked her.

She paused, lifting her head, blinking. 'No, wait,' she said. She had heard something... She turned around, facing Mitch, still holding on to the bear.

'Markovich survived,' she said.

Mitch's brow furrowed. 'I don't think so.' He glanced at the corpse of the man behind him.

'Not this time,' Hallberg said quickly. 'Last time. He

told Church—when the bombs fell, his family died, but he survived.'

'How?' Mitch asked, but before he got his answer, Hallberg was already streaking past him towards the pile of stone where Markovich's house had once been, scrambling up and over the remnants, pulling at them, tearing at the stones with her hands, throwing and hurling pieces of wood behind her, plunging her hands into the smouldering piles with no regard for the lingering heat or hurt.

Mitch loomed behind her. 'What are you looking for?'

Hallberg stopped and looked up at him, breathless. 'The cellar,' she said. 'That's how Markovich made it. So maybe…'

'Church,' Mitch said, eyes widening. He fell to his knees and began hauling at the rock himself, and slowly the other officers around them took note and began heading over, began digging too—removing, piece by piece, what remained of Markovich's house.

They dug frantically, Hallberg soaked with sweat, face caked in dust and soot. She dug her fingers under a chunk of stone as large as her torso, her nails breaking and peeling back as she sank them in. Mitch pulled with her, the two of them giving it everything they had as they heaved the rock up. It balanced on edge for a moment and then tumbled down the pile, coming to rest at the bottom of it.

Hallberg turned her attention back to the hole left behind, a sound of joy and glee leaping from her throat before she could stop it. There in the dirt was a hand—Church's arm, buried almost from the wrist down, but Church's arm nonetheless.

She grabbed it and squeezed, feeling it limp and lifeless.

'Sol!' she yelled. 'Solomon, come on!' She pulled as hard as she could, trying to drag him free, tears flicking from her cheeks and spotting the dusty ground around her. But he was pinned, buried under tonnes and tonnes of debris.

'God damn it!' she pleaded. 'Please. Please, Sol, no…' She stooped forward, the tears rolling thick and fast, and rested her head against his knuckles. 'Please,' she whispered, holding his hand, willing him not to be dead. Willing him back to life.

And then, slowly, as though hearing her prayers, his grip began to tighten around hers.

FORTY-TWO

PRESENT DAY

THE PLANE RATTLED down onto the runway—a chartered twin-prop cargo plane with no seat padding or drink service.

Church had never wanted a whisky so much in his life. He was wrapped in bandages from his head down to his knees. The gash above his brow meant that his entire skull had been wrapped in white, and the stab wound in his side had been stitched and sterilised so he was stable enough for transport—but that was about all he was. Stable. Having a house fall on you was no picnic either, and he'd scarcely made it to the cellar door before the first bomb hit, dropping the ceiling on him and practically crushing him then and there. He'd tumbled into darkness, and the next thing he knew Hallberg's voice was ringing in his head and someone was pulling painfully on his arm.

It was dawn when his face finally broke free of the rubble and they dragged him into the light, coughing, wheezing, bleeding, broken. Cracked ribs, he thought, a pretty bad concussion, and who knew what else. He was in so much pain he couldn't even imagine.

But at least it was over. Well, almost.

As the plane hit the runway, Church groaned and twisted in the seat, strapped to the fuselage on a folding chair.

Mitch smiled at his discomfort. The prick.

But Hallberg reached out and put her hand on his, squeezing tightly as the engines began spooling down and the pilot guided them towards the tiny terminal building at the private airfield they'd landed at.

Church could only hold his head back, eyes closed, and breathe through it, the roiling waves of pain radiating through him almost enough to make him vomit.

They slowed to a halt and Hallberg rose, approaching the door, turning the handle to unlock it and pushing it forward to form the stairs down to the runway.

Mitch got himself up and helped Church to his feet, still grinning as Church hissed and swore under his breath.

'Come on, you big fucker,' he chuckled. 'Stop putting it on—you're getting no sympathy from me.'

'I got stabbed,' Church grumbled, forcing himself upright.

'Jesus, Church, who hasn't been stabbed? I never knew you to be such an attention whore,' Mitch said, draping Church's arm across his shoulders and shaking his head.

'I will bite you,' Church threatened. 'My mouth's not injured.'

'Don't I know it!' Mitch laughed. 'We couldn't have been that lucky, could we?'

Even Hallberg afforded a smirk at that one.

Night had already fallen again and Church could feel the gentle, cold winter breeze on his face as he moved gingerly forward. Something he wasn't sure he was ever going to feel again, as Markovich's house came crashing down on his head.

As he reached the door, Mitch paused, unloading him through the narrow gap, letting him take his own weight on the folding handrail of the door-stairs. His hand closed around the rickety metal pole and the whole thing strained as he put his weight on it.

'Hamming it up, are we?' came a voice from below.

He looked up to see Nanna standing there, hands on hips, all but glaring at him.

'You want to fucking help me?' Church asked, putting his foot down on the first step, a bolt of lightning riding through his body. He swayed, almost falling down the rest.

'Not a chance,' Nanna replied. 'You should remember this feeling—might make you think twice before you go running off to kill yourself again.'

Church paused for breath on the second step. 'Why are you even here if you're not going to help?'

'Mostly to berate you for being an idiot,' she retorted.

'I need better friends,' Church mumbled, shaking his head and getting to the ground finally. 'Look, Nan,' he started, 'as glad as I am to see you, I don't think I can take a dressing down—'

But she didn't let him finish, instead stepping forward and wrapping him up so tightly in a bear-hug he thought he was going to pass out.

'You can't keep doing this shit to me,' she whispered into his shoulder. 'I already lost you once. I can't bury you again—I don't have the strength.'

Slowly, Church reached up and held her, weak and tired. He didn't say anything back, didn't make a promise he couldn't keep.

Nanna peeled herself away and wiped off her cheeks, clearing her throat as Mitch and Hallberg stepped down onto the runway next to Church.

Mitch gave Nanna a hug too, and she looked him up and down. 'At least you're in one piece.'

He shrugged. 'I had the sense to stay in the helicopter. I'm too old for this shit,' he said, gesturing to Church. 'Don't know why he's so hell-bent on reliving his glory days all of a sudden.'

'Doesn't feel glorious,' Church mumbled.

Hallberg hovered at his side. 'Let's get you home,' she whispered, gently taking his elbow—seemingly the only one who gave a damn about how he was actually feeling.

'In all seriousness, Sol,' Nanna said then, stepping

back to block his exit path, 'does this mean you're finally going to slow down? Retire, even?' She lowered her head, hunting for his eyes.

'Yeah,' he replied, glancing not at Nanna, but at Hallberg instead. 'Maybe.'

Nanna huffed and blinked. 'Stupid question, really, isn't it? You're always going to have something to prove, aren't you? I just wish—God... I just wish I knew what that was.'

Church lingered there for a moment more. He knew exactly what that was. But he didn't think Nanna would, or could, ever understand.

So instead, he just lifted his hand and put it on her shoulder. 'It's good to see you,' he said, mustering all he had for a smile. 'And I'm glad it's finally finished.'

And he really meant that, even if, at the back of his mind, he knew that whatever kind of peace, whatever kind of sanctuary he found... it would never be permanent. It would never last.

No, he'd led too long, too dark a life for that.

His past would always come calling.

His future would always be at stake.

And yet, as he limped on...

He knew he deserved nothing less.

And certainly nothing more.

EPILOGUE I

CHURCH PULLED open the sliding door that led onto Fletcher's little balcony, gritting his teeth against the pain in his side—the strain of just opening a simple door almost too much for him—and stepped into the cold winter air.

It was dark, and the city lights glittered in the distance, the din of London echoing up from the streets below, the smell of the place—of concrete and car exhausts, of nine million people—invading his senses.

He eased himself down onto her rail and reached under his ribs, touching at the lumpy, poorly knitted flesh. Field-stitched and healing badly, it was still giving him grief weeks on. He didn't like being injured, and though the doctor Hallberg had made him see told him it could be months before he was 'fighting fit' again, that turn of phrase had earned a harsh look from Hallberg.

But despite that, he wanted to be. Couldn't shake the

feeling that something was coming. But what, he didn't know.

The door opened behind him and Fletcher stepped out, swearing softly against the cold, wrapping her cardigan around herself.

She approached the rail, turning and leaning against it. 'You're not cold?'

Church looked down at his arms, the hair stood on end at the temperature. But no, he couldn't feel it. His mind was too occupied. He shook his head, looking up at her. Her pale complexion, her rosy cheeks, her dark eyes, black hair pulled back into a loose ponytail. She looked harrowed by this experience. By Church's stories, his recounting of what happened in Kosovo all those years ago. The response Fletcher got from the initial article had publishers, editors, clamouring for more. For a bigger piece. The whole story.

She couldn't do it without Church, she said.

He'd given in. Maybe he wanted to clear his conscience. Maybe he wanted her to tell him, after it was all out there, that he did all he could.

But with each word, she looked at him with a little less warmth, a little more fear. And she was looking at him now with something else. Something like pity. Something Church didn't like.

'I know it's a lot,' she said then, reaching out and putting her hand on his arm.

He detected a little hesitation, like she had to force herself to touch him. For a brief moment, years ago, he thought they might have been… something. But now, she could hardly stand to touch him, let alone anything else.

'But,' she went on, 'it's for the best. I promise.'

Church just hummed a non-response. *The best for who?* Her, definitely. Him, who could say?

He just wanted it all to be over. But as he stared out at the city, he knew it wasn't. It was a cesspool of crime and violence. A festering pit of simmering hatred ready to boil over at any moment. Gangs. Terrorists. Killers on the streets looking to take a life. Killers in Westminster looking to ruin millions. The city, the world—it felt like it was rotting from the inside out.

Church was alive—barely—but how many others were, too? How many of the men he'd killed, he'd crossed, were out there now, plotting their revenge. Like Dragan. How many of his ilk were stalking the shadows this very moment, waiting for their moment to make him bleed? To make the world bleed?

He narrowed his eyes and Fletcher leaned in slightly.

'What can you see?' she asked.

'Nothing.' Church pushed himself up from the rail, eyes fixed on the darkened skyline in the distance. He dug his fingers into the fading scar on his ribs—the pain good, reminding him what awaited if he let his guard down. A mistake he'd not quickly make again.

'It's quiet,' he said, turning away from Fletcher and drawing in a long, difficult breath. 'For now.'

EPILOGUE II

The winter sun was low and bright, the air cold, the trees bare around Mitch's farm.

They were sitting outside at a wooden table, a cafetière of strong coffee between them, the grounds steeping before the plunger was pushed.

'I'm just saying,' Mitch said, 'I think she likes you.'

'Can we not, please?' Church said back, staring into the pale blue sky.

'I saw it. When she thought you were dead... she was devastated.'

'I hope you were too. But does that mean you also fancy me?' Church arched an eyebrow, looking over at Mitch.

'You wish,' Mitch laughed, reaching out and slowly repressing the plunger.

Church thought on it a little. It had crossed his mind. He couldn't lie about that. He let out a little sigh. She was twenty years younger than him. Hell, her father was probably his age. He couldn't deny she was attractive, but he had no intention of pursuing it. Or of giving her the wrong idea.

'I know you think you're too old for her—' Mitch began.

'Do you now?' Church interrupted.

'Yeah, of course. Hell, you probably are. But you know Mick Jagger's eighty or something and his girlfriend is twenty. A ballerina, supposedly.'

'Fucking hell,' Church muttered. Not at the age gap, but at the inanity of the conversation. 'Access to the internet has made you stupider, I swear to God.'

'Hallberg's older than that. And you're younger than Mick. She's got a big job, she's intelligent, older than her years.'

'Older than her years? You sure you're not eighty?' Church asked Mitch, wishing he'd pour the coffee already. He adjusted himself on his chair, wrapped up in a thick wool-lined bomber jacket. But even through it, he could feel the cold—the stab wound in his side seeming to be a barometer for it these days. If it hurt, it was cold.

'You were gone a long time, Sol. Society's more accepting of this kind of stuff now. It's a new world. Scary, different, but you shouldn't feel so pressured to conform to old societal conventions,' Mitch dithered in, finally pouring them two cups.

'You got a gun on you?' Church asked, leaning

forward and taking his drink. 'I think I'd like to blow my brains out.'

'You deserve happiness, that's all I'm saying.'

'You're saying a lot more than that. Most of it complete bollocks, mate.' Church sipped the coffee, the hot liquid warming him.

'Yeah, well—'

Church's phone began buzzing on the table in front of him and cut Mitch off. He reached for it quickly, glad, for once, that it was ringing. He looked at the number and answered.

'Fletcher,' he said, voice stricken with relief. 'Save me.'

'Church—what's wrong?'

'I've fallen into a wormhole and seemingly surfaced in a dimension where eighty-year-olds are having it off with twenty-year-old ballerinas and Mitch seems very interested in that fact.'

He sneered at Church and gave him the finger.

'You mean Mick Jagger? Yeah, that's fucked up,' Fletcher said. 'Glad to know it's nothing serious, though.'

'So what's going on?' Church asked, reading the apprehension in her voice.

'I just got a strange email—about you.'

'About me?' Church straightened in his chair and Mitch leaned in, the playful banter all at once gone between them.

'Yeah, from someone anonymous saying they

wanted to get in touch with you. Asking for your email, your phone number.'

Church put his cup down and adjusted himself in the chair. 'You didn't give it, did you?'

'Of course not,' she said, offended. 'I never give up my sources, and I didn't even name you on that article. He must have gone back through my older publications and found the one on Walter Blackthorn, seen your video, your face. Put two and two together that you were my source for the Kosovo article, too.'

'My face,' Church muttered.

She sighed. 'Yeah, I thought that too. This guy knows you by sight. Scary thought for a special forces soldier, right?'

'Mmm,' was all Church responded with. A noise more than a word.

'He said he needed to speak to you urgently. A matter of life and death,' the email said.

'That narrows it down,' Church replied, taking another sip of coffee. It was rapidly cooling in the cold winter air.

'He also said…'

'What, Fletcher?'

'That it was about righting the wrongs of your pasts. About erasing the sins committed during the war.'

'The Kosovo War?' Church asked, brow crumpling.

'No,' Fletcher said, the words almost sticking in her throat. 'Iraq. The email said you met in Basra?'

Church's blood ran a little colder.

'The email said that he was sorry. That he finally

understands. And that… you're the only one who can help him.' She cleared her throat. 'What do you want me to do?'

Church thought about that. There were a lot of things he wanted to say. Foremost of which was to tell this guy to shove it up his arse. Church needed the time. Needed the rest. Needed the peace. But if this anonymous contact was talking about Basra… then it couldn't be anything good.

Nothing good happened in that place.

Nothing.

Teeth gritted, Church decided. 'Set up a meeting,' he said.

'You sure?' Fletcher confirmed.

'I am.'

'Where?' she asked.

'Somewhere open. Somewhere I can get a good look at this guy through the scope of a rifle.'

'And what if you don't like what you see?'

Church lifted, and then drained, the last of his coffee, the last remnants of warmth clinging desperately to the liquid.

'Come on, Fletcher,' Church said with a little smile. 'You know that's the kind of question that can make you an accessory.'

She let out a wry little laugh. 'Jesus, how did I get mixed up in all this shit?'

Church's smile widened. 'Last time I checked, you're the one who put yourself in the middle of it all.'

'And regretting every second of it,' Fletcher laughed.

'Yeah, until the next story comes along. Then, like always,' he said, looking out over the bare, skeletal trees in front of him, stock still in the frigid, biting air. 'You won't be able to resist.'

AUTHOR'S NOTE

Hey, reader!

Thanks so much for reading *The Fury*. I hope you enjoyed digging into Solomon's world—and his past, too. I'm so, so enjoying writing this series, and getting the opportunity to immerse myself in some history as I'm crafting these stories, learning more about our world and the events that have shaped it… It's humbling.

The idea for this book came to me pretty suddenly. Not lightning-bolt style inspiration, but more of a scratching at the back of the mind that couldn't be ignored. I was watching a political debate, and one of the pundits made the point that NATO was an organisation of peace that had never committed an aggressive action. His opponent laughed and said, "You never heard of the Yugoslavian War?"

And I thought to myself, no, I never have. I began reading about the dissolution of Yugoslavia and the resulting conflicts. It was 1991 when the country began

breaking apart, with Slovenia, Croatia, Bosnia and
Herzegovina, and Macedonia seceding. Serbia and
Montenegro remained and were still referred to as
Yugoslavia until 2006, when the union finally dissolved
completely. But why? The Cold War, and the resulting
break-up of the Soviet Union.

But let's roll back slightly to Yugoslavia's founding,
just to get the full picture. Yugoslavia was formed in
1918 after the end of World War I, as the Kingdom of
Serbs, Croats and Slovenes. In 1929 it was renamed the
Kingdom of Yugoslavia. During World War II, it was
invaded by the Axis powers and occupied until 1943,
when the Communist-led Partisan resistance proclaimed
it the Democratic Federal Yugoslavia with the backing
of the Allies. In 1944, King Peter II, living in exile
(coincidentally), gave his recognition to the Anti-Fascist
Council for the National Liberation of Yugoslavia as the
official government. Following the end of the war in
1945, a parliamentary election established the
Constituent Assembly of Yugoslavia. This officially
abolished monarchical rule, paving the way for a forty-
year reign of the Communist party in the country.

During this time, Josip Broz Tito ruled the country
from 1944 until his death in 1980—first as Prime
Minister and then as President. In 1963, the country was
renamed yet again (and for the final time), becoming the
Socialist Federal Republic of Yugoslavia, and comprised
six constituent republics: Bosnia and Herzegovina,
Croatia, Macedonia, Montenegro, Slovenia, and Serbia.
Within Serbia were two socialist autonomous provinces:

Vojvodina and Kosovo. They were technically equal members of the federation, but following Tito's death, political and economic tensions rose, ultimately resulting in widespread ultra-nationalism and ethnic conflicts across the country.

Kosovo was largely populated by ethnic Albanians, and the Kosovo War itself was fuelled by the unbridled racism the Kosovar Albanians faced, officially breaking out in 1998. But we're getting slightly ahead of ourselves, as this wasn't the only conflict. In fact, it was the last of many.

After Tito died in 1980, wars broke out as new regimes attempted to replace the old, with the republics of Yugoslavia trying to install their own military, police, and political forces in place of the unified Yugoslavian institutions. This happened across Yugoslavia over the ten years following Tito's demise, and then, in 1991, Yugoslavia began to collapse completely when the Cold War ended. As a socialist one-party state, it was officially neutral during the Cold War, but because of its similar political and economic systems to the Soviet Union, events across the border influenced Yugoslavia greatly. In 1986, Mikhail Gorbachev introduced liberalising reforms in the Soviet Union, and other communist countries soon followed, heavily influenced by the Soviet Union's looming shadow to the east.

Then, in 1989, the Berlin Wall fell, uniting West and East Germany in a historic step forward for the country. As Eastern Europe began to haul itself out of its stagnated socialist quagmire, Yugoslavians began calling out for the same thing. By 1991, as the Soviet Union collapsed, so did Yugoslavia.

In 1990, Croatia's attempted forced replacement of the police sparked the beginning of the Yugoslav Wars. A similar action in Bosnia and Herzegovina ignited a war there that lasted more than three years. During these bloody conflicts, almost all of the Serbs living in these regions fled to Serbia. Eventually, Croatia, Bosnia and Herzegovina, and Macedonia were the first republics to declare independence in 1991. And when I say bloody, I mean bloody. The Bosnian War, beginning in 1992, claimed the lives of 100,000 people, an estimated 61% of whom were Bosniaks. The Serbians, as in Kosovo later, engaged in widespread ethnic cleansing in their controlled territories, and in 1995 committed the worst of these acts.

The Srebrenica genocide occurred in July 1995, during which Republika Srpska forces killed around 8,000 Bosniak civilians. This event forced NATO to intervene on the Bosniak-Croat side, leading to the signing of the Dayton Peace Agreements in December 1995. However, this didn't include Kosovo or the oppression ethnic Albanians were also facing at the hands of the Yugoslav military.

During this time, tensions continued to brew across the border in Serbia and Kosovo. Ethnic Albanians in Kosovo felt autonomy was not enough and demanded Kosovo become a constituent republic with a right to separate from the last remnants of Yugoslavia—at that time Serbia and Montenegro.

The KLA—the Kosovo Liberation Army, an Albanian separatist militia fighting for Kosovan independence—began funnelling weapons to their fighters through Albania, arming themselves for the fight to come, and for the next three years, things steadily escalated.

In February 1998, small-scale conflicts exploded into full-blown war. The KLA began targeting Yugoslav authorities in Kosovo, and in response, Kosovo saw a massive increase in the presence of Serbian paramilitaries and soldiers, who immediately pursued retribution against KLA sympathisers and political figures aligned with the KLA's goals. This ultimately claimed the lives of up to 2,000 civilians and KLA fighters and displaced around 370,000 Kosovan Albanians who felt compelled to flee their homes or face persecution and death, further fuelling the rage of KLA forces in Kosovo.

As the war wore on, with both sides striking at each other at every opportunity, Yugoslav forces began engaging in widespread ethnic cleansing, sweeping across the country in a ruthless campaign of repression and murder. Estimates put the death toll at 13,535 (as noted in the 2015 Kosovo Memory Book). Of these thirteen thousand, more than ten thousand were ethnic Albanians, and of those ten thousand, eight thousand were civilians killed by Serbian forces.

However, over a million (estimated between 1.2–1.4 million) Kosovan Albanians were displaced during the war, and only once it ended did they begin to return.

As we explored in this book, NATO officially

entered the conflict on March 24th, 1999, when Operation Allied Force began, and bombers took off from neighbouring countries to make their first bombing runs.

The initial goal was cited as destroying Yugoslav air defences and high-value military targets, but initially it didn't go well. Milošević (the Serbian president) resisted, and despite NATO brass believing he would surrender in days (if not hours), the bombing went on for 78 days.

NATO began narrowing its focus from large-scale military targets to smaller ones, hitting ground units, tanks, and individual artillery pieces. The bombings were heavily constrained, as they needed to be sanctioned by all nineteen NATO member states.

Ultimately, the operation was a complete fucking mess.

In May of 1999, a NATO bomber accidentally attacked an Albanian refugee convoy, mistaking it for a Yugoslav military convoy, killing fifty people. The same month, NATO bombs hit the Chinese embassy in Belgrade, killing three Chinese journalists and sparking outrage from the Chinese government. NATO claimed it was bad intel supplied by the CIA that led to this 'mistake', but rumours swirled that it was deliberate, as the Chinese embassy was suspected of relaying Yugoslav army radio signals. Later in May, NATO bombed the Dubrava prison in Kosovo, killing ninety-five civilians.

With the bombings going poorly, NATO countries began considering full-scale ground operations, with the then British Prime Minister, Tony Blair, a strong voice in pushing that agenda. US President Clinton was reluctant to commit troops, but instead authorised a CIA operation to look into ways to topple the Yugoslav government from within (this was a big inspiration for the story of this book).

Milošević was holding out hope that Russia would come to Serbia's aid if NATO put troops in Kosovo. Ultimately, Russia did not intervene, and eventually Milošević accepted conditions offered by a Finnish-Russian mediation team, agreeing to allow UN-led NATO troops into Kosovo.

Following this, Norwegian and British Special Forces worked directly with the KLA (another huge inspiration for this book—I simply messed with the timelines a little), and were the first troops to cross the border into Kosovo on a peacekeeping mission.

On June 9th, 1999, Milošević accepted terms and ended the fighting, and on June 10th air operations were officially suspended. On the 12th of June, the NATO-led peacekeeping Kosovo Force (KFOR), consisting of 30,000 soldiers, began entering Kosovo.

On the same day, Norwegian Forsvarets Spesialkommando (FSK) soldiers, alongside British SAS 22 Regiment, were the first to enter Pristina.

I, of course, took some liberties in telling this story. Officially, there's no record of the SAS being in Kosovo prior to June of 1999. But with the Americans exploring clandestine operations in Serbia prior to these dates, and Tony Blair pushing strongly for British military action, it's not hard to imagine something like this might have happened.

The SAS played a big part in the Bosnian War as UK Liaison Officers, wearing UN berets and carrying UN-issue rifles to blend in. They were covertly inserted in an intelligence-gathering capacity, but saw plenty of action as they worked in high-conflict zones. Following the conclusion of the conflict, the SAS returned to Bosnia to hunt suspected war criminals who had engaged in ethnic cleansing. One such mission was codenamed Operation Tango, and saw the SAS pursuing Milan Kovačević, who had been responsible for rounding up Muslims for internment camps, where they were starved and beaten to death.

The SAS tracked Kovačević to Prijedor Hospital, posed as Red Cross officials, and talked their way inside with pistols concealed beneath their clothing. They found and arrested Kovačević, extracting him via helicopter and then by C130 to The Hague to face trial. He later died in custody from a suspected heart attack. Weird, eh?

The second target in Operation Tango was Simo Drljača, a former police chief suspected of organising the ethnic cleansing of Prijedor's Muslim population, among other crimes. As the first extraction team entered the hospital to pick up Kovačević, a second team approached Drljača at the Prijedor reservoir, where he was fishing. Not prepared to go quietly, Drljača opened fire on the SAS, wounding one. The SAS returned fire, killing him.

Operation Ensue saw the pursuit of Stevan Todorović, a Serb wanted for war crimes committed during the ethnic cleansing of Bosanski Šamac in April 1992. This mission took place in Serbia, where they tracked him to a remote cabin. They stormed the building, taking Todorović by night. Bound and gagged, he was transported by 4x4 to the Drina River, loaded into a Zodiac inflatable boat, and transported across the border into Bosnia, where he was then transferred by helicopter to Tuzla, where he was formally arrested.

Strangely, a public announcement was made that Todorović had been taken by the SAS inside Serbia (somewhere they shouldn't have been). This was highly unusual, but it was suspected it was done deliberately to let the Serbs know there was nowhere to hide that the SAS couldn't reach.

It's this kind of thing that I find so exciting, so interesting. It's these kinds of stories that I think are amazing, carried out by heroes. I mean, come on—SAS soldiers hunting war criminals responsible for ethnic cleansing, behind enemy lines? That's book-worthy right there!

These are stories of heroes, and I love being able to tell a version of them. I've got no military experience, but I hope my admiration and respect for these men bleed through these pages, through every word.

It's not my intention to sanitise or romanticise. I try to balance excitement and action with the reality of these wars—with their darkness. I try to bring a little bit of information, some kind of education, exploring these dark corners of our history, the ones we're so eager to forget.

I encourage you to go out, learn more about what happened in Croatia, Bosnia, and Kosovo. It's hugely interesting, and those people—the ones who survived, the ones who didn't—deserve to have their stories, their lives, known.

If you read the epilogue, you know we're headed to Basra next—Iraq, 2005. Like all wars, that one was bloody, terrible, harrowing. I won't spoil anything for you, as I think it's going to be a real rollercoaster and a hell of a read (if it comes together!).

So sit back, buckle up, and get ready. Because there's more Church coming.

Lots more.

And we've got no intention of slowing down.

In fact…

We're just getting started.

See you then—

Dan

THANKS FOR READING

Reviews are the best way to support authors you like. They help other readers discover new writers, and they tell Amazon that books are worth reading! Just leaving a rating or a few words is immensely helpful to indie authors like myself, so if you enjoyed *The Exile,* please consider leaving me a rating or review when you have a second.

And if you'd like to reach out to me to let me know what you thought of this book, please do! I respond to all reader emails and messages when I can and I love hearing from you.

To stay up to date with all things Solomon Church and Morgan Greene, find me on Facebook as Morgan Greene Author, or head to my website: *morgangreene. co.uk*

SOLOMON CHURCH WILL RETURN

April 2004. The city of Fallujah, Iraq, is at boiling point.

Four Blackwater USA contractors are ambushed and murdered by Sunni insurgents. The Americans are mutilated, burned alive, and hung from a bridge over the Euphrates. The images are broadcast worldwide. The message is clear. The response can only be one thing: all-out war.

The U.S. launches Operation Vigilant Resolve, dispatching an army of Marines to seize control of the city and wipe out the Al-Qaeda-backed insurgency by any means necessary. What follows is one of the bloodiest battles of the Iraq War.

But the fight can't be won.

As the civilian death toll rises and political pressure mounts, U.S. forces are ordered to withdraw—leaving Fallujah in the hands of the very men they came to destroy. The insurgents waste no time. They dig in. They fortify. And they prepare for the next wave.

In the chaos of withdrawal, a CIA weapons cache vanishes. Classified ordnance, untraceable arms, surveillance gear—gone. The only personnel who knew the cache's location are dead. If those weapons fall into the wrong hands, retaking the city becomes impossible. But losing them publicly would trigger a political firestorm.

The US sends in a two-person CIA team—covert, deniable—to track the weapons and retrieve them before they surface. But Fallujah is a warzone now and danger lurks in every alleyway.

While pursuing a lead, the team is ambushed by Tariq al-Aswad, an extremist cell determined to find the weapons and rise through the ranks of Al Qaeda. A vicious firefight ensues, the agents' Marine escorts killed, the team scattered, divided. One agent disappears. The other barely escapes.

Reeling and desperate to find his missing analyst, he knows that he needs to act fast, and locate her before Tariq al-Aswad do. If he doesn't, they'll make her suffer a fate a thousand times worse than death. But if he reports this failing up the chain, he knows the CIA will abandon the op, and their agent in favour of deniability.

He searches for an answer, for help. And in a chance encounter, meets Solomon Church.

Together, they decide to go back into Fallujah. Back into hell.

The clock is ticking. The stakes are high.

And if they fail… The tide of war could turn altogether.

The Outcast is available now. Secure your copy today!

Made in United States
Orlando, FL
12 June 2025

62068426R00233